Black Nab
A DCI Finnegan Yorkshire Crime Thriller
Ely North

Red Handed Print

Contact ely@elynorthcrimefiction.com

Cover design by Cherie Chapman/Chapman & Wilder
Cover image © Stephen Smith / Alamy Stock Photo

Disclaimer: This is a work of fiction. Names, characters, businesses, places, events, locales, and incidents are either the products of the author's imagination or used in a fictitious manner. Any resemblance to actual persons, living or dead, or actual events is purely coincidental.

Published by Red Handed Print

First Edition

Kindle e-book ISBN-13: 978-0-6452904-6-2

Paperback ISBN-13: 978-0-6452904-7-9

Prologue

Ode To Black Nab

In 1539, cruel Henry, the bells did grab
His boat and Jack Tars, not sail too far
Before they hit Black Nab
It stands there as protector, of air, and land, and sea
Repulsing all invasion, as long as it may be
When you gaze upon the bay, young lassie, and young lad
Pay homage to your sentry... your guardian, old Black Nab
anon.

1

Friday 20th February 10:45 pm

Shirley Fox places the empty gin and tonic glass on the table and says goodnight to her friends. It will be the last time she sees them.

Faux cheek to cheek kisses are exchanged.

'You must be mad, walking,' Claire says. 'It's bloody freezing out there.'

Shirley slides into her parka, pulls the zipper up.

'I'd call it bracing. Anyway, there's something romantic about walking arm in arm with Dudley up the old steps, past the church, and abbey silhouetted in lights. It's atmospheric.'

'Romantic? Atmospheric?' Mandy scoffs.

'You know what they say, girls; if you don't stoke the fire, it will go out,' Shirley replies with an impish grin.

'If you were married to my old man, you'd be throwing a bucket of water on the fire,' Mandy jokes as the other two women snort with laughter.

Shirley turns to leave. 'I'll see you Sunday lunchtime if you decide to go to The Malting Pot for a drink. Me and Dudley will be there from about midday. See ya!'

Mandy and Claire witness their friend disappear through the pub door.

'Do you think she was quiet tonight?' Mandy quizzes.

Claire ponders the question. 'A little. I think she's had a tough week.'

'Hmm... maybe. Right, one more before we hit the road?'

'Aye, why not,' Claire replies as Mandy collects the empties and heads towards the sparsely populated bar.

Shirley Fox saunters up Church Lane, breathing in the crisp night air, as the waves continue their incessant clamour far below.

She peers at the steps ahead, expecting Dudley and Tyson to materialise at any moment. There's no sign of them.

An orange glow from a replica Victorian gaslight bathes the ancient cobbled street in a ghostly orange hue.

The moon hangs low, morbid, almost ashamed.

Movement, slight, nothing more than a fleeting shadow. A tingle shoots down her spine. Stomach involuntarily knots.

Stop it, Shirl. You're spooking yourself. You've walked this way a hundred times before. Anyway, Dudley will be already coming down the steps and Tyson will scare off any creeps.

Placing a hand on the railing, she pauses, staring up at the steep incline. Still no sign of Dudley and the dog. She wavers on the bottom step as she fumbles for her phone.

Senses something behind her but doesn't have time to react.

A hand grabs her face. Rag shoved over mouth and nose. A strong chemical smell. She struggles and tries to scream. Only muffled, muted cries emanate. Woozy darkness approaches. She fights back, spins around. Two fearful eyes glare at her through the slits in the mask. Struggles. Rips at the woollen hat pulled low. It comes free. Sees her attacker.

'You... but why?' she gasps.

The blow to the side of the head doesn't hurt. It merely shocks her. Senses blur, mind dizzy.

She falls. Instinctively throws her arms out in front. Her chin and front teeth graze the stone step. Heavy footsteps thunder down from above.

Desperately tries to remain conscious. A gentle hand turns her onto her back. She's safe.

It must be Dudley. Why doesn't he speak? Where's Tyson?

The caring hands, wrapped in supple leather, encircle her neck then harden.

Gurgling.

Another unseen face behind a ski mask as the pressure on her throat increases.

The only thing she controls—her eyes.

Anger, the last emotion she'll experience as she glares at the attacker.

How dare you deprive me of life, of love, of ever seeing my daughter again. You have no right!

He reads her rage and leans forward. Sympathises with her predicament. It was not meant to be this way.

Whispers gently into her ear as the first attacker trembles violently, a spectator.

'Prosti, spi seychas. It's nothing personal.'

Nothing personal! I don't think you can get more personal than taking my life. At least let me see your face, you coward!

Hands desperately claw at his head, but he's too strong. The bottom of the mask rides up slightly and uncovers his neck.

Her eyes fall upon the delicate symbol etched into skin. A flower with creamy white petals encircling yellow florets attached to a green stalk.

Beauty on a beast.

Her eyes flicker as life, with all its sorrows and splendour, ebbs away.

You may take my life, but I won't go. I'll be with you every waking moment and in your nightmares. I won't go! I'm not ready! It's not my time!

2

Six Months Later - Sunday 16th August 9:50 pm

A vehicle creeps up alongside the diesel bowser. The rumble of the throaty engine dies. Occupants—silent. Their eyes, sharp as a hungry falcon, scrutinise their hunting ground. Windows down, the sweet scent of cut grass permeates the air.

In front, a white Vauxhall Viva, parked. Its elderly driver in the store pressing his bank card against the payment terminal. Only one attendant. Nothing more than a boy, maybe his first job, night shift at a service station. Ten minutes until his night ends and he can reconcile the till, lock up, go home.

The two men in the Land Rover Defender wait. Cool, calm, hardened. Woolly hats pulled down over their eyebrows, black nitrile gloves cover their hands.

Get a move on, grandad, the driver thinks, impatient, edgy.

The old man exits the store and ambles to his car, oblivious of the battered four-wheel drive. He gets in, starts the engine. A man in the vehicle behind steps out of the passenger side and removes the diesel cap. A truck with blazing headlights thunders by with scant regard for the speed limit. Its blinding lights momentarily illuminate the deserted countryside.

The Vauxhall pulls sedately onto the main road and trundles away. Rear red lights twinkle as they recede.

Diesel gurgles into the fuel tank as the click, click, click of the bowser racks up money. The passenger replaces the nozzle, screws the fuel cap on, slaps the side panel. A plume of dirty smoke from the exhaust accompanies a cough and splutter from the engine, pungent, aromatic.

He walks towards the store, his hiking rucksack contradictory with the time and place.

The Land Rover pulls hard and slow to the right, then straightens, partially blocking the store window. A sideways glance from the driver at the young lad behind the counter.

He barely looks up as the man dressed in black saunters in. Unaware as he pulls down his Sherpa balaclava. Unsuspecting as he extracts the twin-barrelled sawn-off shotgun deftly from the backpack.

The driver smirks and swallows hard, his mouth as dry as sandpaper.

The attendant's mind-numbingly tedious night is over as he stares down the barrel of two cold, dark holes.

He takes the note handed to him.

He reads, clenching his bowels.

He shakes as he thinks of his mother.

He speaks, stutteringly.

Apologises for the fact there's not much cash. It's been a quiet night and most people pay by card—like it's his fault.

The man places the rucksack on the counter as the boy stuffs notes into it.

He asks a dumb question.

The man shakes his head.

Of course I don't want the fucking coins!

Why do they always ask that?

Maybe I should write it on the note... next time.

He nods towards the cigarette kiosk and glances out the window. Nothing apart from the guttural throb of the diesel engine.

The boy fumbles packets of cigarettes and tobacco pouches into the bag. His eyes comprehend the warnings—Smoking Kills.

Hands the bag over, sniffles.

The man flips the note over and pushes it in his face. The boy nods, understanding—*do nothing for ten minutes... otherwise!*

He hoists the backpack on, sticks the gun under his armpit, pulls at the zipper on his jacket, turns, stops.

Picks up three Mars bars, drops two into his jacket pocket and tosses the other one to the lad.

Eyes smile behind the mask.

3

Sunday 16th August 11:55 pm – Whitby, UK

Dudley Fox picks up the TV remote control and presses the channel button. The evening news is replaced by a celebrity chef, frying fish in a griddle pan.

"Salmon fillets only need three to four minutes per side. Maybe a minute or so longer on the skin. We want to get that skin nice and crispy."

He flicks the TV off and huffs. 'Damn cooking programmes, it's all that's on these days.'

Tyson throws him a sad look from his dog bed, as Dudley addresses the empty chair where his wife used to sit.

'Okay Shirley, it's time for bed,' he says as he glances at the clock on the wall.

He walks over to her chair, picks up a red, heart-shaped silk cushion, and fluffs it up before placing it lovingly down against the back of the chair. Grabbing his mobile phone off the mantelpiece, he types a new, but predictable, text message.

> `Goodnight Shirley. Sleep`
> `tight. I love and miss you.`

As he hits the send button, there's an immediate ping, followed by a vibration as Shirley's phone rattles on the coffee table next to her chair. A smile drifts across his weary face. It's a familiar routine which plays out every night.

The first couple of times he texted his wife a goodnight message, he felt foolish, almost ashamed of his unusual behaviour, but those feelings soon passed. It didn't take long before it became a nightly ritual. For some reason, it comforted him. He knew the truth. He was an intelligent man who had no time for God or superstitions, a man of science, and yet the simple nightly text message gave him an earthly connection with her.

Stepping from the shower, he grabs a fluffy towel and dries in front of the bathroom mirror. The reflection that bounces back makes him wince. There's no point denying it. The trauma has taken its toll. Six months ago he was a fit, energetic, middle-aged man who ran daily, worked out at the gym three times a week, and spent many weekends walking in the Dales, or the Lake District with Shirley.

His diet was high in fresh fruit and vegetables, lean meat, and whole grains. He didn't smoke and only imbibed occasionally; a Sunday afternoon at the local Malting Pot brewery enjoying a couple of pints of beer, or a glass of red wine at dinner parties, a nip of single malt at Christmas. That life was gone, changed forever on a cold February night. Good habits traded for bad. His healthy diet replaced by takeaways and ready-made meals, exercise traded for lethargy and saturnine introspection. His only exertion was walking Tyson once a day.

Drinking was the main problem. It had crept up on him, like Shirley's killer had crept up on her. He was going through a half-bottle of scotch every day, sometimes more, as he ruminated over old photos and tried to quash the guilt.

It didn't take long for his weight to increase. His healthy countenance replaced by drawn, grey skin across his face, rather like a side of beef that's boiled rather than roasted.

The truth is, there are only two things keeping him going; his daughter, and the burning desire to find Shirley's killer!

In the bedroom, he places his phone on the bedside cabinet, flings the covers back on the bed and slips under them. This is the worst part of the day. Alone, contemplating. Thinking what might have been had he not left his phone in the kitchen and fallen asleep in front of the television on that Friday night.

He'd berated himself for six months on his error, a simple error, a human error that would forever haunt him during his nightmares and through his waking hell.

'You stupid bloody fool, Dudley. You stupid, stupid, bloody fool. Please forgive me, Shirley?' he murmurs into the damp pillow.

His thoughts turn to his daughter, Amber, in the hope it will bring some relief, a sliver of happiness, but it doesn't.

She was in her final year of university when it happened. Shirley had already noticed a few telltale signs when Amber occasionally ventured home for a weekend. The permanently dilated pupils, the slight bruises on her inner forearms, the way she'd stagger in as dawn broke and sleep for most of the day, only to wake exhausted and with little appetite. Then miraculously, by the time evening came around, she'd come to life and be full of zest and nervous, radiant energy. Shirley had noted her suspicions to Dudley, but he had merely laughed it off.

'She's twenty-one years old, Shirl. If you can't go out partying until all hours and have a good time when you're young—then when can you?'

He winces at his past words and can now clearly see what Shirley had seen then. After innumerable sombre thoughts and stabs of remorse, sleep finally slides through him like a shot of anaesthetic. His eyes close, the pain ends.

———◦———

Bing! Bing!

His heart thumps into his chest as adrenalin and cortisone flood his body. Bolting upright, he flicks on the lamp, grabs his phone and stares at it. There's a message. He checks the time—1:15 am. He immediately thinks of Amber as panic claws at his insides. She knows not to ring late as it brings back memories of that black night six months ago. Scrabbling for his spectacles, he fumbles them onto his head with trembling hands. He punches in his four digit security code and the phone opens for him. At first, he's confused before nausea overwhelms him.

It's a text message... from his dead wife!

4

On the west cliff of Whitby, less than five miles away from Dudley Fox's home on the east cliff, another person is having trouble sleeping.

Frank Finnegan rolls out of bed and shuffles into his tartan slippers. He creeps quietly from the bedroom, making a mental note not to stand on the creaky floorboard. The last thing he wants to do is disturb his wife.

In the kitchen he pulls the plastic tub from the cupboard which houses assorted over-the-counter medicines. With double the recommended dose of liquid antacid dispensed, he necks it down in one.

'Oh, that's better. It's working already,' he murmurs as blessed relief enters his stomach.

As he replaces the plastic tub, the pitter patter of claws on the varnished cork tiles has him glancing over his shoulder. The dog stares up at him and whimpers as she wags her tail in expectation. Frank fixes her with a severe frown. The dog takes a tentative step back and emits a high-pitched whine as she cocks her head to one side and blinks. Frank's resolve wavers.

'Foxtrot, you'll be the death of me. If Meera finds out I've given you a midnight treat, she'll have my guts for garters,' he whispers, imploringly.

The dog tilts its head to the other side. Its eyes widen.

'You little bugger! You always know how to melt my heart. Okay, but not a word to Meera, right?'

Throwing the Jack Russell a chewy stick, he flicks the kitchen light off and creeps up the stairs.

He attempts to climb into bed as silently as possible, but his stout physique is too much for the bed frame to remain silent.

'Heartburn?' Meera states, patently wide awake.

'Sorry, love. Didn't mean to disturb you.'

'I told you not to have that second helping of meat and potato pie.'

'It's your fault.'

'How's that?'

'If you didn't make the finest meat and tattie pie in the world, then I wouldn't have gone back for seconds.'

'I'll try harder to make it less palatable next time.'

'Don't you bloody dare!'

'You're supposed to be on a diet. Anyway, it's not just the pie, is it?'

'What do you mean?'

'It's the bloody job!' she hisses.

'Please Meera, don't start on that again. My mind's made up.'

Meera switches on her bedside lamp, fluffs up her pillow and stares down at her husband.

'Frank, you're fifty-eight, overweight, have numerous health issues, and you're consumed with your work. It's not a good outlook. You could have taken early retirement three years ago, with a good pension. The house is paid off. We have a nice nest egg put aside and I earn reasonable money at the hospice.'

'And what would I bloody do in retirement?' he grumbles.

'You have your allotment, your fishing.'

'Aye, but they're for my downtime; a chance to forget and relax. They don't give me the mental stimulation I crave.'

'What about the Sudoku and the cryptic crosswords?'

'Sudoku and the Guardian's cryptic crossword do not give me the same thrill as chasing villains and low-life.'

'It's thrills you're after, is it?'

'I didn't mean it like that. Catching rotten apples and putting them away is all I've known for the last thirty-odd years since I joined the force. It's in my blood.'

A heavy silence ensues for a good few minutes as his wife silently bristles.

'Meera, hear me out for a moment.'

'Go on,' she says, folding her arms across her chest.

He turns to her. 'I know you only have my welfare at heart. And I appreciate that... I really do. You care for me, you love me; we've been together since we were childhood sweethearts. But...'

'Here we go.'

'But... when I'm on a case whether it be an armed robbery, a violent assault, or a murder, I come alive, my brain comes *alive*.

Every perpetrator of a crime leaves a clue—always. Sometimes they leave many clues, and those people are easy to find. Then there are those smarter ones who don't appear to leave any trail. They're the ones I love. My real-life cryptic crosswords. If I give the job away, then I lose that.'

Meera turns to him and snuggles her head into his chest, defeated by his honesty.

'I know. I'm sorry for badgering you, but you've worked so hard for so long that I want you to enjoy the next twenty, thirty years without putting yourself in danger, getting shot at again, working the long hours and stressing about things.'

'I tell you what, when I turn sixty, we'll take ourselves away, somewhere exotic for a fortnight's holiday, and I'll reassess.'

'Ooh! Somewhere exotic. You mean the Maldives or Honolulu?'

'I was thinking more like Cleethorpes or Clacton.'

'Very funny,' she yawns as she pulls away and turns her lamp off.

'Night love.'

'Night, Frank.'

Silence descends like a heavy shroud as thoughts bounce around Frank's head.

'Oh, I forgot to mention,' Meera begins.

'What?'

'I bumped into Dudley Fox today as I was coming out of St Mary's.'

'How was he? Did you speak to him?'

'Yes. He didn't seem to hear me at first. Lost in a world of his own.'

'Hardly surprising.'

'He must have been walking his dog on the beach as the bottom of his trousers were wet.'

'Spoken like a true copper's wife.'

'He cut a sorry figure. A shadow of his former self.'

'I know. I feel for him.'

'Is the case still open?'

'Yes, of course it is. Nearly six months since it happened. It's been scaled right back, of course.'

'Any progress?'

'None, not a sausage. A crime with no motive, no witnesses, no evidence, and no CCTV footage—just a dead body. I'm missing something.'

'And you still think Dudley had nothing to do with it?'

'Why would you ask that?'

'Oh, the gossip around town at the time.'

'And that's what it was—gossip. No, me and Zac put Dudley through the ringer. We investigated every possible angle, analysed his phone, his computer, his movements, his friends, his acquaintances. Over thirty hours of questioning. He had nothing to gain by her death; there was no life insurance on her. The house was already paid off. I threw everything at him, and at a time when he was in shock and grieving. Christ, I hate myself for it some days.'

'You were only doing your job, Frank. He was an obvious suspect.'

'He was the only bloody suspect! They had the perfect marriage, according to everyone.'

'There's no such thing as a perfect marriage,' Meera yawns.

'Oi, what's that supposed to mean? What about our marriage?'

'Keep your hair on. I was only joking.'

'Hmm...' Frank grizzles as he turns onto his side.

'You're not too close to it, are you? I mean, we weren't friends, but we did occasionally associate with them at the bowls club.'

'No. I can separate personal from police business. It sounds cliched, but when you've been in the job as long as I have, you develop a sixth sense for these things. I'm telling you—Dudley Fox did not murder his wife. But whichever bastard did, I'll catch him... or her, come hell or high water. My only regret is we don't have the death penalty. What's the point of throwing someone in jail for twenty to thirty years? It costs millions to the taxpayer, which could be better spent creating jobs for young kids or going into hospitals. If someone kills—intentionally, then they should pay the ultimate price—end of story.'

'And would you volunteer to be the one who gave a lethal injection, or opened the trap door to another living human being?'

'Too bloody right I would!'

'And what if, after a year or so, some new evidence emerged which proved they weren't the killer—how would you feel?'

'Extremely unlikely these days, with DNA analysis and modern policing methods.'

'So, you're saying there's never, ever, a miscarriage of justice in the twenty-first century?'

'No... I'm not saying that unequivocally. Of course, there can always be corrupt people in the police and witnesses who are desperate to implicate someone for their own advantage. All I'm saying is it's extremely unlikely.'

'But still a possibility?'

'Yes, an extremely slim possibility. The whole is greater than the sum of its parts. If one innocent person dies but fifty murdering bastards never get to walk the streets again, then it's a price worth paying.'

'And if it was our daughter who was innocently euthanised or strapped into an electric chair?'

Frank stiffens with emotion. 'That's cruel, and uncalled for Meera.'

She already bitterly regrets her remark. 'I'm sorry Frank, you're right. It was thoughtless of me.'

Tension lingers in the air as Meera desperately tries to think of something to say to change the route of her husband's thoughts.

'Is it tomorrow your new sergeant starts?'

'Aye. Although technically it's today,' he replies morosely, still thinking of his daughter as he glances at the clock.

'So, who is he? Promotion or transfer?'

Frank pulls himself away from his morbid thoughts as he curses himself for eating a second helping of the pie.

'She's a transfer... from the west midlands. Twenty-nine. She has a good report. Street-wise, keen, all that stuff.'

'My, my, a she! What's her name?'

'Prisha Kumar—detective sergeant of four years.'

Meera laughs out loud. 'Oh my God! A woman of ethnicity under the tutelage of DCI Frank Finnegan in Whitby, North Yorkshire. Whatever is the world coming to?'

Frank assumes his wife is trying to wind him up but still responds indignantly.

'I don't care what colour, size, or shape they are, or where they come from as long as they have an eye for detail, can read body language and are hungry, then I'm fine to work with.'

'Don't forget punctual.'

'Oh, yes, and punctual.'

'And smartly dressed and have good table manners.'

'That goes without saying.'

'Poor girl doesn't know what she's letting herself in for. Goodnight, love. Sleep tight and stop worrying. I love you... despite all your faults, you're a good man.'

'A good man? Me, the executioner?' he says followed by a chuckle.

As she snuggles into her pillow, he follows her and plants a tender kiss on the nape of her neck.

His wife shivers and wriggles as Frank slumps onto his back and trawls through the Fox investigation in his head once again.

'Frank?'

'What now? I thought you'd gone back off.'

'Your decision not to retire has nothing to do with the Fox case... has it?'

'No.'

'Even the best fisherman can let one slip through the net sometimes. It's not how you'll be remembered.'

'Night, Meera.'

5

Dudley Fox, shaking, and still nauseous, sniffs and wipes the tears from his cheek and reads the message again for the tenth time.

> Goodnight, Dudley, I miss you too. I will always love you.

Who would do such a thing? Do they know the grief this is causing me?

After Shirley had gone, her phone kept receiving calls and texts from various people. The dentist's secretary to confirm an appointment. A pair of shoes she'd dropped off at a cobbler to get the heel fixed. Gym membership renewal. Old friends from the past who had obviously not heard the news. Dudley eventually barred all incoming calls apart from his own. He'd even put a block on Amber. Not that his daughter would have been as stupid or maudlin enough to ring her mother's phone.

But now, someone, somewhere, must have hacked into Shirley's mobile. He eventually types a reply.

> BASTARD! Who is this? You sick scumbag! I've had to endure almost six months of unbearable grief and you think it's funny to pull a stunt like this? When I find out who you are your life won't be worth living!

Hitting the send arrow, he instantly hears his wife's phone ping in the living room downstairs. He enters the bathroom and throws water over his face. There's no chance of sleep now. Another bleep from his phone and his anger returns as he marches into the bedroom and puts his glasses on. Another message from the hacker.

> Sorry Dudley. I never meant to upset you. I didn't realise I'd been gone so long. There's no such thing as time where I am. It seems like yesterday since we parted.

He types angrily, creating spelling mistakes he'd normally rectify.

> Fick you! I'm goin straight to the plice tomorrow. You are goig to regrwt this!

A few seconds pass before another ping lights up his mobile. The message has a laughing smiley face followed by an embarrassed smiley face.

> Sorry to laugh, but you really need to spellcheck before you hit send… that's not like you, Dudley. It really is me, your wife, Shirley!

Dudley's mind is racing and planning. It's been a long time since he employed the grey matter, but for the first time in an age, he feels he has a purpose.

Okay, come on Dudley… think! I need to engage. Get whoever it is into a conversation, and maybe they'll divulge something about their identity. One silly slip up and I'll have them.

He types his question, calm and rational.

> **If it is Shirley, do you mind answering a few questions?**

A reply comes back within seconds.

> **Fire away**

He makes his way downstairs into the living room and fills a small tumbler with a generous drop of single malt whisky. The liquid burns his throat as he takes a seat and ponders his question, then types.

> **What was our favourite Christmas film?**

Shirley's phone pings and rattles on the little coffee table. A few seconds pass.

> **It's a Wonderful Life**

Dudley is surprised, but only for a moment.

Lucky guess. That particular film is probably on the top of most people's lists, especially from our generation.

> Next question, what famous line from the film did I sometimes say to you?

The reply takes a little longer this time.

> Do you want the moon, Shirley? Just say the word and I'll throw a lasso around it for you.

Dudley can't help but smile at the correct answer, as the texter falls into his trap.

You're not as clever as you think you are, you fool. You've now narrowed down the suspects from potentially hundreds to maybe no more than half a dozen. Shirley would have only shared that piece of information with a handful of close friends. Now to play my game.

> You're on a roll. Last question for tonight, Shirl. Where do I keep your wedding ring?

Dudley is the only person in the world who knows the secret location. He smashes his whisky back and pours a refill, smiling smugly as the seconds tick by.

'What's wrong?' he calls out. 'Cat got your tongue?'

Tyson eyes him warily from his bed as Dudley makes a mental list of Shirley's close friends and work colleagues. He'll make damn sure he calls or visits them later in the day. An aching weariness overtakes him as the whisky takes effect.

The clock on the mantlepiece beats out its unending march as all life infinitesimally ebbs away. Eventually, his phone asks for his attention once more.

'About time,' he grumbles to himself as he slips his spectacles on. 'This should be fun.'

> Sorry about that, Dudley. Something happened and my connection with you faded

'Yeah, right? Of course it did. You spineless coward. Well, I'm onto you now. Here's a little something to give *you* a sleepless night.'

Before he can type his reply, insinuating he has a good idea who the texter is, a new message drops in.

> You now keep my wedding ring under *your* pillow

His hand involuntarily trembles. The phone drops to the floor as if it were a bar of molten lead. Dizziness fogs his mind, his legs buckle. He steadies himself against the drinks cabinet.

'You can't know that! Only I know that, only I know that!' he screams.

6

Monday 17th August 8:22 am

DCI Frank Finnegan glances at the clock on the wall and huffs, annoyed.

'Give me strength... not another slacker, please God,' he murmurs under his breath.

Muted voices from the CID room has him lifting his head to stare through his office window. A young woman with jet-black hair pulled into a tight ponytail is talking with DS Cartwright. He responds by nodding towards Frank's office. She turns on her heels and heads his way. Frank studies her for a second before focusing his attention back on Cartwright. He's ogling her, admiring her frame, her rear, her upright, and confident disposition.

Sleazy little git!

Frank has little time for Jason Cartwright. He'd like to get rid of him but doesn't have the heart, nor the means. Slovenly, tardy, sexist and worst of all—he's a terrible copper. If they stuck him in Broadmoor for a week, he still wouldn't be able to spot a criminal. To Cartwright, it was simply a job. It paid the bills and maybe his mates respected or feared him a little more. There were a lot like him on the force. It was harder to get out of the police than into it. Dead wood, treading water, was how Frank referred to their type.

The woman knocks on the door.

'Come in,' Frank testily shouts as he studies the latest overnight reports.

'Detective Sergeant Kumar reporting for duty, sir,' she says with a confident, excited voice accompanied by a broad smile.

Finnegan leans back in his plump leather chair and nods at the clock on the wall.

'What's that, Sergeant Kumar?'

'A wall... sir?'

'Very funny, but what's hanging from the wall?'

She scans the room. 'You have a calendar, a whiteboard, some sticky-notes, a poster of Lynda La Plante... for some bizarre reason, a clock, and some undistinguishable stains... which to the untrained eye looks like congealed blood or possibly tomato sauce. I could get forensics to analyse it, to be sure.'

Frank suppresses a smirk and pulls his sternest face.

'Smartarses don't last too long around this station, so drop the attitude. It doesn't work with me. You're twenty minutes late!'

The grin drops from her face. 'Sorry guv, but the desk sergeant insisted on giving me a whirlwind tour of the station.'

'Did he indeed.'

'Only the basics. Toilets, kitchen, interview rooms. He also introduced me to a few people. Probably trying to make a newcomer feel welcome on their first day,' she explains, pointedly.

Frank folds his arms and studies her intently. She's a sharp wire, this one. Sassy, smart, not afraid of authority, a dry sense of humour... in other words, a regal pain in the backside. Just what I need, like a hole in the head.

'Right, come on, let's go. We've wasted enough time,' Frank says as he lurches from his chair, grabs his weather-beaten overcoat and heads out of the door. They clatter down the stairs and out into the carpark.

'And another thing—don't call me guv! You're not working for the met; you're in Whitby, North Yorkshire.'

'Noted, chief inspector. How would you like me to address you?' she replies tartly, as Frank leads the way to a grubby unmarked Ford Focus in dire need of a wash.

'When around the public, you address me as inspector, sir, or boss. Around other officers, you can call me boss or Frank.'

'That's very progressive of you, Frank.'

He stops dead in his tracks and eyeballs her. 'Okay, I've told you once, I won't tell you again—drop the attitude. You've had a bollocking for being late, take it on the chin, and move on. You're twenty-nine, not nineteen. I don't want pouting sulks and snarky comments from people on my team. Do I make myself clear?'

He senses a moment of resistance before she drops her eyes to the ground for an instant before immediately raising them and staring proudly into his face.

'Perfectly clear, Frank. We've got off on the wrong foot. My fault. Can we wipe the slate clean and start again?'

He offers her a wry smile. 'Aye, fair enough. Welcome aboard, Prisha. Let's hope it's a long and happy working relationship. Hop in.'

As he slides into the driver's seat, he's oblivious to the eye-roll his new DS makes to the heavens.

The car pulls out onto a narrow road.

'So, what's the go, Frank?'

'Another petrol station robbery, overnight. It's been the sixth this year in North Yorkshire. Last year they were targeting Northumbria. Looks to me like it's the same gang slowly working down the coast. Clever. Moving their way around the country. Another ten years and they'll be back where they started from. Well, I aim to end their little game before it gets out of our jurisdiction.'

'How do they operate?'

'There's two of them. One never gets out from behind the wheel. The other is average height, five-nine, five-ten, athletically built, but not over-the-top. Typically, late at night about ten, ten-thirty they roll in, fill up with diesel, then the athletic guy walks into the store with a large rucksack and a rolled up ski mask. As he enters, he pulls down the mask, draws a sawn-off twelve-bore from the rucksack, then hands the cashier a note.'

'Saying?'

'Empty the till and deposit all cigarettes and tobacco into the bag. Never speaks.'

'Seems a little low-tech, boss.'

'Aye, low-tech, but effective. Depending on the petrol station, they can get away with anything from a few grand to over ten. Mind you, that's retail value for the cigarettes and tobacco. On the streets, it would be half that price. So far, they've only targeted stations that are in remote places. No towns or cities where there'd be a lot more people around.'

'Do we have an ID on the vehicle?'

'An old Land Rover Defender. Early 2000 model. Light green or bluey grey colour. No number plates.'

'There can't be too many of them around. Sounds like a farm vehicle.'

'Or a builders run-around. Bastards. It's bad enough that people have to work for the minimum wage in a dead-end job without having the bejeezus scared out of them late on a night with a sawn-off shotgun pointing at their noggin.'

'Any assaults?'

'Not yet.'

'With the gunman not talking, it could mean he's foreign.'

'Possibly. Unless it's a ruse.'

'So where are we heading?'

'Service station, near Scaling Reservoir on the A171. About a twenty minute drive.'

After garnering little additional evidence from the manager of the petrol station, or the traumatised attendant on duty the previous night, Frank offers them the usual spiel and makes his way outside with Prisha in tow.

'Not much to add from what uniform gave us, boss. Apart from one, or both of them have a sweet tooth.'

'Who can resist a Mars bar?' Frank replies as he wanders over to the bowser where the getaway vehicle was parked and crouches down to inspect the concrete. 'It's only a matter of time before they slip up. Right, come on, let's get back to the station.'

They climb into the car and set off.

'What other cases are on the go at the moment?' Prisha asks.

'Too many,' Frank responds wearily as he manoeuvres onto the main road. 'There's a serious assault from a couple of weeks back that left a young man in a coma. A stolen shipment of gin from a local business, estimated at over fifty grand. Or at least that's what they say. Probably bumping it up for the insurance. But the big one is an unsolved murder from six months ago. A woman by the name of Shirley Fox—murdered on a cold February evening not long after she left the Prince of Wales public house.'

'Where's that?'

'East side of the river. Below the abbey. I'll take you there later, but when you get back to the station, I want you to go over the case file. There's a hell of a lot to get through.'

'Any other details you can give me?'

'Shirley was fifty-four years old. There were no witnesses. No obvious motive. Hardly any forensics of any note and no CCTV footage.'

'Curious. Was she married?'

'Yes, to Dudley Fox.'

'And he had an alibi?'

Frank appears to lose patience. 'Prisha, I want you to go over the case file for two reasons; one, to get up to speed with the investigation, and two, a fresh pair of eyes on the details. If I tell you everything I know, I could unwittingly let my opinions sway your interpretation of the facts.'

'Sorry, boss. I was just wanting to get a head start,' she replies as she stares at the rolling North Sea in the distance, nestled between verdant fields and a pale sapphire sky.

Frank turns to her and smiles. 'I'm sorry. Apparently, according to my wife, I can sometimes come across as brusque. I'm not really. It's simply the Yorkshire way to be forthright.'

'No need to apologise. I have a thick skin.'

He smiles at her. 'Your partner should be at the station by now. I'll introduce you when we get back.'

'And who would that be?'

'DS Zac Stoker. Sad business,' he adds wistfully. 'He took two weeks' leave to spend some time with his mother. She was taken into a hospice a few weeks ago.'

'Oh dear. How is she?'

'She passed away peacefully last week.'

Stilted silence follows.

'What's he like?'

'Zac? He's a damn fine detective... in the making. Still some way to go, but he's a good egg. A big family man.'

'How old is he?'

'Thirty three. Been a DS for three years.'

'Similarities to myself.'

'You have a couple of years on him in the experience stakes. He has passed his inspectors' exam, though. How about you?'

'Passed it last year.'

'What was your score?'

'Eighty-nine per cent.'

'Holy thunder! That's classed as exceptional.'

'Apparently.'

7

Frank checks his watch and peers out of his office window into the large, soulless office. DS Zac Stoker and DS Kumar are in animated conversation as they point at a computer screen. He smiles to himself.

'Looks like they've hit it off.'

He pulls on his jacket and marches into the room.

'How are you going?' he asks Prisha.

'There's a lot to get through, boss. It will take me some days to get up to speed.'

'There's only so much you can glean from words on a computer screen. Come on, let's go for a little drive, then a walk.'

———◇———

They amble across the car park towards the unmarked pool car.

'Where are we going?' Prisha asks.

'I'll show you where he lives.'

'Where who lives?'

'Dudley Fox. What are your first thoughts about the case?'

Prisha mentally recaps what she's learnt so far, as she hops into the car and fastens her seatbelt.

'Shirley Fox used to meet up with three close friends on a Friday night once a month at the Prince Of Wales pub. It was a regular occurrence, one which had been going on for years. On Friday 20th February this year, she met with Claire Rowan and Mandy Dempsey in the pub at approximately 7:30 pm. Another friend, Libby... erm...'

'Libby Hobson,' Frank interjects.

'Yes, Libby Hobson wasn't present, as she was unwell. Shirley and her husband had a routine established for her nights out. Fifteen minutes before she was ready to leave the pub, she'd always text him. If the weather was bad, Dudley would drive, park up and meet her inside the pub. If the weather was fine, then he'd walk the back way, past the abbey, to meet her with their dog, usually arriving as Shirley left the pub or a little further on up Church Lane.

On the night of her murder, she sent a text to Dudley at 10:31 pm. It read—setting off in 15–walking. She said goodnight to her friends at 10:45 pm and left the pub by herself. The weather was good. Cold, but clear skies and a full moon. Her body was found at 11:03 pm at the bottom of the 199 Steps by a young couple who raised the alarm. She had a gash to the side of her head and had been strangled. She died of asphyxiation.

Dudley Fox never arrived that night because he'd fallen asleep in front of the TV and his phone, which he usually kept on charge in the living room, was on charge in the kitchen.

Therefore, he never heard the phone beep when Shirley's text arrived. There was no sign of sexual assault or robbery.'

Frank arches his eyebrows. 'You have good recall, sergeant.'

'Thank you, sir.'

'And what are your instincts telling you?'

'I think Dudley's alibi is weak, and as there are no other suspects, then...'

Frank interrupts her. 'And absolutely no evidence against him.'

'Not yet.'

'Don't fall into the trap that I did.'

'What trap?'

'Concluding that because there are no other suspects, and Dudley's alibi is impossible to prove, then he must be the killer. Tunnel vision is the Achilles' heel of many investigations.'

'As I said, I've only read the prominent parts of the case so far.'

Frank drives towards the River Esk and heads over Whitby Swing Bridge, then takes a right turn onto Church Street. They begin a gentle ascent with the murky green river to their right.

'It's hard to go anywhere in Whitby without getting beautiful views,' Prisha murmurs.

'Most of the town is built on the edge of two cliffs—the east and the west. Wait till winter comes around and it's blowing a gale with a biting wind coming in off the North Sea. Then maybe you won't find it as alluring. It can chill you to the bone in seconds.'

'I'm actually looking forward to it. Rugged and windswept and not as many tourists. It will feel like I've got the whole place to myself.'

Frank chuckles. 'You're an old romantic at heart, sergeant.'

The car takes a couple of lefts and turns onto St Mary's Archway. 'He lives up here on the left, number thirty-three.'

The car slows as they both peer out at the house.

'I'm a little surprised,' Prisha states.

'About?'

'I thought Dudley Fox was some bigwig scientist at Menwith Hill?'

'He is.'

'I'd have thought he would have something more palatial. This looks like ex-council housing.'

'I suppose he wasn't always a big shot. He probably bought it years ago when he got his first job after university. Homes are strange beasts. They hold a lot of memories. Some people don't like to let go, even if they can afford something grander. Anyway, it's a tidy little area with stunning aspects, and only a stone's throw from the hustle and bustle of the town centre. It backs onto the grounds of the abbey.'

They complete a loop of the small estate and pull back onto the main road.

'Okay, get your stopwatch out,' Frank says as he parks up in the community centre car park not more than a five-minute stroll from Dudley's house.

'What are we doing?' Prisha asks as she pulls her phone out and taps at an app on her screen.

'We're going to take the walk that Dudley usually took when he went to meet his wife. I've done this walk twice, from Dudley's place. At a steady pace, it takes ten minutes to reach the Prince of Wales, where Shirley Fox spent the evening. If you dawdle, which is what we are going to do now, it takes about fifteen.'

'Because of the dog?' Prisha says as she starts the timer on her mobile.

'Yes.'

'Why are we starting here?'

'Discretion. If Dudley sees us setting off from his house, it will only cause him more anguish and God knows he's been through enough of that.'

8

They follow the road to a T-junction and turn left, heading towards Whitby Abbey and the coast. After a few minutes' gentle stroll, they pass the Malting Pot brewery, then enter the turning area behind the abbey where the road officially ends.

'I've only been here a week and I've already fallen head over heels in love with the place,' Prisha gushes as she marvels at the ancient buildings and monuments. 'It's swimming in history. I could cut the atmosphere with a knife.'

'Into history, are you?'

'Yes, it's a side-hobby of mine.'

'You need to get together with my wife, Meera—she's a history buff. There's nothing she doesn't know about this place. She'd be delighted to show you around.'

'I take it you don't share her passion?'

They pass by a wrought-iron gate supported by ageless stone pillars which leads them into the graveyard of the Church of St Mary.

'No, can't say I do. What's in the past belongs in the past. Life's too short to be mithering with what's already been and gone. I'll stick to my allotment, and crosswords for my entertainment.'

They follow the main pathway, passing replica Victorian era gaslights and weathered gravestones leaning at sleepy angles. Prisha gazes to her left where a couple of Clydesdale horses are happily standing in a small paddock peering over a high stone wall at the continuous stream of tourists and passers-by. In the distance, the sun floods the undulating, fertile moors in golden shafts.

'Have you lived here all your life, Frank?'

'Not quite. I was born in Scotland, raised in Yorkshire. My father was Irish and my mother Welsh.'

Prisha grins. 'Holy moly! You're a mongrel, Frank.'

He chortles. 'Aye, you're not the first to say that. I started on the force when I turned eighteen. Moved to Whitby once I'd tied the knot with Meera. We lived in a place near to where you are now, up on the west cliff, close to the Whalebone Arch. Of course, I bet your place has undergone a renovation and is all nice and modern. Our first place didn't have any hot water or gas heating. Flagstone floors, damp on the walls, doors with gaps down the side where the wind blew in.'

'It sounds kind of romantic for a newlywed couple.'

Frank comes to an abrupt halt and stares at her.

'Romantic? Have you got rocks in your head?'

Prisha chortles. 'I'm sure if I posed the same question to Meera, she'd have a different interpretation.'

They continue walking. 'Aye, I dare say she would. But she has a tendency to peer back on the past with rosy-coloured spectacles.'

'Surely, you must have some fond memories of those times?'

'We didn't have a telly and not much brass, so we had to make our own entertainment.'

'Like board games and things?'

'Aye, that and sex.'

Prisha slaps him on the arm with the back of her hand.

'Frank!' she exclaims in mock horror.

'What? You don't think it was your generation who invented it, do you?'

'Can we change the subject, please?'

'It was you who asked.'

They come to the end of the narrow path and gaze at the intimidating 199 Steps.

'So these are the famous steps,' Prisha says.

'That's right. Bloody things,' he grumbles.

'What's the matter?'

'It's not too bad going down, but coming back up is a different kettle of fish. I should have known better.'

'You can always take a breather on one of the benches.'

'No. My father used to say it was bad luck to sit on the coffin benches.'

'The what?'

'Coffin benches. In the olden days, the pallbearers would carry the coffin up the steps to the church. The benches were to rest the coffin on and give the fellas a break.'

'It's very macabre and gothic,' Prisha says. 'But fascinating.'

As they reach the bottom, Frank nods at the last few steps.

'And this is where Shirley Fox met her end,' he says wistfully.

Prisha studies the area. 'Whereabouts exactly?'

Frank dodges a mob of tourists as they bustle past eating ice creams.

'Her head was on the fourth step next to the first railing post. Her feet were touching the bottom step. She was lying diagonally.'

'Any idea what weapon was used to cause the blow to the side of the head?'

'Something blunt. A cosh or possibly a torch.'

'Was she lying face up or face down?'

'Face up. There was an abrasion on her chin and hands, and a chipped front tooth.'

'That would suggest she fell face first, and broke her fall with her hands,' Prisha says, crouching. 'The blow to the head was probably not hard enough to knock her out, just daze her.'

'That's what we believe.'

'Which means the killer then turned her over to strangle her.'

An old couple with two dogs on leads stare with goggle eyes at Prisha and give her a wide berth as they pass.

'It appears that way.'

'Hell of a risk. And it rules out robbery. If they were after her handbag or phone, she'd have already been incapacitated from the blow. Why strangle her?'

'Could have been sexually motivated. There are a lot of dark alleys around here.'

'Meaning he may have intended to drag her out of the way but got disturbed.'

'It's one possibility.'

'Poor woman. What a way to go.'

'Aye, it's a rum do.'

9

I've had a dream run, which bodes well. Although, I don't believe in good luck, or coincidence. Fate does not pave the way of our destiny—planning does.

There has been little traffic on the one main road and virtually none on the back lanes.

I pull up in front of a farm gate, alight, and unhook the chain. The steel gate squeaks and groans its annoyance as I thrust it open. The disturbance attracts the attention of a small herd of cattle in the adjoining field which eye me suspiciously. They can't give witness statements, so I'm safe. I jump back behind the wheel and drive slowly through.

The dilapidated hay barn is two hundred yards ahead. Overgrown gorse bushes running along the perimeter obscure me from the holiday park further along the coast to the northwest. To the south and east, nothing but fields. Behind me, a few distant hills dotted with farm buildings. Dead ahead... the barren North Sea.

I am invisible!

There's only a couple of weeks left of the school holidays and although today's mission is risky, it's the best chance in a long time, and maybe the last opportunity until next year's summer holidays. I realise it's a long shot, and deep down, I don't really hold out much hope, but the adrenalin is surging through my veins, making me feel alive.

There is much at stake. If it goes wrong, I'll go down for a long time. Yet, the pot of shimmering gold that awaits me, if successful, is too tempting.

Everything has been so meticulously planned, I feel confident I can pull it off. Not necessarily today, but at some point.

An endeavour like this takes patience and nerves of steel. And the good thing is, I can always pull the plug at any moment if things unravel. All my actions will all appear completely innocent. No one harmed, no one suspicious. It just means the operation will have to be mothballed to let a bit of time pass between events. There's no rush.

I reverse into the shed and park up alongside a stack of hay bales and turn the engine off, leaving the keys in. I get out and slide open the side door.

'Come on little fellow,' I encourage. The puppy tentatively moves forward, slightly nervous, suspicious. I hold my hand out and he licks it as his tail wags furiously. Attaching a lead, I gently lift him from the vehicle and place him on the grass. He doesn't waste any time in relieving himself against the back wheel. I zip up my jacket to obscure the binoculars and set off towards the cliffs.

Turning the centre wheel on the binoculars, the lenses home in, bringing the girls into sharp focus. It's a fitting backdrop. Innocence in the foreground and the dark menacing silhouette of Black Nab in the background.

My heart is racing like I've taken a snort of amphetamine. But this feeling is better than any drug I've ever experienced. The excitement, mixed with fear, takes my breath away. They clamber over rocks, heading towards the bottom of the cliff. I scan up and down the beach, but cannot spot any adult that appears to be accompanying them. There are a couple of dog walkers far to the west, a woman sunbathing, and a family ambling along on the shoreline. None can see the girls from their vantage point.

It's decision time! I'll never get a better opportunity than this. Chance and fortune have favoured me. Can I hold my nerve?

I can pull out at any point... until I've handed them the drinks.

Their laughter and giggles drift to me on a gentle breeze coming off the sea as they begin the ascent. My conscience stabs at my soul as I wrestle with the known consequences.

Yes, it will be an ordeal for them, but a short-lived one. Yes, their parents will suffer. Friends, relatives, acquaintances will all experience it. The fear, the terror, the unknown.

The elixir of power overwhelms my tormented morality. For once... I am in control!

The reward is too great, too tempting. I deserve this for all the effort I've put in. I've taken a lot of risks and now my payday beckons. Just be strong and relaxed, don't freak them out or make them suspicious. Be my normal, casual, friendly self.

They are halfway up the grassy incline of the cliff. One of them stops, spins around and stares out to sea, while the other peers up to my position. She places a hand to her head, like a salute, to shield the sun. I wave at her. She says something to her friend. Now they both stare at me as I wave again. There's a brief pause until they recognise me and call my name, waving back, but venturing no further. Time for my secret weapon. I lift the dog up, grab his paw, and now he waves at them. Excited shrieks follow as they move with urgency upwards and onwards.

They reach me, puffing and panting. They're not concerned with me in the slightest, as my genial smile puts them at ease. They pat and cuddle the dog as I place him on the ground.

'Is it a he or a she?'

'It's a he. Bobby.'

'I didn't know you had a dog?'

'I didn't. Not until yesterday when I saw the suitcase.'

The girls stare at me, confused.

'Suitcase?' one of them asks. 'What do you mean?'

'You know the big oak tree near the main gate?'

'Yes.'

'I spotted an old suitcase.'

They both clasp their hands over their mouths as their eyes widen.

'No, please! Don't tell me it's true?'

'Initially, I thought someone had dumped it as we get a lot of rubbish thrown into the grounds. Bin bags, mattresses, boxes of bottles. It's too much trouble for some lazy sods to go to the council tip. They assume some other muggins will clean it up for them. I got out and went to pick up the suitcase. As I neared, I heard a whimper.'

The girls shut their eyes and shake their heads.

'Oh no! How could they? To such a beautiful and adorable puppy.'

They both drop to their knees and shower the dog in hugs and kisses.

'When I opened the suitcase, there he was. A little distressed but overall, safe and well.'

'What are you going to do with him?'

'Are you keeping him?'

I chuckle. 'Oh, yes. I've fallen in love with him.'

'What type of dog is he?'

That's a good question, and one I don't have a definitive answer to. The dog's breed was never considered in the master-plan. First error.

'Erm... not sure. He's definitely a terrier of some sort. Could be a Heinz.'

'A Heinz?' she asks.

'Yeah. Fifty-seven varieties.'

They both giggle.

It's still not too late to call the whole thing off. Nothing untoward has happened yet. But then again, I'm on a roll.

'The sad thing was, he wasn't alone.'

'What do you mean?'

'He had a brother and sister curled up next to him. They were sleepier, whereas this little fellow was a bundle of energy,' I add, rubbing the puppy's back vigorously.

'What, you mean there are two others like him?'

'Yep.'

'Where are they now?'

'Safe and warm. Probably snuggled on the thick woollen blankets I laid out for them. All I've got to do is find good homes for his brother and sister,' I add with an air of concern.

The girls grab each other in excitement.

'I've been asking mam and dad for ages if I can get a dog!' one of them cries.

'Me too! But they always say no.'

'If I can't find good homes for them, they'll have to go to the shelter.'

'You mean the RSPCA?'

'Yeah. I'll hate myself for doing it as they only keep them for so long before... well, you know.'

'No, what?'

'Come on, girls, use your imagination. I don't want to spell it out, but what usually happens to animals that are unwanted, unloved?'

Their wails of anguish and distress actually pull at my heart strings, which is ridiculous as the whole thing is fabricated—well, apart from Bobby or whatever the dog's real name is.

'No, no, no, you can't do that!'

'I won't have any other choice. Having Bobby is going to be a handful for me. I certainly can't manage another two.'

I make a deliberate play of glancing at my watch. 'Right, I better head off. I only get an hour for lunch, and I've already used up twenty minutes. See you later, girls!' I turn to leave, dragging the dog behind me.

'Wait!'

'What?'

'Can you take us to see them?'

'The other two puppies?'

'Yes!' they both yell in unison.

I frown and tilt my head to one side.

'Please! We beg you!'

I slump and relent.

'Only if it's okay with your parents. Where are they? Who did you come to the beach with?'

'Just my mam. She's sunbathing on the beach.'

'Fine. Call her and see if you've got permission. You both know me, so tell her who I am and where I'm taking you both. You can't be too careful these days.'

This is the critical juncture. What they say next will either abort the mission, or it will be full steam ahead. I've been

55

quietly assessing them, and I've not yet noticed a teenage girl's ever-present accessory on either of them.

'We don't have our phones with us. Mam made us leave them in her bag after I dropped mine in the water last year.'

Has this been pre-ordained? Surely, it's written in the stars. Things are moving quickly. No phone means no GPS tracking and no contact. This could not have been scripted better. It's decision time—stick or twist?

'I could use your phone to call her?' she suggests, gazing at me with wide, brown eyes, full of innocence and anticipation.

How much innocence will be left if I carry out the plan?

Another act of serendipity materialises as I realise I've left my phone in the car on the passenger seat. If I'd had it on me, they'd have spotted it bulging out of my back pocket.

The perfect storm gathers pace.

'Sorry, I left my phone at work. Not to worry, eh, maybe another time.'

'When are you taking them to the RSPCA?'

I shrug as I walk away again. 'Maybe tomorrow. I can't keep them at work. I could get the sack.'

The girls fall into a frenzied whispered discussion as I saunter off.

'How long will it take to get us back here?' she calls out.

I stop, turn, smile.

'Just over ten minutes there, ten minutes back, and five minutes with the puppies. You'll be back here in less than half-an-hour.'

The girls are in the back seats in a state of giddy excitement as they mollycoddle Bobby, talking at ten to the dozen. I start the engine.

'Are either of you thirsty? It's getting warm, and I noticed you don't have any water with you?'

'I'm gagging!'

'No, I'm good,' she says, stroking Bobby who is tired and ready for a sleep.

I pull out the cartons, remove the straws from the plastic wrappers and pierce the foil cap.

'Here you go. Drink this.'

'Ooh, ta.' She grabs it and sucks studiously on the straw.

'No thanks. I'm not thirsty,' the other insists.

'It doesn't matter. Take it and drink. Remember what you're always being told—keep your fluids up. You may think you're not thirsty, but you probably are.'

She reluctantly accepts the drink and lethargically sips at it. The other girl emits a small burp then apologises.

'Pardon me. All gone.'

I hold my hand out as she passes the empty carton back to me.

That's it. I've passed the point of no-return. There are no mitigating circumstances for drugging a thirteen-year-old girl. I'm guilty and if caught, I'll be looking at a minimum of ten to twelve behind bars, even if I don't take it any further. And now, another blip in the plan. The other girl is not interested in drinking. I need to remain calm.

'Come on, hurry up with your drink. I'm not setting off until it's finished.'

'Why?'

'Drinks in moving vehicles don't mix—spillage? Come on, get it down, it won't kill you,' I say, adding a chuckle and a caring smile for good measure.

She reluctantly obliges as she refocuses her attention onto the dog, who is now drifting into sleep.

'Okay, have you both got your seatbelts on?'

'Yes,' they both reply. I manoeuvre out of the shed and trundle slowly over the grass towards the open gate as my eyes scan back and forth between the rearview mirror and the field ahead.

She yawns, stretches, her eyes flicker. The other one is wide awake.

I near the gate and realise I can't be on the open road with two visible teenage girls in the back.

'Why are you stopping?'

'Sorry. It's not running right. I think I might have a flat.'

I jump out, adrenalin pumping and kick at the rear-offside tyre.

'Nothing wrong with that one!' I shout.

I lift my head and peer inside. Some good news, some bad. One girl is nearly asleep, the other is wide awake.

I take my time to inspect the other tyres before I hop back in.

'Is one of them flat?' she asks, stroking Bobby.

'No, all good,' I say turning around to witness one of them descend into sleep.

'I can't wait to see the puppies,' she says with a yawn, eyelids flickering.

I edge out of the entrance and stop. She yawns. My phone pings. I glance at it. A text from my aunty. I check the mirror. She's sporting a puzzled expression.

'I thought you said you'd left your phone at work?'

I laugh—unconvincingly. She detects the lie and immediately assesses her environment. She doesn't like what she sees. Confusion gives way to perception as she stares at her comatose best friend, the dog, her surroundings.

'I think I'd like to get out now,' she declares, heroically, but pathetically, as she tries the child-locked handle of the door.

Too late now for her and me.

'Hey, chill. Ten minutes and we'll be with the puppies. Why don't you rest your head? You look exhausted. I'll wake you when we get there.'

Her eyes try to fight the tiredness, but it's a losing battle. She gives me one last glare. She knows what I'm about and there's nothing she can do about it as she flops back into the seat.

I give it a minute or two, then lay the girls on the floor of the vehicle and cover them with a picnic blanket which was given to me by my aunty for my twenty-first birthday. I've never used it before. First time for everything. It's come in very handy.

Perfect... almost. Phase one complete. It was the hardest part. The next two stages should be a breeze. I'm buzzing!

10

Prisha stares down at the spot where Shirley Fox had the life squeezed out of her. She carefully does a three-sixty taking in the lay of the land.

'And nobody saw a thing,' she mutters to herself.

'Come on, let's get a bite to eat and we can discuss it,' Frank says as he takes her gently by the arm and coaxes her away.

'So where is the pub, the Prince of Wales?'

'Down here.'

They walk on no more than fifty yards and Frank nods towards it.

'Good grief, hidden away right on the bend of the road.'

She turns around and stares back at the murder scene.

'A blind spot, to anyone sitting in the Prince Of Wales,' she says. 'But what about the Lodge Inn?' she says indicating to another tiny pub directly opposite to where Shirley Fox was slain and adjacent to the Prince Of Wales. 'I cannot believe no one would have seen or heard anything from that vantage point.'

'You're correct... if it had been open. The brewery closed it down and put it on the market eighteen months back. It's only recently reopened.'

They edge sideways towards the pub where Shirley had her last ever drink.

Prisha pulls her phone out and stops the timer. 'Twelve minutes and forty-five seconds, minus a couple of minutes when we stopped at the steps.'

'Plus another five minutes for Dudley to get from his house to where we started at the community centre. That's nearly bang on fifteen minutes.'

'Which corresponds with Dudley's, and Shirley's friends accounts. Hmm...'

They enter the threshold of the pub and make their way to the bar, which is moderately busy.

'We're lucky, looks like we got here before the lunchtime rush. They do good grub here—you up for a bite to eat?'

'Yes, I am actually.'

'What are you drinking?' Frank asks as he pulls his bank card from his wallet.

'An orange juice, thanks.'

'Good choice. That means I can get a pint and you're driving back to the station.'

Frank orders the drinks as Prisha studies the bar menu.

'I'll go for the smoke salmon on rye with cream cheese and capers.'

The barman returns with the orange juice and an amber pint with a creamy head of Whitby Whaler bitter.

'Could I order the smoked salmon and cream cheese and I'll have four rounds of dripping on bread, thanks,' Frank says passing the barman his bank card.

Prisha eyes Frank suspiciously. 'Frank, please tell that isn't what I think it is?'

'I don't know what you mean.'

'Dripping on bread—is that fat?'

'Yes, beef fat to be precise, on white bread and lathered in salt. It goes perfect with a pint of bitter.'

She slaps her forehead with her palm. 'For God's sake, Frank! You need to start looking after yourself.'

He smirks. 'Calm the farm. I'm as fit as a fiddle.'

Instead of taking a seat on the westerly aspect of the pub, where they could have taken in harbour views, Prisha insists on sitting on the east side so she can stare out at the street where Shirley Fox met her end, even though she cannot see her final resting spot. Frank finds her request a tad ghoulish but reluctantly agrees.

'I take it you've watched the limited CCTV footage we obtained on the night,' Frank says as he takes a satisfying gulp of ale.

'Yes. There wasn't much of it.'

'No. The jewellers across the road, their security camera was on the blink. Footage from here showed her leaving the pub, but once she'd rounded the bend, she was out of sight. The only other footage was from the abbey. The only people it recorded was the young couple who found the body.'

'And you don't suspect them?'

'No. They're just kids. Both badly shaken up. Of course we checked them out but no connections or motives whatsoever.'

'What about house to house enquiries?'

'As you can see most of the downstairs properties are shops, so they close about six. A lot of the rooms above the shops are holiday rentals. All the holidaymakers were out and about enjoying Whitby's nightlife at the time of Shirley's death. Everyone was accounted for.'

'What about the house nearest to where her body was found?'

'A holiday rental as well, but it had been unoccupied for a few weeks as there was renovation work going on. The elderly woman who owns it lives in Bristol. She has a nephew who manages it for her.'

'Did he have an alibi?'

'Yes. Everyone we interviewed had alibis.'

The distant echo of a disembodied voice, via a loudspeaker distracts Frank. He cocks his head to one side like a dog that's heard a meow.

'What is it, boss?'

'Shush.'

A moment later, a rapid electronic beep can be distinctly heard.

'The lifeboat's being launched,' Frank says as their food is delivered. He takes a large bite of his dripping on bread and washes it down with another hefty slug of beer. 'Probably holidaymakers who have got themselves into trouble,' he remarks without too much concern.

He holds a sandwich triangle towards Prisha.

'Try it.'

Prisha turns her nose up in disgust. 'You've got to be joking. White bread, fat, and salt. It's enough to give you a heart attack before you leave the pub.'

Frank chuckles. 'You don't know what you're missing out on. Mind you, if my wife found out she'd have my guts for garters. She's got me on another bloody diet. As much as it goes against the grain to tell my officers to forget what they've witnessed—you've seen nothing—right?'

'Yes, Frank. I've seen nothing,'

She smiles with a slight shake of the head as her thoughts return to Shirley Fox.

'Were there any sexual assault cases either before or since Shirley's murder?'

'Only domestic related.'

'Only?'

'Sorry. I didn't mean to imply it as a lesser offence. I was indicating they weren't random assaults on strangers. The victim and perpetrator were either living together or had recently separated.'

'It could have been an out-of-towner; in which case we wouldn't have noticed a pattern. A random, opportunist attack.'

'Possibly. But murder is a big step up from sexual assault.'

'If he wasn't local, we don't know if he's murdered before.'

'Fair point, but why do you keep saying—he?'

'Just going on stats, boss. I know you've ruled out Dudley Fox as a suspect, but you'd be well aware that a high percentage of homicides are committed by people who the victim knew, more often than not a partner or close family member.'

'Yes. I'm aware of the statistics.'

11

After dinner they spend the next forty minutes exploring the tiny alleyways and hidey-holes in the vicinity until they find themselves on Collier's Hope, the harbour beach situated between the east and west piers. Prisha gazes forlornly out at the grey, brackish water, as gentle waves tumble onto the sand, disturbing the dirty tide mark. An air-sea-rescue helicopter hovers in the distance before banking sharply and heading off down the coast.

'That doesn't bode well,' Frank reflects.

Prisha turns to him. 'This place is a rabbit warren. There's a dozen different ways to get to the spot where Shirley was murdered without being seen. They could have come up through the town or sidled along the river to this beach. They could have come down by the side of the abbey or even climbed the cliff.'

'Yes. Which leads me to believe it had to be someone with extensive local knowledge so probably rules out holidaymakers. Come on, let's head back. I'm not looking forward to those bloody steps, I can tell you.'

They have to stop twice for Frank to catch his breath as they climb the arduous ascent towards Whitby Abbey.

'Anyone for dripping on bread?' Prisha says with a cheeky grin.

Frank half lifts his head and chucks her a withering glance.

'There's a cruel streak to you, sergeant. You'd do well to keep it in check,' he replies with a weary smile.

As they pass through the gateway and enter the abbey carpark, Prisha comes to a halt.

'I'll finish studying the case file when I get back, boss.'

'Good,' Frank pants.

'There is one minor thing which I noticed.'

'What?'

'Shirley Fox was supposed to meet with three friends that night but she only met with two; Claire Rowan and Mandy Dempsey.'

'That's right. Shirley's best friend was Libby Hobson. She texted Shirley earlier in the day to say she was coming down with a cold and was taking to her bed.'

They saunter on sidestepping droves of tourists who are making their way from the abbey, heading towards the old town.

Frank spots an ice cream van.

'Fancy a cone?'

'Yeah, why not. I'll have a ninety-nine.'

As they join the short queue, a young boy sitting on the ground next to the van catches Frank's attention.

'Look at that lad,' he murmurs to Prisha. 'Poor bugger's got a face like a slapped arse.'

He pays for three ice cream cones and wanders over to the morose looking boy.

'Here you go, sunshine. Get your laughing gear around this,' Frank says with a chuckle offering him the cone.

The boy is hesitant until he notices Prisha sidle up to Frank. He jumps to his feet and takes the cone.

'Thanks, mister.'

'Why the glum face?'

'My brother won't let me play with him. He's got some new mates and they're playing on the beach.'

'Ha! My brother used to pull that stunt on me. Do you know what I used to do?'

'No, what?'

'I'd make my own fun up, create my own adventure. You on holiday here?'

'Yeah. Staying at the holiday park on the clifftop.'

'Get yourself over the bridge and onto the front. Plenty of amusement arcades over there to cheer you up. Here, take this and make it last.'

He pulls a tenner from his pocket and pushes it onto the boy.

'Aw! Cheers mister!' he cries as he grabs the note and heads off with a spring in his step.

'That was very generous of you, Frank.'

'Not really. What's a tenner worth these days? Anyway, I can't bear to see unhappy kids. There's enough time to be miserable when you're an adult. Childhood should be all about fun, freedom, and exploration. It's precious.'

They casually saunter on.

'I've read the interviews from Claire Rowan and Mandy Dempsey who were in the pub with Shirley that night, but I couldn't see the interview with Libby. I'd have thought the main people involved would have been prioritised at the top of the case file. Maybe, I haven't got to it yet,' she adds as an afterthought.

'She wasn't interviewed. Not officially. I called her, and she confirmed what we already knew.'

Prisha lets out a huff of surprise and indignation which is not lost on Frank.

'Sergeant, if we interviewed *everybody* who wasn't in the pub that night then we'd have needed a thousand coppers and ten bloody years.'

'Hmm...'

'And what does that mean?'

Prisha falls silent, not wanting to throw correct procedure in her new boss's face, especially on her first day.

'Come on lass, spit it out. I encourage all my officers to be forthright with me, as I am with them. If you've got something on your mind, then let's hear it.'

'Okay,' she says gazing into his eyes. 'For one, it's slack police work. It's a loose end. And for another, it throws up other possibilities.'

'Such as?'

Prisha thinks for a moment as her imagination works overtime.

'What if the reason Dudley Fox didn't meet his wife that night was because he was having an affair with Libby Hobson, and they were together?'

'If he was, which I'm ninety-nine per cent certain he wasn't, then it would exonerate them both from the crime, wouldn't it? I'm not interested in extra-marital affairs, sergeant, I'm interested in the killer, or killers.'

'It's still a line of enquiry. Bumping off your partner to be with the person you truly love is not unheard of, and Dudley's alibi is weak. What if Dudley did actually meet his wife that night? She confronts him about Libby, they get into a fight, and he kills her.'

'You've seen where he lives on the Archway. It's a giant crescent. Houses opposite and side by side, over a hundred of the buggers. They were all door knocked and no one saw Dudley walking his dog, although many said it wasn't uncommon for them to notice him out for a late night stroll with Tyson, but not on the night of Shirley's death.'

'You said his back garden looks out onto the abbey?'

'Yes.'

'Then maybe he didn't follow the road but cut through the abbey grounds?'

'Which would have taken him right past the CCTV on the abbey.'

Prisha puckers her lips and drops the thread. They walk on in silence. Frank's conscience is pricking him. His sergeant has a valid point—it was slack policing and a loose end.

A murder with no witnesses was always intensive on police time, not only the door-to-door knocking of the locals but also every caravan park, static home, and campsite in the area. Still, it was no excuse and one he intended to remedy, even if it meant losing face in front of his new officer.

12

Frank and Prisha stroll towards the double glass doors of the station.

'Thanks for lunch and the ice cream, Frank.'

He smiles at her. 'It's my pleasure. By the way, it's called dinner around these parts.'

'Sorry?'

'We have breakfast, dinner, tea, and supper, oh, and elevenses.'

'I'll bear that in mind, sir.'

Frank opens the door and makes a beeline to the desk sergeant.

'I heard the siren earlier. What's happened?' he asks, as Prisha heads towards the stairwell.

The sergeant winces and takes a sharp intake of breath.

'Got a nines at about eleven twenty. Two thirteen-year-old girls have gone missing from Saltwick Bay. The mother was there with her daughter, and her daughter's best mate from about ten. They all sunbathed for a while until the girls decided to go for a walk.'

'Which direction?'

'East to explore Black Nab. Anyway, the mother was becoming concerned by about eleven and went to search for them, but couldn't see them anywhere. She called 999, and we had two special constables in the area. They were on the scene within about fifteen minutes and raised the alarm. The coastguard and lifeboat were onto it within minutes. They have two boats out and air-sea-rescue looking for them. A handful of local fishermen are also out in their boats.'

'Hell, that's no good. Although, the sea is like a millpond. Did the girls not answer their phones?'

'They left them with the mother. We have six officers down there now scouring the beach, along with the parents and some members of the public. I'm liaising with the coastguard, but so far, no sighting.'

Frank glances at the clock on the wall. 'We still have plenty of daylight left. The coastguard do a good job so let's keep our fingers crossed.'

'Yes. There but for the grace of God, go I,' the desk sergeant murmurs as he thinks of his own children.

'Were they strong swimmers?'

'Details are sketchy at the moment as the first responders are still on the beach. But from what they said over the radio, the girls were competent, if not Olympic contenders. We'll know more once the search finishes for the night and their reports are submitted.'

'Family liaison officer?'

'On the beach with the parents.'

'Good. Not my domain, but keep me informed if you hear anything.'

'Will do, Frank.'

13

Frank sucks the last of the juice from the pork bone, then scoops up the remnants of pineapple rice onto his fork and shovels it into his mouth.

Meera emits a long chuckle. 'Something tells me you enjoyed it?'

Frank pushes the empty plate away. 'Meera, I love everything you cook, but sticky jerk and brown sugar ribs with pineapple rice is your pièce de résistance. It's nearly as good as my roast beef and Yorkshire puds.'

Meera stands and collects the plates. 'Ha! Nearly as good, indeed. Now, don't sit there man, you can help with the clean-up.'

'I've had a busy day,' he laments as he presses the remote control and the local news blinks onto the TV screen.

'And don't you think I've also had a busy day at the hospice? It's not only physically tiring but mentally. Molly is going downhill day by day. It's only a matter of time. I've seen it too many times before. When she talks about her childhood, she's lucid, articulate; her eyes sparkle as she comes alive. When I ask her what she wants for tea, all she repeats is "don't worry,

Arthur's getting fish and chips." I know I've done the job for over thirty years, but it doesn't get any easier when you know they're on the way out.'

'How old is she?' Frank asks as he reluctantly follows his wife into the kitchen.

'Ninety-four.'

'Holy shite! She's had a bloody good innings.'

'And there's no need for that language, Frank Finnegan! I've told you before, I don't want cursing in this house. You're not at the station now.'

As she scrapes food remnants into the bin, he inches up behind and drapes his arms around her, then rests his head on her shoulder.

He takes a deep breath. 'What would I do without you? You make everything worthwhile.'

She puts the plates down and turns around, kissing him gently on the lips as her arms cradle his neck.

'Now don't you go getting all frisky, old man, because that is not on the menu tonight.' She grips him in a firm embrace. 'And how was your day?' she adds, pulling away.

'Oh... yeah,' he replies, opening the dishwasher.

'I see. Not good, but not bad.'

'The new girl, Prisha, is sharp. So that's good. Another petrol station robbery and no leads, so that's bad. Oh, and two young girls went missing off Saltwick Bay mid-morning. The coastguard are on to it, but if they haven't found them by now, then I fear the worst.'

'Sweet Lord, let them be safe,' Meera whispers. 'I heard the helicopter earlier, but assumed it was a vessel in distress or something. We'll pray for the girls before bed.'

'Your prayers won't help them. Only bloody good fortune.'

She flicks him on the backside with a damp tea towel as he's bent over stacking the plates.

'Heathen! The Lord can perform miracles.'

'Can he? Then maybe I should get him on my team as a consultant because I could do with some divine intervention.'

As he slams the dishwasher door shut and presses the start button, the voice from the TV distracts him. He re-enters the dining room as footage of the local lifeboat, coastguard, and helicopter flash across the screen.

"The girls went missing about 11 am and despite an intensive sea search by the coastguard and lifeboat, and a ground search by police, family, and members of the public, the girls have yet to be found. And now, to today's other top stories."

He shuts the TV down and picks up The Guardian newspaper and quickly flicks to the crossword.

'Don't suppose there's any pudding on the go?' he shouts towards the kitchen.

'No! You're on a diet, remember? Puddings are off the menu for the month. I'll make you a cup of green tea. It supposedly aids digestion.'

'Great... green tea and another thing missing from the menu,' he mutters to himself as he reaches for a pen, then studies the first cryptic clue.

"Willie sings a song to Hardy—but not Oliver."

'Oh, come on, that's too easy. Give me something to stimulate the grey matter,' he says as he inks "Nelson" into the white boxes. 'Willie Nelson, Thomas Masterman Hardy of Lord Nelson fame. Is this The Guardian or The Beano?'

14

Tuesday 18th August 7:45 am

Frank kisses his wife on the cheek. 'Bye, love. Have a good day.'

'And you, too. Be careful. I'll see you tonight,' she calls after him as he ambles happily down the narrow brick path that cuts a swathe through a manicured lawn bedecked on its boundaries by a myriad of blooming flowers.

'Foxgloves look magnificent,' he mumbles to himself.

'Should I get something for tea or are you cooking?'

Frank pulls open his car door and turns to his wife.

'I was thinking of fish and chips,' he replies, hoping his wife's mind is still a little groggy so early in the morning.

'Oh no, you don't. You can buy some wet fish and shallow fry.'

'Homemade chips?' he enquires expectantly.

'No! You can make a nice salad to go with it.'

'Yes, Meera.' He starts the engine and takes in the magnificent views over Whitby sea front. 'Looks like another day in paradise, or as near as damn it.'

He's a little surprised to see a lot more cars than usual parked up at the back of the station.

'Eh up, something's going on,' he murmurs as he navigates the car into a parking bay.

He grabs his briefcase and tub of sandwiches from the passenger seat and alights, before noticing the superintendent's car parked in a reserved spot.

'Oh, hell! What does she want?' he curses as he realises something big must have happened overnight. Heading towards the building, he checks his phone for any missed calls or texts, but there's nothing.

The desk sergeant is not in his usual seat. Instead, a young, uniformed female constable is staffing the area.

'Morning, sir,' the young woman greets him with a smile.

'Morning, constable. Any news on the missing girls?'

Disappointment replaces her smile. 'I'm afraid not, sir. They resumed the search at first light.'

'Hmm...' Frank grunts. 'I noticed the superintendent's car in the carpark.'

'Yes, sir.'

'Any idea why she's honoured us with a visit?'

The constable shrugs. 'Not the foggiest, unless it's to do with the girls.'

'That's the coastguard's job,' Frank says as he hurries through the double doors and climbs the back stairs.

In the CID room he's pleased to witness Prisha, Zac and two detective constables busy at their computers and it's still ten minutes before their shift starts.

'Ah! This is what I like to see,' he declares. 'The early bird catches the worm.' Everyone looks up from their work, but their expressions telegraph concern.

'The superintendent wants to see you, boss,' Zac states almost apologetically.

'Any idea what it's about?'

Prisha shifts nervously in her seat. 'I think it's best she explains.'

Frank slips out of his lightweight jacket and folds it over his arm. 'I see. Where is she?'

'In your office along with Chief Inspector Pearson, boss.'

'Two bundles of joy for the price of one. Sounds serious,' Frank says with a wry smile as he heads towards his office.

He knocks once on the door and lets himself in. Detective Superintendent Anne Banks is sitting in a chair behind Frank's desk. Chief Inspector Iain Pearson, in charge of uniform, is sitting bolt upright in a chair opposite. Both officers rise to their feet as handshakes are exchanged.

'Ma'am,' Frank nods deferentially towards his superior. 'Iain,' he adds.

'Take a seat, Frank,' Superintendent Banks orders officiously. The offer to take a seat in his own office rankles, but he pushes the grievance aside. To be paid a visit by the chief inspector and the superintendent on the same day is something of a rarity.

'It's about the missing girls,' the superintendent begins. 'We are broadening the line of enquiry to include a land search.'

Frank frowns. 'And why's that?'

The Super pushes a report towards him.

'It's from one of the young special constables who was first on the scene at Saltwick Bay yesterday.'

He quickly scans the report, taking in the salient details and skimming the fluff.

He pushes the report back towards the Super.

'I see. Good police work by the special constable. It certainly opens up new possibilities into the girls' disappearance. Does this mean the sea search has been called off, ma'am?'

'No. There's still a possibility they were swept out to sea, but it's been over twenty hours since the alarm was raised. Something should have turned up by now. The beaches around the coast of the country are heaving with holidaymakers, and so far, nothing has washed up. We'll leave the coastguard to do their job, and we'll do ours. We'll treat this as a major, missing persons search. If the girls weren't washed out to sea, then where are they? I want you to initiate a full scale land search.'

Frank studies the bony facial structure and grey hair of his Super. His relationship with her has always been business-like, professional, mechanical. She's humourless and dour, but fair and reasonable.

'Okay, I'll put a team together immediately, but I'm going to need more resources,' Frank says as he feels a tingle through his body.

'How many have you got in CID at the moment?' she asks

'I have three detective sergeants, four detective constables and myself.'

'You can have three uniformed constables and four special constables from Whitby, and I'll pull in another five officers from Scarborough, York, and Northallerton. Spread the load,' Chief Inspector Anderson says, another sombre individual. 'You're going to need a lot of boots on the ground, Frank, especially with the influx of holidaymakers.'

'Yes. I could do with more bodies than that,' Frank adds thoughtfully as he mentally counts the resources heading his way. 'There's going to be a hell of a lot of door knocking and visiting campgrounds and holiday parks.'

'We could always do with more, Frank,' the Super says coldly. 'But we are spread very thin at this time of year. We had that triple murder over in York a fortnight ago, otherwise I could have drafted in more from there. Anyway, it is what it is. You'll have to make do.'

'Understood, ma'am. But I do need an inspector on the case. We need a chain of command.'

Chief Inspector Anderson uncrosses his legs and laughs.

'You'll be lucky. Inspectors are as rare as rocking horse shit at the moment.'

The Super rises to her feet. 'He's right. You can make one of your sergeants acting DI. Give me a name, Frank, and I'll authorise it and get the paperwork done.'

Frank considers his three options before immediately discounting Jason Cartwright, even though he's the longest serving detective sergeant. It's a tough call, but his decision is made.

———⋅◦⋅———

'Prisha, Zac... in my office, please.' Frank takes his seat behind his desk and pulls up the case file of the missing girls, which has already been updated with photos, particulars, and reports from the two special constables who were first on the scene. The two sergeants enter the office.

'Take a seat,' he says. 'This is now a missing person's investigation and time is of the essence. We've lost nearly a day, which in these situations could be critical. I'm SIO on the case. We've been allocated numerous uniforms from our station and various other locations. Hopefully, all feet should be on the ground by midday, at which point I'll hold a briefing. Unfortunately, I wasn't allocated an inspector, which means, sergeant Kumar, you are promoted to acting detective inspector.'

'But sir, I... I'm obviously honoured, but don't you think Zac should have got the role,' she stammers as she throws Zac an apologetic glance. 'I mean, I've only been here a day. Zac knows the area and has contacts, and...'

Zac's face is like thunder, but he remains silent. Frank holds his hand up and leans forward.

'Prisha, you got the role because you have a few years more experience than Zac. That's the only reason.' He swivels his eyes onto Zac. 'I know this might feel like a kick in the balls, Zac, but I promise you it isn't. You're a good detective, as is Prisha. You'll feel a little hurt, snubbed, but you need to banish those emotions. We have two young girls to find, and that's way more important than bruised egos.'

Zac relaxes and after a moment's reflection, he offers his hand to Prisha.

'Congrats, Prisha. I'm sure you'll do a great job.'

Prisha sheepishly shakes his hand.

'Look on the bright side, Zac; as a sergeant you'll qualify for overtime which the Super's authorised, whereas an inspector will only get time off in lieu.'

Smiles crack on their faces.

'Well... I have been saving for a new car,' Zac says with a chuckle.

'That's the spirit. Anyway, you two will be working closely together. Prisha, you'll be heading up Team A. Zac, you'll be in charge of Team B.'

His attention returns to his computer screen as he re-reads the report from the special constable.

'So, we have a couple of footprints on the cliff east of Saltwick Bay,' he murmurs.

'Yes, boss,' Prisha confirms. 'Forensics have taken some good prints and the girls' parents have confirmed what type of footwear the girls were wearing yesterday.'

Zac continues. 'Emma Tolhurst was wearing a pair of Adidas Superstar trainers and Zoe Clark, a pair of Converse Run Star Motions.'

He pulls out his phone and shows Frank pictures of the footwear he's already downloaded from the internet.

Prisha leans forward and points at one photo. 'As you can see, the Run Stars have a very distinctive sole.'

Frank studies the rows of horizontal and vertical ridges that adorn the sole. 'Hell, do people actually wear those things? They look as uncomfortable as all buggery.'

The two sergeants laugh. 'They're the dog's bollocks,' Zac explains. 'You wouldn't get much change out of a hundred quid.'

'A hundred quid for a pair of pumps,' Frank murmurs, confounded by the modern world.

Prisha points at the photo on Frank's computer screen.

'Anyway, boss, as you can see, the photo the special constable took on her phone of the footprints is almost identical to the Run Stars.'

'Hmm... do we know the girls' shoe sizes?'

'They're both size 7.'

'I see. We need to get a pair of these Run Stars to give to forensics and see if the soles match.'

'Already onto it, boss,' Prisha says, glancing at the clock on the wall. 'I have a list of shoe and sports shops in the area. They open in ten minutes. I'll go myself.'

'Good work all round. Of course, this doesn't mean that we ignore our other pressing cases, in particular the Shirley Fox murder, and the armed robberies, but you're both experienced in working multiple cases at a time. However, finding those girls safe and well takes precedence for the moment. Understood?'

'Yes, boss,' they both nod.

The officers await further instruction as Frank stares at the images of the shoes.

'Inspector Kumar! Are you still here? I thought you had a pair of shoes to collect?'

'Yes, boss. On my way.'

She leaps to her feet and scurries out of the door, with Zac trailing behind.

'Zac, a moment,' Frank calls out. The sergeant stops and eyeballs his boss.

'Yes?'

'Are you okay with this?'

Zac flashes Frank a broad, warm grin. 'Yes, boss. I'm cool. Like you said, it's not about me—it's about the two girls.'

'Good man. Is Kylie Pembroke on duty today?'

'Yes. I saw her walking across the car park not more than ten minutes ago.'

'Can you send her up to me? I want a quick chat.'

'Sure, boss.'

Special Constable Kylie Pembroke is sitting nervously in Frank's office, awaiting his return. She fidgets at her uniform. She's heard differing accounts about DCI Finnegan. Some say he's a grumpy tyrant whose explosive temper can leave some officers in tears. Others say he's a decent, easy-going older man with a sense of humour and a gentle touch. She assumes the truth lies somewhere between.

'Ah! Pembroke,' Frank booms as he ambles into his office, carrying a steaming mug of tea.

'Morning, sir.'

'It's Kylie, isn't it?' She nods, apprehensive. 'Kylie, I've read your report.'

She instinctively feels she may have done something wrong, or left something out, or got the timeline of events muddled up. Frank flops into his leather recliner, which emits a whooshing sound.

'What's wrong?' Frank asks, as he studies her worried expression.

'Nothing, sir.'

'You look like you've lost a shilling and found sixpence.'

The young constable has no idea what that means.

'Sir?'

'Nothing. I've brought you here for a quick chat about yesterday's events and also to congratulate you on a piece of bloody good police work.'

She smiles as relief floods her body, putting her at ease.

'I notice you filed your report at 9:30 pm?'

'Yes, sir.'

'But your shift ended at 3 pm.'

'Sir.'

'That's dedication, especially for an unpaid officer.'

She offers a winsome grin.

Frank studies her report again. 'According to your account, you'd scoured the beach up to three miles east of Saltwick Bay. At about 8 pm, as you were heading back, you climbed the cliff approximately a mile from where the girls were last seen.'

'Yes, sir.'

'Why?'

'I knew there was only an hour's daylight left and I thought if I climbed to the top of the cliff, I'd get a better view.'

Frank nods. 'Go on.'

'About halfway up, I passed over a small stream. It only had a trickle of water in it because of the lack of rain lately. Further on the ground was wet and boggy. That's when I spotted three very distinctive footprints. By the size of them I knew they weren't adult footprints, and neither were they a child's footprint. I got my phone out and took a series of photos. I took my Hi-Viz vest off and placed it over two of the prints and weighed it down with a couple of rocks.'

Frank cracks a wide beam. 'To preserve the site for forensics?'

'Yes sir. The vest was not ideal, but it was the best I had available. I then called control via radio and told them what I'd found, and waited until forensics arrived.'

'Your personal file tells me you've been a special constable for over a year and you're studying archaeology at university.'

'Sir.'

'And when you've got your degree, then what?'

'Not sure yet, sir. I enjoy the police work, but I also enjoy going on archaeological digs.'

'Maybe forensics would suit you?'

'Maybe, sir.'

Frank abruptly lurches from his seat. 'I've had a word with your sergeant, and he's transferred you to my team until further notice. Are you happy with that?'

Pembroke, assuming their little chat is nearing an end, rises.

'Yes sir!' she exclaims, standing a few inches taller as her eyes sparkle with excitement.

'Good. Report to DI Kumar, who will give you further instructions. And well done.'

Kylie Pembroke floats out of the office as though walking on air.

15

Frank stands between a large investigation board and a whiteboard. The first board has a recent picture of Zoe Clark and Emma Tolhurst pinned to its centre. Above it, one word—MISSING!—cut from last night's local newspaper. A red piece of yarn, attached to the pin, stretches out to another pin, stuck into a photo of the sole of a sports shoe, with a neatly typed label underneath which reads—footprints approximately one mile south east of Saltwick Bay Beach, opposite Black Nab, near cliff top. To the left of the board is a printed timeline of the last known movements of the girls.

He gazes at the nineteen officers seated in front of him. All introductions have been made, and he's given a rudimentary overview of the case to date.

'I'll hand you over to DI Kumar,' he says as he takes a seat.

Prisha strides confidently forward, belying her inner turmoil.

'The missing girls are best friends, Zoe Clark, and Emma Tolhurst, both thirteen years old. They attend Carston Hall Public Girls School about fifteen minutes from Whitby, near Robin Hood's Bay.'

Prisha picks up a ruler and points at the timeline on the board and a photocopied zoomed in map of the area.

'At around 9:30 am yesterday, Sarah Clark, her daughter—Zoe Clark, and Zoe's best friend—Emma Tolhurst parked at the abbey pay and display car park and paid for three hours' parking.

They proceeded along the Cleveland Way towards Saltwick Bay Holiday Park, about a mile in distance, or twenty minutes' walk at a gentle pace. A little way past the holiday park is a set of steps leading down to a sandy beach. The time is now approximately 9:55 am.

They spread out beach towels. Sarah Clark read a book as the girls chatted. Within ten minutes, the girls were bored and informed Sarah Clark they were going for a walk to look at Black Nab—a large rock feature about a hundred yards off the coast and roughly five hundred yards from where Mrs Clark was sunbathing. The girls set off along the beach in an easterly direction. It's now approximately 10:05 am.

Sarah Clark told the girls not to be too long as they needed to set off back to the car about twelve-fifteen.

An important side note: neither of the girls had their mobile phones with them. Sarah Clark made them leave their phones with her, as the last phone Zoe Clark had was ruined when she dropped it in the sea last year.'

She glances at Frank for affirmation as her nerves ease, becoming ever more confident. Frank gives her a slow blink and an almost imperceptible nod.

'At 11 am Sarah Clark was becoming slightly concerned the girls hadn't returned, so went searching for them. By 11:20 am, and with no sightings, she panicked and called 999.'

'Lucky she didn't leave her phone behind,' DS Cartwright notes as he munches on a jam donut.

Prisha ignores him and continues.

'Emergency services informed us of the situation at 11:23. Two special constables were on their rounds close to the abbey and were dispatched to the scene, arriving there at 11:39.

One of the attending officers, Special Constable Pembroke, tried to calm the mother and asked if the girls had been wearing swimming costumes. The mother confirmed they were wearing costumes underneath their clothes. Both girls could swim but were not strong swimmers. The mother gave a detailed description of what the girls were wearing, including their footwear. By this time, about a dozen members of the public were also engaged in the search.

At 11:41, Special Constable Pembroke radioed through the information about the girls wearing swimming costumes, at which point the alarm was raised with the Coastguard Rescue Service and the local lifeboat. The coastguard, air-sea-rescue, lifeboat, and numerous fishing vessels took part in the search until dusk and resumed their search at first light this morning. However, let's step back in time a few hours.

At around 8:00 pm Special Constable Pembroke climbed a rocky spur further down the coast to get a better vantage point of the area. During her ascent, she came across three well-defined footprints. Their size indicated to her they could belong to an adolescent, and they had a distinctive marking. A marking she recognised as she has the same make of shoes as Zoe, although she wasn't wearing them at the time. She relayed this finding to control who organised a team of forensics, who eventually went out there to take imprints.'

She pauses and takes a sip of water.

'Any questions so far?'

A young constable, drafted in from York, raises his hand. Prisha nods at him.

'How far along were the footprints from where the mother had been sunbathing?'

'About a mile as the crow flies, but on foot maybe a mile and a half.'

'What's at the top of the rocky spur?'

Prisha glances at Pembroke.

'Kylie?' she says.

Kylie Pembroke reluctantly stands up. 'Erm... there's the walking track—Cleveland Way. To the south, south east, and west are open fields dotted with a few farms with the A171 in the distance. To the northwest, you're looking back on Whitby. It's fairly isolated, apart from the walkers along the coastal path.'

Another arm goes up, this time by a detective constable.

'Boss,' he says, referring to Prisha, who is slightly taken aback by the title. 'What about witnesses? Did anyone see the girls?'

Prisha holds her arm out to Zac.

'I'll let DS Stoker answer that.'

Zac makes his way to the front of the room and stands at the opposite end of the whiteboard to his colleague.

'So far, we have nothing. There weren't many people on the beach at that time of day and you've got to remember this isn't Whitby's main beach. Only the locals know about it and those staying in Saltwick Bay. Plus, it's not the greatest beach. A patch of sand and then it's all rocks. As for any walkers who were passing at the time, well, they're going to be hard to track down. We're hoping the media release may jog someone's memory.'

He points at the map.

'The sandy beach at the bay isn't huge. You could walk it in maybe five, eight minutes. Where the sand ends, it's replaced by rocks, as the coastline juts out into the sea. At high tide, it's impassable, but at low tide, it's perfectly safe, apart from slippery rocks and occasional rockfalls.

It's frequented by a lot of fossil hunters. As Prisha noted, Black Nab is a tall, naturally formed geographical feature standing about one hundred yards from the cliffs. I've checked with the coastguard and low tide yesterday was at 11:05 am, high tide at 17:17 pm.'

He jabs a finger into the map.

'The girls were still in the line of sight of Sarah Clark as they walked around Black Nab. The next time she looked, they'd disappeared from view. She assumed they'd wandered further along the beach, beyond the rocky spur which blocked her vision.'

The questions flow as another uniformed constable, from outside Whitby, raises his hand.

'Looking at the timeline, the girls left the mother at about ten and she raised the alarm at eleven twenty.'

'Correct,' Zac confirms.

'But realistically, if the girls went missing, what time do you think it was?'

'Hard to say,' Zac replies.

Special Constable Pembroke rises to her feet. 'I can try to narrow it down,' she says tentatively.

No one opposes her. She strides forward and places a finger on the map.

'I know Saltwick Bay well. From where Sarah Clark was relaxing, a walk to the rocky spur would take a gentle twenty minutes. The spur is not too arduous, apart from the bottom section, which is slippery, so you have to go slowly. It took me about ten minutes to reach the place where I found the footprints and it would be another five minutes to the top. All up, it would have taken about thirty-five minutes.'

'So the earliest time they could have reached that point, *if* they went directly there, would have been 10:40 am,' Zac elaborates. 'But we need to be cautious about exact times. I'd suggest an hour's timeframe between 10:30 and 11:30 am is when the girls disappeared.'

'I agree,' Frank says.

DS Cartwright stands up, clearly unimpressed with proceedings and directs his question to Frank.

'Boss, aren't we jumping the gun a little? Two girls wearing swimming costumes disappear off a beach. The most obvious explanation is they got into difficulties and were washed out to sea. Three footprints, which may or may not be theirs, doesn't mean they climbed the spur and disappeared. They could have climbed the cliff, come back down, then got into trouble in the water.'

Frank ambles to the front again, wary of how much time is being chewed up.

'As Zac explained, the tide was well on its way out when the girls set off. The swell was nearly non-existent, conditions calm, barely a breeze. There is always a chance one of them got into difficulties in the water—but both of them at the same time? These aren't toddlers we're dealing with.'

'And Sarah Clark said it would be extremely out of character for either girl to go for a swim. They'd paddle and splash each other, but that's all,' Prisha adds.

'Still, boss,' DS cartwright moans, not convinced.

'Cartwright, we are simply covering all bases. If the footprints hadn't been discovered, then this would have been left to the coastguard. However, if forensics come back with a positive ID on the prints compared to the shoes either girl was wearing, then we have to accept the possibility their disappearance was not via the sea... but by land.'

'Is there a chance they were abducted?' another uniformed constable enquires.

Frank rubs at the stubble on his chin. 'It's one of many possibilities. They may have met up with friends. They could have walked further down the coast, got too close to the edge, and been caught in a landslip that buried them alive. Let's not rule anything in or out at this stage.'

He claps his hands together to indicate it's time for action.

'Okay, listen up, everyone. Team A will be headed by DI Kumar; Team B by DS Stoker.' He turns to Prisha. 'I want your team to focus on friends, family, siblings, boyfriends... or girlfriends. You need to go to the girls' school and get a list of close friends, and question all the teachers who aren't on holiday, and anyone else who works at the school. We need to find out what sort of kids they're really like. Are they the type to do a runner? Have they been in trouble before? Are they risk-takers? Also, dig deeper with the parents and close family members, but go easy.'

'Yes, boss.'

'Oh and check the sex offenders' register and get a list of anyone within a twenty-mile radius and interview them. Anyone who doesn't have a verifiable alibi, bring them in for questioning.'

'Boss.'

'DS Stoker, your team is going to do a lot of the grunt work. I want every house east of the river door knocked, that includes holiday parks, campgrounds, hotels, farms, B&Bs. All names and addresses are to be meticulously catalogued. Anyone who isn't home, make a note and follow up later. Once you've organised that, you can help Prisha with the interviews.'

'Sir.'

Frank focuses his attention on the rest of the team.

'You'll be pleased to know the Super has authorised overtime.'

A loud cheer erupts as Frank grins at them.

'Mercenaries,' he mutters. 'However,' he yells above the din, 'I don't want anyone working eighteen hour shifts. You need to be fresh and alert. You're no use to me or the team if you turn up to work after four hours sleep and haven't eaten in twenty hours. Do your job, go home, rest, eat, hydrate, sleep then get back here at 7:30 am, sharp! Do I make myself clear?'

'Yes, boss!'

'And Cartwright?'

'Yes?'

'You're on the graveyard shift.'

'Aw! Come off it boss. I'm in a darts team and we're into finals week.'

'I don't care if you're in the world donut eating championships! You're on night shift. And this goes to you and anyone else: when I'm not on duty, you can ring me any time of day or night. But I'll warn you; if you wake me up on a trifling matter, then woe betide you—I'll have your guts for garters! At my age, I need my beauty sleep.

And lastly, let's remember what this is about. Two young girls, who've barely begun life, are missing. It's our job to reunite them with their parents—the sooner the better. Right, let's get cracking. Good luck team.'

Good-natured banter and laughter breaks out as Frank marches back to his office amidst a flurry of activity.

16

Prisha pulls into the palatial driveway of Carston Hall School. As the tyres crunch over pebbles, she admires the rich greenery of trees which cloister the avenue. Shafts of sunlight filter through like golden, spidery fingers.

When she transferred from West Midlands Police to North Yorkshire, she was expecting the occasional mugging, robbery, burglary. After all, it has one of the lowest crime rates in the country and yet barely a day into the job and she's investigating a murder, a series of armed robberies and now, two girls who have mysteriously disappeared.

Charles Murray is the deputy principal of Carston Hall, an exclusive girls' public school. She talked briefly with him an hour ago to organise her visit. It's an old anachronism—public school, what it really means is it's a private school and if you want to send your little darlings here, then you better have some serious money.

As she rounds a bend, a man is standing on stone steps, awaiting her arrival. She assumes it's Charles Murray. The driveway was impressive, but the giant building behind him is breathtaking. It is more like a country house, which wouldn't be out of place in a Jane Austen novel or Downton Abbey episode.

As she alights from the car, he's already on her, shaking her hand, offering a warm smile.

'Ah, DI Kumar, I take it? Charles Murray. Pleased to meet you.'

'Likewise.'

'Follow me.' He briskly turns around and heads to the enormous entrance. 'I see you came in an unmarked car.'

'Yes. I'm CID. We always use unmarked vehicles.'

'Good, good. I was hoping you'd be discreet.'

She hurries to catch up with him.

'Discreet?'

He stops. 'Yes.'

He drops his head and takes a quick look around, although the place is empty apart from a pair of peacocks strutting through the extensive gardens.

'Having blue flashing lights and sirens wailing is not a good look for the school. I'd rather keep things low key.'

Prisha narrows her gaze, which leaves him in no doubt about her reaction.

'That's not to say I don't appreciate the full gravity of the situation and, of course, I, all staff, and students will assist the police in any way we can to help expedite the issue.'

She's already taken a dislike to the man.

Expedite the issue? We're not investigating a broken down photocopier, or a leaky cistern—these are two girls we are talking about; two girls who could be in danger, if the worst has not already happened.

The inside of the building is in keeping with the outside appearance. Oak panels, old dusty paintings of landscapes, highly polished wooden floors with a swathe of Paisley carpet running down the middle, ornate vases, and ancient heirlooms adorn the hallway.

'This place must be what... early Victorian?' she enquires.

As they stride up a circular staircase, the deputy principal comes alive.

'It's late Georgian—1815, to be precise. Lord Carston built it for his family. He was an early industrialist. The building became a girls' school in 1919, not long after women first got the vote. In fact, we name our sports houses after four prominent suffragettes; Fawcett, Pankhurst, Davison, and Singh.'

By the time they reach his office, Prisha has undergone a crash course in the history of Carston Hall and some of the glittering illuminati who have graced its hallowed corridors.

They enter a large room with magnificent views of the extensive gardens which surround the school. A row of three enlarged framed photographs line the back wall portraying different buildings. In the foreground is a group of smiling kids. In two of the photos, they are sporting walking gear, and in the other, they are wearing wetsuits. Charles Murray is front and centre surrounded by the children, albeit when he was younger.

'They all look happy,' she says, pointing to one of the photos.

'Yes. We'd just got back from an overnight trek on the moors when that picture was taken, so everyone was quite relieved. That's Westerdale Grange.'

Her eyes flit to the next photo and the kids in wetsuits.

'And this?' she asks.

'That's our beach retreat.'

He makes it sound like an old wooden shack when, in fact, it's a glorious old manor house.

'And where's that?'

'Cornelian Manor is a few miles north of Cayton Beach, which has some of the finest surfing on the east coast. We have six retreats in all. Four in North Yorkshire, one in Scotland and one in the Lake District. We use them for outdoor pursuits; fell-walking, kayaking, mountain-biking, surfing, that sort of thing.'

Lucky for some.

'From your website, I understand this is also a boarding school?'

'That's correct.'

'How many boarders?'

'We have twenty-two. Although, we only have eight permanent boarders, and only four are with us at the moment.'

'Sorry, I don't understand.'

'We accommodate day girls... those who bus in each day. Then there are the term boarders—those who board with us during the school term. And we have permanent boarders who are with us all year round.'

She's shocked. 'Are you telling me some girls spend the entire year here?'

He smiles in a patronising manner. 'Yes. Not many, just the eight, like I said. I understand you must find it old-fashioned, Inspector Kumar, but I've crunched the numbers and the ones who are permanent boarders achieve a far higher success rate than the temporary boarders, and higher again compared to the day girls.'

'But what about family time? Birthdays, Christmas, Easter, holidays?'

'Some parents see that as an unnecessary distraction from their children's studies.'

'And do you see it as an unnecessary distraction... to be with family?' she asks.

He offers her a seat and smiles. 'I'm not one to stand in judgement... tea?'

'What? Erm, yes, black, no sugar, thanks.'

She tries to refocus on the two missing girls. There's no need to become riled by privilege, and what she would call child abuse by dumping your kids in an overbearing environment and forgetting about them, all in the name of education.

'It shocked me when I saw the reports yesterday about the missing girls,' he states as he prepares the tea. 'Terrible business. Still no news?'

'I'm afraid not, although we are widening our investigation. That's why I'm here.'

He appears to freeze for a moment before picking the kettle up.

'Widening your investigation?'

'Yes. We are not entirely certain the girls were swept out to sea. There is a possibility they went missing on land.'

'I see. And what makes you think that?'

'I'm not at liberty to say.'

He places the tea down on the leather bound desk in front of her. His hand trembles slightly, making the cup rattle in the saucer. Prisha studies him. He's tall, lean, and handsome in an old-fashioned way. But he's also ugly. Some people say you should ignore looks and go for personality—a lesson she's yet to learn. He sits down opposite and lifts the lid on a laptop as she pulls out a notepad.

'How many students attend Carston Hall?'

'Three-hundred and eighty, last year. Next term, four hundred and twelve, which is pushing our upper limit.'

'And how many teachers?'

'Twenty-five full time, fifteen part-time, plus numerous private tutors who are on call for those who need a push up the ladder. Of course, those numbers don't include myself or the principal.'

'What about ancillary staff?'

'An accountant, a media manager, a head receptionist, three support staff, a site manager—or caretaker in the old money; a part-time gardener; two part-time cleaners; a boarding manager, and two boarding assistants—typically ex-students who are in a gap year.'

'I take it all staff are police checked and have their working with children licence?'

He sits upright and freezes for a split second before his head snaps violently to one side.

'Of course, inspector! Even contractors who enter the grounds to do maintenance work have to produce their credentials to me before they begin work. We have a reputation to preserve. That's why this business isn't good for anybody.'

This guy beggars belief. 'You think the school being mentioned in the media reports could have an adverse effect?'

'Yes. Parents can be fickle, especially when they're paying a lot of money for their child's education. The sooner the girls are found, the better for all.'

'Safe and well?'

'Sorry?'

'The sooner the girls are found... safe and well?'

He shuffles in his chair. 'Yes, that goes without saying. My primary concern is the girls' welfare. My secondary concern is for the school's reputation.'

'On the phone, you said the principal was on holiday.'

'Yes, she is.'

'Have you contacted her?'

'I've tried calling twice, but unfortunately her phone appears to be out of range.'

'Where's she holidaying?'

'Africa—on safari.'

'Of course.' *How the other half live.* 'I'm going to need a list of...'

He interrupts her as his fingers hammer at the keyboard on his laptop. 'I've already pre-empted you, inspector. I take it you'll require names, addresses, and phone numbers of all staff and students.'

'Not all staff and students. We don't have the resources for that, but if you could give me a list of all students in the girls' homeroom and all the teachers who taught them last year, that will do for the moment. If any names crop up, not on the list, then I'll call you for their details.'

'Certainly.'

With a few more clicks of the mouse, the inkjet printer comes to life as he beams at her.

'I'm a bit of a wizard with spreadsheets.'

He walks over to the printer and retrieves the printout.

'Have you ever taken Zoe or Emma for classes?'

'No. Not that I can recall. I only fill in when a teacher is off sick.'

'But you know the girls?'

He shrugs as he hands her the list. 'I recognise their faces. But honestly, I can't say I've had any interaction with them.'

'I see. I'm trying to build up a picture of their personalities.'

He pulls open an old wooden filing cabinet and retrieves two folders.

'This is their end-of-year reports from their home teacher, Miss Butler.'

He sits down and studies the documents before pushing them across to her.

'As you can see, they appear to be diligent and hardworking girls without being outstanding. Behaviour appears to be good with only one misdemeanour recorded throughout the year for Zoe Clark.'

She skims across the grades and the summary by their teacher.

'It doesn't state what the misdemeanour was?'

'No. It must have been a very minor infraction that was dealt with by Miss Butler. If it had been serious, then Zoe would have been sent to me to deal with it.'

'What do you class as a minor infraction?'

He takes a gulp of tea. 'Oh, it's typically something to do with school uniform. The girls like to wear their dresses short. It's school policy that the hem of the dress is below the knee.'

'Who are on the school grounds at the moment?'

'Myself, the four boarders, two boarding assistants, and Mr Bridges. Everyone else is away. There's still another two and a half weeks before the new school year starts. About a week before school resumes, teachers will start drifting back in to prepare for the forthcoming term.'

'And Mr Bridges is?'

'Oh, sorry, the site manager.'

'Caretaker?'

'Yes.'

'And what's he like?'

'Excellent, I cannot fault the man. He's diligent, punctual and can turn his hand to almost anything.'

'Such as?'

'Blocked toilets, broken desks, sticky doors, even minor electrical work. This is what he calls his busiest time of year. When the school is deserted, he can come and go unimpeded.'

'Do you know Zoe and Emma's parents—Mr and Mrs Clark and Mr and Mrs Tolhurst?'

A head shake follows. 'I'm afraid I'm not being much use to you, inspector.'

'How much are day fees for the year?'

'They start at eight-thousand pounds for year sevens and rise incrementally, finishing at twelve thousand pounds for year twelves. Of course, that's indexed to inflation.'

She takes a sharp intake of breath. 'That's a lot of money to find out of a household budget.'

'I'm afraid a good education costs money—it always has. I can tell by your face you don't agree with me.'

'I believe education should be free for all, and that everyone should start on the same level playing field.'

He chuckles. 'Ah, an old-fashioned socialist.'

'Not at all. I don't have a preference for any political party. They're all a shower of... well, you know.' She finishes the last dregs of tea. 'Have either parents ever struggled with the school fees?'

He retrieves another couple of folders from the filing cabinet, and quickly reads them.

'The Clarks—no. Mr Clark is a partner for a prestigious accounting firm. In fact, last year they paid their fees upfront and so qualified for a five per cent discount.'

He studies the other folder.

'Ah, yes, I remember now. The Tolhurst's pay by instalment, every two weeks. It helps spread the load. The father visited me at the beginning of term two last year. He asked if he could defer a month's payment and have it distributed over the rest of the year.'

'Did you agree?'

He throws an annoyed glance her way. 'Of course. We may be a business, but we're not unreasonable.'

'Did he state why he couldn't meet that month's payment?'

'Yes,' he begins tentatively, 'as I recall, he had something wrong with his taxi. Needed a new part or something and it was quite expensive.'

'Did they meet the rest of their instalments?'

'Yes. No issues.'

Prisha laughs wryly to herself.

'Did I say something funny, inspector?'

'Sorry, no. I'm just amused at the irony.'

'What irony?'

'The rich guy getting a discount. You'd think the discount would go to the poorer family.'

He appears irritated, so she decides to cut her losses. She rises and grabs the printout of names.

'Thanks for your time, Mr Murray. You've been very helpful. If you could direct me to the boarding house and Mr Bridges, I'd be grateful.'

He walks to the window and points at a long row of converted barns across from a large playground.

'Those are the boarding rooms across the yard next to the stables.'

'The girls have their own horses?'

'The school has twelve ponies. There're miles and miles of trail rides around these parts.'

'I had to make do with My Little Pony in the back garden,' she murmurs. 'And where can I find Mr Bridges?'

He points his finger to the floor. 'He's directly below, far below. His workshop is in the cellar.'

As she strides towards the door, she realises she hasn't asked him the most important question.

'One last question, Mr Murray; can you tell me where you were yesterday between 10:30 and 11:30 am?'

'I was here all day. I arrived just after nine and left about five-fifteen.'

'You didn't leave the school grounds at any time?'

He pauses, thoughtfully. 'No.'

'And can anyone verify you were here between those specific times?'

'Yes. I have a catch up meeting every day at 10:30 with the boarding assistants.'

'How long do the meetings typically last?'

'It can vary. Yesterday, I'd say it was about twenty minutes.'

'Thank you for your time, Mr Murray. I'll be in touch if I require any further information. Here's my card. If you think of anything else that may assist in the investigation, then please call me. Oh, by the way, when you did teach, what was your main subject?'

'Chemistry and political history.'

17

She pulls the door shut behind her as she leaves the boarding rooms and heads across the yard to the caretaker's workshop. As she glances up at the imposing Carston Hall, she notices the deputy principal staring down at her, three stories above. He quickly moves back from the window and out of sight.

Thirty minutes with two of the four boarders and their assistants yielded nothing. The boarders are two to three years older than Zoe and Emma and didn't know them personally, although they recognised their faces from the TV. As for the assistants—same story. They confirmed the meeting with the deputy principal yesterday at ten-thirty, although they said it barely lasted ten minutes, not twenty.

Even though none of them knew the missing girls, they were all visibly upset, with two of them breaking into tears. A noticeable difference in reaction compared to that of Charles Murray.

As she trots down the stone steps to the cellar, she calls out.

'Hello, Mr Bridges?'

'Hello,' a soft male voice replies.

She enters the workshop, which is gloomy and smells of old wood and paint.

'Can I help you?'

A man of average height appears. He's youngish, maybe late twenties-early thirties. His close cropped hair sits above attractive features, and his body is muscular in an athletic way. He throws Prisha a smile, which, if she were in a bar, would have her fluttering her eyelashes back at him. Her heart skips a beat.

'You're Mr Bridges?'

'Yes. But please call me Mark. Mr Bridges sounds like a stuffy old geography teacher.'

'Hi, I'm DI Kumar from North Yorkshire Police.'

She holds her ID in front of him.

'That says detective sergeant, not inspector,' he adds with a chuckle.

She blushes. 'Ahem, I'm acting inspector, as of earlier today.'

'I'm ribbing you, inspector.' A deep frown replaces his genial smile. 'I take it you're here about Zoe and Emma, the missing girls?'

'Yes. Do you mind if I ask you a few questions?'

'Not at all, as long as you've cleared it with Twitchy.'

'Twitchy?'

'Mr Murray, deputy principal.'

'Oh, yes. I spoke with him recently. He seemed a little jittery. Is he always like that?'

He sits down on the edge of an old desk and places his hands in his lap.

'He can be a bit intense, highly strung. But he's not a bad old stick.'

'Do you know the missing girls?'

'No. I recognised their faces from last night's newspaper.'

He nods towards the desk where the girls' smiling faces are peering out below a headline that reads, "MISSING! LOST AT SEA!"

She shakes her head. 'Looks like even local newspapers are going down the tabloid sensationalist route these days.'

'I guess they need to do something to arrest their dwindling sales.'

'So, you didn't know the girls?'

'No. I may have said hello or good morning to them at some point, but that's all.'

'Had you heard any rumours about them? Any playground tittle-tattle about clandestine boyfriends or secret hideaways?'

He shakes his head. 'No. This is an all-girls school inspector. If I took notice of all the rumours and petty disputes, I'd never get any work done.'

A shrill ringing startles her. Bridges casually looks to a shelf where an old-fashioned phone is demanding attention.

'Excuse me. That's the bat phone. Looks like Twitchy wants me for something.' He picks up the receiver. 'Good afternoon, Mr Murray. Yes, yes… I see. I did actually hear a brief thunderstorm on Sunday night, so that could be the reason. If the electricity supply was interrupted, then you know how temperamental it can be. I have been telling you to get a new

117

system for a while now. Yes... I know, it's on the list. I'll pop up in twenty to check it out. Yes, she's here with me now,' he adds as he turns and flashes that damned boyish grin at her.

'Okay. Bye.' He hangs up.

'I can see you're busy, Mr... Mark. One last question and I'll let you get on with your day.'

'Fire away.'

'Can you tell me where you were yesterday between 10:30 am 11:30 am?'

'I was here. Arrived about eight and left around four-thirty. Didn't leave the grounds.'

'Did anyone see you?'

He shrugs nonchalantly. 'There's only been the boarders and Twitchy here for the last few weeks. Oh, wait. I noticed two of the girls saddling up yesterday. Can't be certain of the exact time, but it wasn't long before I had my dinner. Not sure if they noticed me or not.'

Frank's explanation about Yorkshire vernacular flashes across her mind.

'When you say dinner, you mean lunch?'

'No. I mean dinner. You may call it lunch, but you're in Yorkshire now. When in Rome...'

He throws her another irresistible beam.

'Ahem... yes. What time did you stop for dinner?'

'It's always same time—midday.'

'So you possibly saw the girls saddling up somewhere between eleven thirty and twelve?'

He scrunches his nose up. 'Maybe ten minutes earlier, but don't quote me on that.'

'Thanks for your time, Mark,' she says, handing him her card. 'If anything else comes to mind, please call me, no matter how trivial it may seem.'

'I certainly will. And good luck finding the girls. Call it intuition, but I get a sense they're still alive somewhere.'

'We can but hope for the best. Goodbye.'

18

Frank sticks two fingers between the Venetian blinds and surveys the incident room. It's quiet. There's one DC and two civvies typing away at desks. He's spent the last two hours updating reports, replying to emails, and trying to keep on top of the paperwork, which multiplies quicker than he can get through it.

He's frustrated. It's a big investigation, and he's itching to use his vast experience and sharp mind to make a breakthrough, but there's not much he can do until his detectives return and feed him the information they've collected.

He's also hungry, having devoured his packed lunch by mid-morning. He glances at his watch—ten past two. His team won't start drifting back in for at least another two hours.

'Bugger it! I need some fresh air and a bite to eat.'

He hurries through the incident room, calling out to the constable as he does so.

'Constable, I'm taking some air for a while. I'll be back in forty. If anyone wants me—tell them to phone.'

'Yes, boss.'

As he ambles along the street that leads to the town centre, he tries to trick his mind to stop thinking about the case. He focuses on the sights, sounds, and smells that assail him. The unremitting high-pitched squeal of seagulls; the hum of constant traffic; the distant strains of the amusement arcades with their screeching horns, whistles, and sirens.

Waiting at a pedestrian crossing, a sweet sugary waft of freshly cooked donuts tickles his nostrils. It's instantly obliterated as a large dustbin lorry trundles by belching out diesel fumes. Crossing the road, he cuts away from the main drag and follows a backstreet heading towards his secret haven—Miserly Joe's Cafe.

As the hustle and bustle of the tourist trade fades away, he takes another turn down a shabby lane lined with old decrepit houses and a few industrial workshops. Entering the café, he's greeted by the ever smiling face of Jenny, the establishment's proprietor, chief cook, and bottle washer.

'Hello, stranger!' she cries with mock surprise.

'Jenny,' he nods, offering her a warm grin.

'I thought you must have carked it.'

'Thanks for your concern. I've been very busy, that's all.'

'Really? Are you sure that wife of yours hasn't got you on another diet?' she says, following up with a cackling laugh.

Frank is affronted at the suggestion. 'Couldn't be further from the truth, Jenny,' he lies. 'Anyway, I wear the trousers in our marriage, and she knows it, and I'll eat whatever I damn well please. Now, do you serve food here as well as insults, or am I wasting my time?'

'Touchy, touchy. What do you want, the full mashings?'

Frank studies the assortment of goodies keeping warm in bain-maries behind the glass frontage. Bacon, sausage, baked beans, chips, scrambled egg, fried tomatoes, fried bread, black-pudding. He considers the delicacies for a moment while his mouth salivates.

'Ahem, no. I'm just after a snack. A cheese toastie will do.'

'I tell you what I do have; your favourite pork pies came in a few hours ago. I have them out the back.'

Frank cracks a huge beam. 'Now you're talking, Jenny. Are they the big ones?'

She nods.

'Smashing! One pork pie and a large mug of strong tea, please.

'That will be four-pounds-fifty.'

Frank pulls a note from his pocket and hands it over. 'You do realise I'm a police officer and I could arrest you for daylight robbery,' he states with a grave expression.

Jenny scoffs. 'Trouble with you, Frank, you're still stuck in the nineties.'

Frank takes a quick glance around the room. 'Much like your interior designer.'

She slides the note into the cash register but doesn't hand him any change, then disappears out the back.

'Keep the change,' he quips.

She returns in a jiffy and hands Frank a cracked plate with a pie sitting proudly in the middle.

'Here you go, Frank.' Her cheerful demeanour dissipates as she leans forward. 'I've read about the missing girls. Any news?' she whispers.

'Not yet, I'm afraid.'

'I heard some of the men talking earlier. They reckon that someone's done away with them.'

'It's a small town and gossip spreads like wildfire, especially in this place,' he says ruefully.

'But do you think someone has got them? I mean, if they were washed out to sea, their bodies should've turned up by now.'

'Jenny, we have every available officer on the job, and I'm sure we'll know something in a day or two.'

She appears pensive at his words. 'Two days! Could be too bloody late by then.'

'Thanks for the reminder. Now, if you don't mind, I'd like to eat my pie in relative peace.'

He turns and finds himself a table in a quiet corner.

The cafe is rundown and threadbare. Old tables are covered in chipped Formica, surrounded by plastic school chairs drained of their once vibrant colour. The floor is in a good need of a mop and a window cleaner hasn't been seen for many a year. All the same, Frank loves the cafe. It's frequented by what he terms the real people of the town, fishermen, promenade stallholders, bin men, council workers. It's a place where you can fill your stomach and relax with no one giving you so much as a second glance.

He takes a knife and carefully slices down the middle of the pie, smiling at the gently cracking sound of the tan coloured pastry. Flakes fall onto the plate. He slices the pie into quarters and squirts a dollop of brown sauce onto the side of his plate.

'It's a shame to eat you,' he murmurs. A familiar sight in the street diverts his attention. 'Hell's bloody bells! What's she doing here?' he yelps in muted fashion as he grabs a discarded newspaper, spreads it wide, and slinks behind it.

Lowering the paper, his eyes peep over the top as he follows his wife's figure down the street. He rises and peers out of the grimy window until she turns a corner and disappears.

'Phew! Talk about too close for comfort.'

'How's the pie?' Jenny cackles. 'And your trousers?'

19

Prisha parks next to a white Subaru Impreza stationed outside a closed garage door. The house, a three storey semi-detached, is relatively new. When her transfer to North Yorkshire was signed off on, she'd spent a lot of time house hunting in Whitby, online. This type of house would be worth about four-hundred-thousand. Obviously, schoolteachers at Carston Hall must get paid a pretty penny.

As she knocks on the front door, she observes the rest of the street. It's situated a stone's throw from the River Esk, and has a rural feel even though it's less than a ten-minute walk to the town centre. Oddly enough, it's also within spitting distance of the police station.

The front door is flung open, and she's confronted with a tall, attractive woman dressed in active wear. Her jet-black hair is pulled back into a sharp ponytail, highlighting her pale skin and high cheekbones.

'Miss Tiffany Butler?' she enquires, flashing her ID.

'Inspector Kumar, please come in,' she offers as she stands aside.

'How did you know it was me?'

'Mr Murray called me earlier. I'm not expecting anyone else. Also, I saw you in your car assessing my house, probably wondering how a relatively young teacher could afford such a place.'

This woman is savvy.

'It never crossed my mind.'

She emits a haughty laugh. 'Really!'

She leads Prisha into her living room where a vacuum cleaner is standing next to a mop and bucket. Scanning the room brings her to the conclusion she's a neat freak. Everything is modern and clean. A bookshelf is meticulously arranged by author last name. Air freshener diffusers are abundant, filling the house with exquisite fragrances; lavender, rose petal, cedarwood. Prisha makes a mental note to purloin the idea for her own flat.

'Can I get you a refreshment? Tea, coffee, mineral water?'

She sits down on a sleek, black leather couch. 'No thanks.'

Miss Butler takes a chair opposite and clasps her hands together, appearing bright, bubbly, lively—not the way she'd expect a teacher to react when two of her students have gone missing.

Prisha pulls out her notebook and pen.

'I'm like my mother,' she confesses.

'Pardon?' Prisha says.

'My mother. In times of crises, she would always busy herself. Cooking, cleaning, making endless cups of tea. She wasn't one to wallow. For better or for worse, I'm the same. That's why

I'm cleaning and trying to sound positive. Inside, I'm a bag of nerves.'

She's doing well to hide it. 'Yes, ahem... well...'

'Inspector, please throw as many questions as you can at me. I want to help find Zoe and Emma as much as anyone. I've already concluded the police think they may not have lost their lives at sea, and that maybe something more nefarious has occurred.'

Prisha relaxes into the couch and fixes her with a steady eye, hoping she'll calm down a little and let her get on with her job.

'Miss Butler...'

'Please call me Tiffany.'

'Tiffany, I have a lot to get through.'

'Sorry,' she says with an apologetic wince.

'I'm trying to get an idea of Zoe's and Emma's personalities, and so far, I've drawn a blank. I've spoken to the deputy principal, the boarders, the assistants, and the caretaker—Mark Bridges. None of them know the girls—personally—although, all recognise their photos in the media.'

'I can certainly help you out there. I'm not only their homeroom teacher but also head of year, and I took them for maths and financial economics last school year.'

There's an awkward silence as they gaze at each other. Prisha wonders whether she's lost her power of communication today.

'Tiffany... their personality traits?'

'Oh, sorry, yes.' She nods and closes her eyes. 'Well... they are definitely besties.'

'Yes. We've already ascertained that.'

'No, I mean like *really, really,* best friends. Zoe and Emma came to Carston Hall last year—their first year. Before that they were at a local comprehensive school—i.e. a state run school. I'd say that ninety per cent of pupils at Carston Hall came from private schools.'

'Meaning, it was a big adjustment for them and in this new environment, their friendship grew even stronger?'

'Exactly. I think Zoe's father is an accountant, and Emma's father is a taxi driver. The girls weren't used to people who had their own horses, holidayed in St Tropez, and had connections to royalty.'

'Fish out of water?'

She nods thoughtfully. 'And to throw out another cliché—birds of a feather flock together. Initially, they were well behind in their studies. But as the year progressed, they caught up—slightly. Emma Tolhurst is from Caribbean heritage and from my experience, they have a very strong work ethic. They are strivers. I think she pulled Zoe along in her slipstream. You probably went through a similar thing—being from ethnic heritage. Are you Indian or Pakistani?'

'I'm British. My parents were born in Pakistan.'

'Muslim, Hindu, or Christian?'

'Muslim—my parents, that is. I'm agnostic.'

She drops her head to one side and pushes out her bottom lip as though contemplating what horse to bet on.

'I'm sorry. Was that racist of me?' she adds, reticently.

'Racist—no. Tactless—possibly, but I have a thick skin. Can we refocus on Zoe and Emma?'

'Of course... sorry. They didn't really mingle or make new friends. It was them against the world sort of attitude. I've seen it before. As the years pass, the girls get to know one another and by the time they leave, a lot of new friendships have formed.'

Prisha tries again. 'Miss Butler... Tiffany, tell me about their personalities?'

'Typical thirteen-year-old girls; loud, excitable. Fireballs of unbridled energy—surely you remember that age?'

She does, but it's fading fast sitting there trying to elicit useful information from Tiffany Butler.

'Were they secretive, promiscuous, manipulative? Did they mention boys, girls, relationships they could have been involved in?'

As she rocks back and guffaws, Prisha feels the onset of a headache.

'Good lord, no! In fact, I'd say they'd be the last two to become sexually active.'

Odd thing to say. 'Why's that?'

'Both girls are attractive and physically mature—but emotionally—they're rather naïve.'

'In the end-of-year school report, that Mr Murray showed me, you had to reprimand Zoe last year for some minor indiscretion. Can you tell me what it was?'

Her head tilts to the left as she stares at the ceiling.

'Sorry, I can't recall. I teach a lot of girls throughout the year and there are always one or two who play up. I like to deal with it myself, in house, instead of sending them to Mr Murray.'

'Why?'

Her hands clap together again. 'Erm... well... some girls find him a little creepy.'

'In what way?'

'You've met him. Didn't you notice?'

'No.'

'I hate to disparage a colleague, but he sort of mentally undresses you.'

'Do you know if he's married?'

'Divorced, I think... or at least separated.'

She pulls out the spreadsheet of contacts that Charles Murray printed off and hands it to her.

'There are a lot of names on this list. Can you take a look and highlight any pupils that Zoe and Emma interacted with? It could save me some time.'

'Certainly.'

She pulls on a pair of spectacles, picks up a pen, and studies the record. A dog yaps incessantly from either out the back or from next-door. The seconds tick by. She makes a few marks on the paper and hands it back.

'There are four girls who may be able to help you. They seemed to get on well enough.'

'Thank you. Do you have a partner, Miss Butler?'

'No. Although I'm not sure what that's got to do with anything,' she replies curtly.

Prisha disregards her obvious annoyance at the question.

'One final question; can you tell me your whereabouts yesterday between 10:30 and 11:30 am?'

'Yes. I was at Frodsham Health Spa from ten until two. It's my guilty pleasure. I'm a member there and treat myself at the end of every school term. I went in the flotation tank, then had a massage, and a manicure and pedicure.'

'A flotation tank?'

'Yes. It's a large tank full of warm salty water which enables you to float. When you close the lid, it's like being back in the womb. It's very therapeutic. You should try it sometime. I felt like a million dollars when I came out until I heard the news about Emma and Zoe.'

She escorts Prisha to the front door as the yapping from the dog gets more frenetic.

'Is the barking dog yours?'

'No. It's next-doors.'

'Doesn't it get on your nerves?'

'No. It's a puppy. It only barks when the owner is getting ready to take it for a walk.'

Prisha hands her card over, gives the usual spiel, and leaves.

20

Frank finishes talking with Prisha and Zac in his office as the incident room fills up with the rest of the team. It's already past seven in the evening and Frank wants to complete the day's briefing and send everyone home.

'No breakthrough as such, but a lot of good information. Let's do it.'

The three of them stride into the main room, which is burbling with tired voices.

'Okay everyone—heads up. We'll go through what we've got.'

Frank grabs a marker pen and takes up position on one side of the whiteboard while Prisha and Zac take the opposite end.

'Zac, why don't you start?'

Zac takes a step forward. 'Sure, boss. No luck on a positive sighting of the girls. I questioned the parents this afternoon and they all have watertight alibis to their whereabouts around the time of the disappearance. Neither of the girls have siblings and neither the Clark nor the Tolhurst families have close relatives in the area. We have a list of grandparents, and aunties and uncles we'll check out tomorrow.

We've door knocked over three-hundred houses—that includes cabins, campsites, tents, B&Bs, holiday rentals, and caravans. We'll continue tomorrow.

Digital forensics have gone through the girls' phones and checked social media, email, and any other communication apps and came up with nothing untoward. No cyber-bullying, no stalking, no strangers contacting them. Everything appears to be perfectly legit. They also verified, via Google Timeline, the girls' phones were at the beach yesterday during the time of their disappearance. Forensics are now performing a deep search of the phones to check deleted messages, photos, etcetera and should have a report for us by tomorrow.

Moving on. This afternoon a group of twenty volunteers from a local walking and rock climbing club, chaperoned by Special Constable Pembroke, walked the beach and the coastal path as far as Robin Hood's Bay. There's no sign of coastal erosion or landslips and nothing relating to the girls washed up onshore.'

A uniformed constable sticks his hand up. 'Sarge, how come they only checked out the area east of Saltwick Bay?'

He's met by a series of groans and a few derisible jeers.

'I take it you haven't been to Whitby before, constable?'

'No. I prefer Scarborough.'

'Heathen!' someone shouts, to the accompaniment of a few titters.

Zac points at the map. 'Here is Saltwick bay. Northwest of that is an unscalable concrete pier backed up against dangerous cliffs. Further on is the town—east of the river, inundated with holidaymakers. If the girls headed in that direction, we'd have had a hundred sightings by now.'

'Fair enough,' the constable replies sheepishly.

'I do have some positive news, depending on your definition of positive. The three footprints are an exact match to the sports shoes Zoe Clark was wearing. Forensics also went back today, and further up the hill, they found another footprint, but very faint. They can't be positive it's an exact match, but they're about eighty per cent certain.

Close to that footprint, they found dog hair on the grass which is still being analysed. At the moment, this doesn't mean much, as the Cleveland Way walking track is very busy at this time of year, and a lot of walkers take their dogs with them. It could be a red herring, but I thought it warranted a mention.'

Zac takes a step back as Frank finishes scribbling the relevant intel onto the whiteboard.

'Inspector Kumar?' he mutters, with his back to her.

'Boss. I'm afraid there are no positive leads from my team's investigations today. I visited the school and spoke with the deputy principal—Charles Murray, two of the four permanent boarders, their two supervisors, and the caretaker.

All recognised Zoe and Emma, but none had really interacted with either girl. The boarders were a few years older, so that's understandable, and the deputy is more of an admin person—think of him like a police superintendent.'

A few boos go up around the room. Frank spins around, angry.

'Oi, you lot! Show some bloody respect! Superintendent Banks wasn't parachuted into her job. She did it the hard way; uniform, DC, DS, DI, DCI—remember that. Carry on, inspector.'

'Ahem, yes... boss. I also questioned the girls' form teacher—Miss Tiffany Butler. She said the girls were confident, bubbly, energetic but also rather insular as they'd moved from comprehensive to private school last year. This seems to have reinforced their bond. As for intimate relationships, Miss Butler was extremely doubtful. Said the girls were emotionally immature.'

A detective constable raises her arm. 'What about alibis, boss?'

'Okay, alibis. Tiffany Butler said she was at Frodsham Spa between ten and two yesterday. I've not corroborated that yet. I'll check it out tomorrow.

Charles Murray had a meeting with the boarding supervisors—two ex-students—at ten-thirty yesterday. He said the meeting went on for about twenty minutes, the girls were adamant it was about ten minutes.

I timed the drive from Carston Hall to Falcon Lane, which is the closest road to Saltwick Bay Beach. It took twenty minutes exactly—going at the speed limit.

Our cut off time for the girls' disappearance is 11:30 am. If Charles Murray finished his meeting at ten-twenty, jumped in his car, then he could have been at Falcon Lane by eleven. The walk across the fields from Falcon Lane to where the footprints were found takes fifteen minutes—which puts him right in our timeframe.

Having said that, I don't believe he's a suspect. He was initially more concerned about the undue publicity and possible detriment it could have on the school's reputation than about the girls' welfare.

As an aside, Tiffany Butler said some girls found Charles Murray creepy. An ogler apparently, although I didn't pick that up speaking to him. He was odd, but not in that way.

The caretaker, Mark Bridges said he was at the school all day leaving about 4:30 pm. A couple of girls who were saddling horses at the stables may have seen him around eleven thirty give or take. I haven't been able to verify that yet, as the girls were out on a trail ride earlier. I'll check with them tomorrow. But Bridges was helpful, relaxed, and showed genuine concern. As for the others, the boarders, and their supervisors all vouched for each other.'

Frank turns to her. 'Child sex offenders?'

'Checked that, boss. Only two within a twenty-mile radius that have done time for child abuse.

One reported to Whitby Police, as they are supposed to do when leaving the area. He's visiting his sister in Southampton for two weeks. That was five days ago. It's been verified by the local uniforms in Southampton.

The other is Alfred Bramwell, of 15 Esk Road, Rusholme, about a fifteen minute drive west of here.

Had a hidden camera in his backpack getting upskirts as young girls came down a slide in a local playground. He was sentenced to six years, got out in three.

Low risk, good behaviour... you all know the story. That was ten years ago, and Alfred is now pushing seventy-two-years-old.

Not sure he'd be able to take on two feisty thirteen-year-olds. Plus, it's not his style; he's a voyeur, not an abductor, and he was into pre-pubescent children, not teenagers. But he's still worth checking out, if only to knock him off the list.'

'There are plenty of fit and active seventy-year-olds around, inspector,' Frank comments laconically as he puts more bullet points on the board. 'Don't pre-judge someone based on their age.'

'Yes, boss. We also questioned all the teachers who are not on holiday. Those who have taught Zoe and Emma reiterated what Miss Butler said, i.e. the girls are easy-going, bright, and seemed happy enough. None reported any incidents or misbehaviours during the year. We'll start questioning the girls' classmates tomorrow.'

She throws Frank a glance to indicate she's finished her summary.

Frank turns to face his team, takes a deep breath and sighs.

'I've been in contact with the coastguard throughout the day. They're scaling back their operation at the end of daylight today. They'll continue their search at first light tomorrow, but it will move into a recovery operation, not a search for life.

Most missing persons in a drowning accident are recovered within twenty-four hours and relatively close to the location where they entered the water. It seems increasingly likely the girls disappeared on land.'

He glances at his watch. 'It's over thirty-two hours since their reported disappearance and what do we know?'

'Not bloody much,' some wag from the back mutters.

Frank ignores the comment.

'We have footprints belonging to Zoe Clark as she climbed the rocky spur. We know Zoe and Emma were good kids, not the type to get up to mischief. There is no evidence to suggest either of them were in a relationship, or they were being stalked or coerced into anything.

Let's throw some hypotheticals around. Inspector Kumar?'

'Well... pure speculation, but... the girls climb the hill and spot someone they know. He or she lures them away. The girls aren't stupid and would only go with someone they trusted. Which to me would indicate a family member, a close friend of the family, or someone from school.'

'And what could lure away two thirteen-year-old girls?' Frank prompts, already knowing the answer.

'A dog?' Zac suggests.

'What's better than a dog?' Frank asks.

'A puppy,' Prisha murmurs as she thinks of Tiffany Butler's next-door neighbour's yapping canine.

'And what would be the motive?' Frank prods.

'There's only one plausible motive I can think of, boss,' Zac states with grave concern. 'Sexual.'

Frank paces back and forth, tapping his fingers together.

'I'm not a big fan of statistics, but sometimes they don't lie. Ninety-five per cent of people who sexually abuse children are male. Anyone else with any speculative thoughts?'

A sergeant raises his arm.

'Yes?' Frank says.

'What about the girls' home life? Maybe it isn't as quiet and relaxed as the parents state. Let's say they planned to run away. Maybe they even stashed a bag with a change of clothes and some money somewhere near the rocky spur. If you look at the map, the girls could walk unseen across fields until they reached the A171, then hitch a lift. Which means they could be anywhere in the country by now.'

'Hmm... not bad,' Frank says, rubbing his jowl.

'Except,' Prisha intervenes, 'what teenage girls would pull a stunt like that without taking their mobile phones with them?'

Zac speaks. 'The girls' faces and their disappearance are all over the media. The A171 is a busy road at this time of year, and they'd have been trying to flag a lift down about midday. Surely someone would have seen them?'

'Just saying,' says the DS, almost apologetically.

'No, it's a good theory, and one we shall follow up on,' Frank says, offering his support. 'Zac, organise for the media release to be updated asking if anyone saw two teenage girls hitchhiking on the A171 yesterday. Try to get it out on the late TV and radio bulletins tonight.'

'Yes, boss.'

'Okay, anyone else with any theories?'

'They drowned in the sea yesterday at about 11 am,' a disgruntled uniformed officer mumbles.

'Possibly, constable. But until their bodies are recovered from the water, we are treating this as a missing persons investigation—on land.

Right, I want you all to finish entering your reports into the database, then get yourselves home. I can't tell you what to do while off-duty but if you've got any sense, you'll have a good meal, watch a couple of hours TV, get a relaxing shower then hit the sack so you'll turn up tomorrow morning, refreshed and ready to go again.'

There are a few jokes about getting smashed on whisky and visiting a strip-joint. It eases the tension slightly, but not for long as Frank gives his final thought of the day.

'I don't want to end on a downer, but tomorrow we really need a breakthrough... otherwise, I fear the worst.'

21

Frank wearily opens the door and trudges into the hallway as Foxtrot runs up to him, sniffing his feet and trousers as her tail wags excitedly.

'Is that you, Frank?' Meera calls out.

'No! It's Genghis Khan!' he yells back.

He slips out of his jacket and hangs it over the banister post at the bottom of the staircase.

'Who the bloody hell do you think it is?' he adds, muttering under his breath as he stoops to give his Jack Russell a warm pat and cuddle.

'Did you get the wet fish?'

'Oh, shit the bloody bed,' he murmurs, looking at his watch, then glancing ashamedly at Foxtrot. 'Looks like I could be in the doghouse, pardon the pun.'

The dog cocks her head to one side and whimpers. Frank enters the dining room and calls out.

'Sorry, love. I forgot all about it. I can rustle up a nice cheese and onion omelette if you fancy?'

As he enters the kitchen, he's confronted by his wife, who offers him a wide grin and a peck to the lips.

'Good job I got it then,' she says as she pulls away and drops a fillet of haddock onto a plate of seasoned flour.

'Meera, what would I do without you?'

She cackles loudly as she dusts the flour off the fillet and drops another one into the mix. 'I guess you'd waste away.'

Frank spots the electric chip pan in the corner and it's switched on. That particular appliance has not been gainfully employed for over three months.

'Don't tell me we're having proper chips with it?'

'Correct. And mushy peas.'

Frank embraces his wife from behind and kisses her on the back of the neck.

'Don't you go getting any funny ideas, Frank. I've had a tough day too. Three patients passed away today. It was inevitable, and everyone knew it was coming, but still... it's never easy. A lot of paperwork... and tears. I know we're on a diet, but I thought we could suspend it for one night. I've kept up-to-date with the news and know you've had a tough day as well.'

She carefully places a plate of homemade chips into the fryer, which reacts with spitting, bubbling fury.

'Sorry to hear about the loss, love. How old were they?'

'A lady in her nineties, one in her seventies and...' she sniffs, trying to control the tears, 'a lovely woman who was forty-five. Breast cancer. Three teenage boys and a grieving husband she's left behind.'

'Christ,' Frank whispers. 'That disease is ruthless. No rhyme or reason.'

Meera wipes away a tear and stands tall and proud. 'Okay, enough talk of work. Let's switch off for the rest of the night. You go put your feet up and do your cryptic, and tea will be ready in about fifteen minutes.'

'Thanks, pet. Any chance we can have it on our knee?'

She throws him a disapproving look, but instantly wavers.

'Okay, for tonight, but don't think it's going to become a habit. Meals should be eaten around a table.'

As he leaves the kitchen, he fails to hear the muffled sobs from his wife as she buries her face in a damp tea towel.

———— ❧ ————

Frank drops his knife and fork onto his empty plate.

'That was pure heaven,' he says with obvious satisfaction.

Meera pushes herself up from the settee and collects his plate, stacking it on top of hers.

'We're back on the diet tomorrow, and you're cooking,' she says bullishly.

'I'll do the dishes, love. You rest up.'

'No. I need to keep busy. I'll make us a nice cuppa then I'm going to bed.'

By the time she arrives back with two steaming mugs of tea, Frank has finished the cryptic.

'Too easy,' he says with a huff as he tosses the paper to one side. 'I might have to buy The Times. The Guardian doesn't cut it anymore. Maybe they've changed their crossword compiler?'

'Or maybe you've outgrown The Guardian.'

Frank glances at the clock on the wall. 'Do you mind if I put the local news on? It's about to start.'

'Go for it.'

Frank hits the remote and the TV flashes into life. A few seconds later, a brief news bulletin begins.

"The coastguard has scaled back the search for two missing local teenagers off the coast of Whitby.

The two thirteen-year-olds, Zoe Clark, and Emma Tolhurst, disappeared yesterday morning while walking along Saltwick Bay near Black Nab. Initially it was thought the girls may have got into difficulties in the water, but now the police are pursuing another line of investigation.

They believe the girls may have exited the beach onto the Cleveland Way coastal path about a mile east of where they were last seen. The main A171 road is only a short distance away and police are now urging motorists who saw two girls matching their descriptions, hitchhiking along the A171, to contact North Yorkshire Po..."

Frank hits the off button and the innocent faces of the two girls instantly disappear from the screen.

'They're just children,' Meera murmurs sadly, sipping her tea as Foxtrot snuggles closely beside her in the armchair.

'Aye. Innocents abroad,' Frank concurs. 'Zac did a bloody good job to get the media release updated so quickly. I'm not sure it will yield anything apart from a few duff leads, but who knows?'

'I'm surprised you made the new girl acting DI. Zac's been your right-hand man for the last three years. I'd have thought he'd have been given the nod.'

'It was a test,' Frank replies as he stands up and stretches.

'A test?'

'Yes... for both of them. I knew Zac would have slipped into the role of inspector easily, but I wanted to see how Prisha would perform. I also wanted to evaluate Zac's reaction.'

'Reaction?'

'Aye. See if he's made of the right stuff. Being overlooked for the position of DI by a newcomer would have been a kick to the guts for him. A lot of officers would have reacted by being wounded, churlish, throwing banana skins under the new DI's feet. But not Zac. He's taken it on the chin, which is what I hoped. He realises the job is bigger than his ego, something all good coppers need to learn. How many times have I had a right bollocking from the Super?'

'Ha, too many, but I suppose she's only doing her job.'

Frank finishes the dregs of his tea and edges towards the kitchen.

'That's exactly right. I've lost count of the number of times I've walked out of her office with my tail between my legs, but I never let it affect me, or my relationship with her. You've got to be bigger than that. We all stuff up from time to time. It's part of being human.'

'So how is the new girl going? Prisha isn't it?'

'She's doing fine. Sharp as a tack, actually. She pulled me up about something yesterday in relation to the Shirley Fox case.'

'Oh?'

'Something I missed... well, not really missed, but something I meant to check on but never got around to. You know Libby Hobson, don't you?'

'Yes. I wouldn't call us friends, but our paths cross frequently. She's very active in the community. She was a good friend of Shirley Fox and was meant to be in the pub the night Shirley was murdered.'

'That's right. She came down with a cold and cancelled.'

'So?'

'I spoke to her briefly by phone, the day after Shirley's murder, but that was all. I should have really paid a visit and questioned her in a more formal manner.'

Meera scoffs. 'Ha, you don't actually think Libby had anything to do with Shirley's death, do you? She's about five-foot nothing and weighs around seven stone. She wouldn't say boo to a goose.'

'No, I don't think she's directly implicated. The idea is absurd... but something Prisha said.'

'Go on?'

'What if Dudley Fox was late meeting his wife because he was having an affair with Libby Hobson?'

Meera roars with laughter. 'Oh my!' she exclaims.

'What's so funny?' Frank states, appearing hurt.

'The great detective—Frank Finnegan. You obviously don't know, so I'll have to tell you. Libby Hobson is a lesbian and has been in a long-term relationship for at least the last twenty years. It's not something she shouts about from the rooftops, but neither does she hide it.'

'A lesbian?'

'Yes. You know what a lesbian is, don't you?'

Frank rubs thoughtfully at his chin. 'Well I never. Mind you, that doesn't mean she can't change sides occasionally.'

Meera fixes him with a withering glare. 'Change sides? Are you talking about a woman's sexuality or a centre-forward who's on loan to Leeds United?'

'I'm just being...'

'You're being ridiculous, that's what you're being.'

Frank huffs. 'You're right, but that's not the point, is it?'

'What is your point?'

'The fact I didn't investigate her absence from the pub more thoroughly.'

Meera stares into the distance as she strokes Foxtrot on the back. 'As you said a moment ago, we all stuff up sometimes. We're humans, not robots.'

'Aye, I suppose. Right, I'm going to get a shower then hit the sack. You coming?'

'Yes, love. I'll be up in a minute. I just want a little quiet time... if you don't mind.'

Frank kisses her tenderly on the top of her head. 'I understand. Is it about the young woman with breast cancer?'

Meera nods, fighting back the tears. 'Why is life so unfair, Frank?'

'That's one mystery I'll never be able to solve.'

22

Dudley's fingers gently touch the face of Shirley behind the glass frame. He places the wedding photo back on top of the TV and walks to the drinks cabinet.

There's a comforting musicality about the way whisky tumbles into a glass. It's a unique sound unmatched by any other spirit. A gurgling, hypnotic slosh which conjures up flashbacks to black and white espionage films from the sixties; the protagonist sitting at a polished oak table in a large dining room of an English country manor house deciphering code from a Russian informant during the Cold War.

Dudley's in the midst of his own Cold War. He wonders how it will end. He can't imagine Mikhail Gorbachev coming to the rescue and instigating the fall of the Iron Curtain for him.

'Maybe Frank Finnegan is my Mikhail Gorbachev... did you hear that, Shirley? What a joke!'

He swallows his tablets, and his addendum—the lithium drops, collapses onto the settee, stares vacantly at the muted TV, and sips. A picture of the two missing girls flashes up on screen. He turns the volume up and listens to the late night bulletin. As it ends, he's not sure what to think.

'I don't know, Shirley,' he says, talking to her empty chair. 'Sometimes I can't make head nor tail of the world. And me, a scientist. Those two young girls haven't even started living yet. It seems the authorities aren't certain they were in the water after all. If they had been, they'd be long gone by now. I suppose it's good news in a way.'

He grabs the whisky from the table and pours a top up.

'I know, I know, Shirl. I'm drinking too much. Give me a little more time and I'll sort myself out, promise. Mind you, it would help if they found your killer. It would bring some sort of closure. The end of a painful chapter.'

Tyson wanders in, wondering who his master is talking to. He looks around the room, then slinks onto his bed.

'Yes, I hear you—get off the medication, too. I'm not addicted. It helps me sleep, that's all. I'm actually feeling a little better in myself since you sent me that text message the other night.

It's like you really are still here with me. I know it's madness. A man of science can't believe his dead wife can really send text messages to him. Although, there's one thing science has taught me; there are far more things we don't *yet* understand than we do. In fact, there are things we haven't even contemplated because we are unaware of their existence.

It was Donald Rumsfeld who said there are known knowns and known unknowns and, interestingly enough—unknown unknowns. I remember they ridiculed him at the time for talking gibberish. But now I think it was extremely profound.'

He swallows the whisky in one gulp, rises, and places the empty glass on the mantlepiece.

'Yes, I know you disliked the man. That's not my point. What is my point? It's this; communication from beyond the grave, logically, is impossible. And yet, what if there is some life force, or different dimension, we have not yet discovered? A place where the spirit, or soul, migrates to after death. An unknown unknown. We can't explore and analyse the physics behind it if we can't comprehend its existence. What's that? Yes, I am speaking gobbledegook and I really should go to bed.'

He picks up his phone and taps out his goodnight message.

> *Goodnight Shirley. Sleep*
> *tight. I love and miss you*

Her phone vibrates and rattles on the small corner table next to her chair.

'Christ, I hope those two young girls are safe, Shirley. Please let them be safe,' he mumbles as he flicks the lights off and staggers up the stairs.

23

Prisha knows she has a tendency to become obsessed with a case and lose track of time. An hour can fly by in a few minutes.

'Prisha, you waited up for me?'

It's the unmistakable jokey tone of DS Cartwright. She turns and offers him a weary smile.

'Hi Jason. I'm just about to leave.'

She collects her belongings as he takes a chair and pulls a potato cake from a brown paper bag.

'I'll see you tomorrow,' Prisha says.

'Not if I see you first,' he replies, laughing with a mouthful of food.

As she walks home, she thinks of the case. As she makes dinner, she thinks of the case. As she stares blankly at a TV quiz show, she thinks of the case.

Sleep is slow in coming and when it arrives, it's fitful and exhausting as a recurring dream plays in her head.

She's on the beach near Black Nab and has been tasked with collecting every stone and pebble into a pile. It doesn't matter how hard she works and what area she clears, more pebbles appear quicker than she can collect them. It's frustrating and also demeaning that she cannot complete such a straightforward task. An enormous crowd of onlookers gather to watch her. Some laugh and sneer at her pathetic attempts. Just as she makes progress, the tide rushes in and she has to run up a hill to escape danger.

Tossing and turning restlessly, she throws back the sheets and yells.

'Stop it!'

The digital clock tells her it's 3:08 am. Staggering from bed, she lurches towards the window. It's a warm night and her room is stuffy and airless. She pulls at the curtains and slides the window up with some difficulty as she takes in deep gasps of fresh, cooling sea air.

Waves crash on the beach in the distance, but apart from that welcoming sound, all is still as streetlights shimmer and flicker their orange glow. Her racing heart slows as a fine mist falls from the sky. She sticks a hand out as tiny droplets tickle her palm.

Downstairs, she makes a cup of milky hot chocolate before retiring to the bedroom once more. Flicking the bedside lamp on, she plumps up two pillows and rests them against the bedhead before climbing onto the firm mattress. The hot chocolate is comforting as she once again trawls over the case of Zoe and Emma.

There must be something she's missed. It's totally out of character for the girls to wander off and then hitchhike their way to some place—they wouldn't do that, it's not plausible. Two girls of their age from good families can't simply vanish. Families, families... most acts of violence or abduction aren't random. As Frank said, you can't always rely on stats, but sometimes they help focus attention. If the girls were lured away, then they knew the perpetrator, most likely a male.

Stop it, Prisha! It's a bad trait of yours and one that Frank picked up on the other day... my ability to become fixated on one aspect, one suspect, to the detriment of everything else. I have a tendency to arrange the facts to fit the crime instead of letting the facts guide me in the right direction.

I should have gone with Zac when he interviewed the parents. Maybe he missed something? I studied his report and the one from the Family Liaison Officer, but nothing suspicious was gleaned from either... even so, maybe someone's lying?

She checks the clock again. It's red dots showing the inexorable march of time, time the missing girls don't have. Grabbing her phone, she taps at an image. A few seconds later, a grumpy and slightly confused voice answers.

'Bloody hell, Prisha! Do you know what time it is?' Zac whispers angrily.

'Sorry Zac. I couldn't sleep.'

'Well, I bloody could. Hang on, give me a moment. I don't want to wake the missus.'

Muted sounds and heavy sighing are transmitted through the ether as Prisha waits.

'What is it?' he demands.

'I've been thinking about the case.'

'Really? You surprise me,' he states, his tone heavy with sarcasm.

'Is there anything you may have missed when you talked with the parents?'

'You read my report. Why are you ringing me at this hour to question me about it?'

'Sorry. Can you go over it again... for me?'

He emits a resigned sigh down the phone.

'I spoke with the Clark family first. Sarah Clark was obviously on the beach, as she was the one to raise the alarm. John Clark was in a boardroom meeting with his partners at the accountancy firm. The meeting began at ten before being abruptly terminated when John received a call from Sarah at twenty-two minutes past eleven, two minutes after she'd called 999. Mr Clark made his way to the beach to help in the search.

Mrs Tolhurst... Rachel, was working a shift at Tesco's. She started at nine and was there until a uniform went to get her just before midday. Lenny Tolhurst picked up a taxi fare at ten-thirty to take an elderly couple to Holy Island. He only got as far as South Shields, before he received a call from his wife just after twelve.

I checked out everyone's alibis, each one of them having numerous witnesses to their whereabouts. I even got in touch with the couple going to Lindisfarne, who verified Lenny Tolhurst's account.'

'What about relatives?'

'I told everyone at last night's briefing—none live in the area. In fact, the closest relative is Lenny Tolhurst's brother, who lives in Manchester. All other family members from the Clarks and Tolhurst live south of Watford Gap, some in London, some in Brighton, and others in Dorset. Neither of them has a big extended family, and neither family were expecting visitors. Happy now?'

'No... I mean yes.'

'I know what your theory is, about a close family member being the most likely candidate, but in this case it doesn't fit. Whoever took Zoe and Emma it wasn't one of the parents... that's if they were taken. We're not even certain about that, yet. Can I go back to bed now?'

'Yes. Sorry, Zac. It's been preying on my mind all night.'

'You need to take a leaf out of Frank's book and learn to switch off. If you don't get some shut-eye, you'll be bloody useless to everyone tomorrow... I mean today. Right, I'll see you in about four hours... Christ, four bloody hours. Where does the time go?'

'Night Zac.'

The line goes dead as she switches the lamp off and snuggles under the thin duvet. She'll revisit the parents later in the day, to double check, but she'll need to be discreet. No point standing on anyone's toes... especially Zac's.

24

Wednesday 19th August

Emma is scratching around in the cellar. She pushes an ancient archery target out of the way and grabs two old chairs. Dragging them past the camp beds, she stacks them on top of one another and deftly scales the improvised ladder. She peers out of the tiny, cracked window. Her eyes are level with the ground as she gazes at the gravel and a smattering of greenery in the distance. It's all she can see. Glancing over her shoulder at Zoe, she offers her a cheeky grin.

'It's a beautiful day outside.'

'Come down from there. If you fall, you'll kill yourself,' Zoe replies, staring at the two rickety chairs.

Emma performs a false wobble, then leaps from the chairs, landing nimbly on the hard concrete.

'Ta-dah!' she cries, doing a swift pirouette. 'That's what gymnastics does for you. I don't know why you never joined.'

'It's boring,' Zoe gripes as she flops onto her camp bed.

After the momentary distraction, her troubled thoughts return.

'What's he going to do with us? Do you think he's going to come back and rape and murder us?'

Zoe fills the kettle with water from an ancient tap, then strikes a match and lights the small camp stove.

'No. If he wanted to do that, he'd have done it already.'

'Then what's he playing at?' Zoe wails.

'I don't know. Anyway, if he does return, I'll be waiting for him,' she says as she pulls an arrow from the target and runs her fingers through the feathered fletching.

'You couldn't really kill someone, could you?'

'Believe me... yes, I could. If it was a choice between you and me, or him... then he's going down.'

'You're crazy.'

Emma jabs the arrow back into the target, then holds two pot noodles up. 'What do you want, chicken and mushroom or curry flavour?'

'Chicken. They'll be out looking for us, won't they?'

Emma pulls the lids off the pot noodles and empties the sachets of flavourings over the contents.

'Yeah. There'll be a big search party. Police, our parents, friends, locals. It's simply a matter of time.'

'How far do you think he took us?'

'Not sure. I was still half asleep as he dragged us from the boot of the car.'

'It's funny how he didn't say a word to us.'

'Stop talking about it. You'll make yourself worse. We've got food, water, books, a toilet, and beds to sleep on. It could be far worse.'

'I don't see how,' Zoe says as she sobs again. 'I just want to go home.'

Emma sits down beside her friend and cradles her in her arms.

'We'll be home soon. Maybe today or tomorrow, I'm certain.'

'How can you be sure?'

'I feel it—I just know. Hey, how about a game of pat-a-cake?'

'No. It's for kids,' she mumbles.

'We are kids. Come on, we've got to keep occupied.'

She pulls at Emma's hands.

'Pat-a-cake pat-a-cake, baker's man. Bake me a cake as fast as you can. Pat it and roll it, and mark it with zee, and put it in the oven for Zoe and me!'

Zoe breaks out in a giggle as the kettle begins to whistle.

'Right, time for breakfast!'

25

The room is sterile, with magnolia painted breeze block walls. An off-white plastic table is coupled with hard seats. A faint smell of disinfectant lingers in the air.

Dudley checks his watch again. He's waiting for Frank to arrive at work. The desk sergeant said he shouldn't be long, but Dudley is already having second thoughts about the whole thing. If Frank had been in, he imagined he'd saunter down from the CID room and have a quiet word with him in the corner of reception. Now he's sitting here in the interview room, which brings back traumatic memories. The sergeant even searched him before showing him in. He was pleasant enough, but it still doesn't stop Dudley from feeling like a criminal. Maybe he is? Is wasting police time a chargeable offence?

He needs to decide—and fast. Does he tell Frank the truth, or should he stick to his concocted story? He ponders for a moment.

If I exchanged places with Frank, what would I make of my tale? Dudley wonders.

The thing is, Frank, I've been communicating with Shirley via text messages. What? Yes, I realise she died nearly six months ago, but hear me out. It began the night before the two girls went missing, yes that's right, Sunday night or at least very early Monday morning.

At first, I thought it was a sick prank but then I asked her a question that only I know the answer to—but she also knew the answer. That's when I became convinced it was her. It doesn't matter what the question was—that's not why I'm here.

Last night as I climbed into bed, I received another message from her. She gave me some information that could help you with the missing girls. Would he believe it?

Reality hits him in the head like a sledgehammer. Of course he wouldn't! He'd have him committed to the nearest psychiatric hospital! That means he must stick to his fairy story. Just the briefest of bare facts. That's all he needs to know.

———❖———

Dudley is facing the door as the familiar figure of DCI Frank Finnegan walks in.

'Morning Dudley, how's it going?'

'Oh, you know.'

Frank pulls up a seat and slips into it with a weary air.

'I must apologise, Dudley. I have been meaning to call around to keep you updated on the reconstruction video of Shirley's ill-fated night, but I've been snowed under of late. What I can tell you is that a small production team is due up here in a week's time. They've got an actress to play Shirley. Although not her double, there are a lot of similarities; age, looks, height, weight, and of course we'll make sure she's wearing the same clothes as Shirley had on that night.' He suddenly appears alarmed. 'Oh, I must stress they aren't Shirley's real clothes, they're exact duplicates we purchased. We will show the reconstruction on the local news on the sixth-month anniversary of her death, and then on Crimewatch the following Thursday night.'

Dudley nods. 'Let's hope it jogs someone's memory, eh?'

Frank is under a misapprehension. He thinks I'm here about Shirley. It's not too late. I can still back out of this. What if I've imagined the whole thing?

He absentmindedly taps at his phone lying on the table. But he hasn't imagined it. It's in black and white in his text messages. He has a duty to tell him. It could help.

There's an awkward silence.

'Is there anything else you'd like to know about the reconstruction, Dudley?'

He shakes his head. 'No. Actually, Frank, I'm not here about Shirley.'

Surprise adorns Frank's weathered features. 'Then why are you here?'

'I have some information which may help with your search.'

'The search for Shirley's killer?' he replies, with the merest hint of suspicion.

'No, the search for the missing girls—Zoe Clark and Emma Tolhurst.'

26

It's another beautiful, fresh, sunny morning in Whitby as Frank walks into the station. He nods at the desk sergeant.

'Morning,' he says.

'Morning Frank,' the sergeant replies with a wry smile. 'I have someone to see you.'

Frank stops in his tracks. 'What's it about?' he's hoping it's to do with the girls.

'Wouldn't say.'

'Who is it?'

'Dudley Fox. Came in about ten minutes ago. Said he'd wait. I put him in interview room one as he said it was confidential.'

Frank winces as his hopes of an early morning breakthrough on the missing girls evaporates.

'Okay, thanks,' he says, trying to mask his disappointment. Frank knows why Dudley's called in to see him. It's because he was supposed to keep Dudley updated about a forthcoming reconstruction of his wife's last night on earth—and he hasn't. If Dudley were to complain to the superintendent, then Frank would be on the carpet again for another roasting.

He walks into the room and exchanges pleasantries with Dudley before launching into details of the reconstruction. Dudley is tired with deep bags under his eyes and his weight is ballooning. Frank finishes his recap as an uneasy silence descends.

'Is there anything else you'd like to know about the reconstruction, Dudley?'

He shakes his head. 'No. Actually, Frank, I'm not here about Shirley.'

Frank is surprised. 'Then why are you here?'

'I have some information which may help in your search.'

'The search for Shirley's killer?'

'No, the search for the missing girls—Zoe Clark and Emma Tolhurst.'

Frank places two cups of tea onto the table, then returns to the door and quietly closes it before taking his seat.

'So, what have you got?'

'It's probably nothing, and I'd hate to waste your time.'

Frank pushes back in his seat and takes a deep breath.

'Dudley, we don't have much to go on at the moment, so anything you have will be a bonus—bum lead or not,' he replies as he pulls out a notepad and pen.

'The day of the girls' disappearance, Monday, I was out walking Tyson—my dog.'

Frank takes notes and nods, well aware of Dudley's Boxer dog, named after Tyson Fury, the boxer.

'I'm afraid I'm not very observant these days, what with... well, you know. I seem to meander whichever way my feet want to go. Normally, I take Tyson down past St Mary's, then across the bridge to West Cliff Beach and throw a ball for him. But on Monday, I didn't. I followed the road from the abbey down Falcon Lane. I can honestly say I didn't really notice anything or anyone until...'

'Go on, until what?'

'Until the news bulletin last night. It said the police were now focusing their attention on land and the girls may not have gone into the water. Again, being preoccupied with other things, I didn't dwell on the matter... that is, until I took a late night shower and had a sort of flashback from my walk. On Monday morning, when I'd been walking Tyson, I passed a Kombi van parked down a narrow laneway, the one that leads to the Saltwick Bay holiday park.'

'That lane is a dead-end to vehicles. Did you go down it?'

'No. I walked past it, keeping on Falcon Lane.'

'Why did it catch your attention, or at least lodge in your subconscious?'

'Camping at the side of the road is prohibited. It's a bugbear of mine, especially where we live.'

'How do you know they were camping there?'

'I didn't, for sure. It was nothing more than a fleeting thought.'

'How far down the laneway was it?'

'Oh, maybe eighty to a hundred yards.'

'And how was it parked?'

'It was off the road and on the grass verge, hard up against a stone wall.'

'Facing which way?'

'Towards me, towards the T-junction with Falcon Lane. On walking back with Tyson, I noticed it had gone.'

'What time was this?'

'I left the house about ten-thirty, passed the van about eleven and on my return, maybe an hour later, it was gone.'

'Long walk?'

'Yes. I find it helps me relax... to a degree.'

'Did you get the registration?'

'No.'

'Did you see anyone around or inside the vehicle?'

'No.'

'And you saw no one else on your walk, no one you chatted with or said hello to?'

'No. A few cars and caravans passed by, but no one out walking.'

'Did the Kombi pass you?'

'No.'

'Can you describe it?'

'It was white, or maybe light grey, or possibly even very pale blue. A retro type, you know the ones from the sixties with the V shape on the front. I think they're called a Type 2 model.'

Frank scratches at his jaw.

'Any other distinguishing features?'

'Well, here's the thing—one door was orange. Again, it was a fleeting observation. I didn't stop and stare at it and think, that's odd.'

'Which door?'

'Sorry?'

'Which door was orange?'

'Oh, erm... it was the front passenger door... I think.'

'Was the Kombi old, new, refurbished?'

'I couldn't say.'

Frank eyes Dudley suspiciously and scratches the stubble on his chin, then winces as though he has a trapped nerve in his neck.

'Are there any other distinguishing features you can think of?'

'Hell, Frank!' Dudley exclaims, becoming exasperated. 'It had one orange door! If that's not a distinguishing feature, then I don't know what is.'

'Okay, calm down.'

Dudley closes his eyes and sighs. 'Sorry, Frank. That's all I remember. The doctor's got me on medication—antidepressants. They help a little in combating the lows, but the side effects give me a foggy head. I wish I could be of more help.'

He picks his tea up with trembling hands and takes a thirsty gulp. Frank pushes back in his chair, scraping the legs against the floor. He stands and offers his hand.

'Thanks for taking the time to come down and give me the information, Dudley. It may be nothing, but the van was certainly in the right area and at the right time. If anything else springs to mind, then please, call me.'

27

Frank throws open the door to the incident room and strides in. The busy room falls silent. He spots Prisha and Zac huddled around a computer screen.

'Prisha, Zac, can I have a quick word? My office.' It wasn't a request.

Prisha and Zac follow Frank into his office and close the door.

'I've just been given some information from a member of the public. It could be nothing, but it's worth checking out. A white, or very light coloured Kombi van was seen parked in the vicinity of Falcon Lane, near to the Saltwick Bay holiday park at about eleven, Monday morning. That's right in our timeframe and only a mile or so from where the footprints were found. He didn't get the number plate and didn't see anyone in or around the vehicle. It was an older, sixties type model but most importantly, it had one orange door—possibly the front passenger side.'

Zac and Prisha exchange surprised glances.

'Who gave you the info, boss?' Zac queries.

Frank pauses as his eyes dart between his officers.

'Dudley Fox.'

169

———◆———

'Oh, come on, Frank!' Prisha exclaims.

'Come on, what?' Frank snaps as he drops into his chair.

'Dudley Fox! He's already the only suspect we have in his wife's murder, and now he becomes involved in the disappearance of the two girls. It's fishy.'

'What are you implying, Prisha? You think Dudley not only murdered his wife but nearly six months on he decides to abduct two young girls, then present himself to the police with some information.'

'It's not as outlandish as it seems. He could be getting nervous now he knows we are focusing our attention on a land search. He certainly lives in the right spot and would know the area like the back of his hand. The Kombi could be disinformation to throw us off and waste time while he figures his next move.'

'You need to drop this notion about Dudley being his wife's killer. Me and Zac spent over thirty hours questioning him over three days, and not once did he err in retelling his movements of that night. There's not a single scrap of evidence against him, let alone a motive.'

'We have not fully explored the Libby Hobson theory,' Prisha fires back.

Zac pulls a grimace. 'Libby Hobson? What's she got to do with it?'

'Prisha seems to think Dudley may have been having an affair with Shirley's best friend, Libby Hobson, hence the reason she wasn't at the pub that night and the reason Dudley didn't meet his wife.'

'It's possible, sir,' Prisha says as another thought flashes into her head. 'Maybe he paid a hit man. Then lies low for a year or so and finally shacks up with Libby.'

'I see,' Frank thunders. 'So now in your mind it's a crime of passion?'

'It's an avenue which needs to be investigated.'

'My wife has known Libby Hobson for over twenty years, and she assures me there is absolutely no way Dudley and Libby would ever have an affair,' Frank says in a subdued, deep, gruff tone.

'With all due respect, sir, your wife vouching for another woman's integrity is not how we conduct police investigations.'

Frank jumps to his feet and slams his palms on the desk. 'And with slightly less respect, inspector, I don't appreciate your tone!'

Prisha pulls a ferocious pout, folds her arms and stares into the void.

Frank calms and slumps back down. 'The fact is, Libby Hobson is a lesbian and has been in a steady relationship for over twenty years. It's well known within certain circles of the community... circles my wife moves in. Now, can we drop this nonsense about Libby Hobson and focus on the two girls?'

Prisha's face is a picture of shock. It's quickly followed by a crestfallen drop of the head. She closes her eyes.

'Sorry, boss,' she mumbles.

'There's nothing to be sorry about,' Frank says quietly. 'I admire your tenacity and desire to bring a killer to justice, but when a dog has a bone, it can lose sight of the rabbit.'

Zac breaks the stilted silence. 'I'll get uniform to run a PNR check on all Kombi vans registered in the area. That obviously won't pick up any holidaymakers, so I'll put a couple of officers on patrol to check all campsites, farmers' fields, lay-bys. If that Kombi is still in the area, it shouldn't be too hard to find with one orange door.'

'That's the salient point, Zac—if it's still in the area. It could be long gone by now,' Frank says, followed by a long sigh. 'It could be an out-of-towner, an opportunist who accidentally came across the girls and...' he tails off.

'No boss,' Prisha starts. 'Remember what we said in last night's briefing? If the girls were lured away, then it had to be by someone they knew, trusted, which would actually rule out a stranger.'

As Frank processes her words, he becomes reinvigorated and claps his hands together.

'You're right! Zac, get some of your team onto the Kombi sighting, then resume your house to house.'

'Boss.'

'Prisha, what have you got planned?'

'I still have some staff and the two boarders from the school to interview, Alfred Bramwell—the paedo to check out, and a dozen classmates of Zoe's and Emma's. Oh, and Tiffany Butler's alibi at Frodsham Spa to corroborate.'

'You're busy, but all those things can wait. You're coming with me. It won't take long.'

28

Frank and Prisha scurry across the car park with a bounce in their step.

'Where are we going, boss?' Prisha asks.

'To conduct a little experiment.'

Prisha laughs. 'This sounds like fun. Care to elaborate?'

'I want to check out Dudley Fox's Kombi tale.'

'You sound sceptical. If you don't believe him, then why have you got Zac wasting time checking out all the Kombi vans in the area?'

'I never said I don't believe him. But some details were vague in the extreme.'

They jump into the Ford Focus, which is littered with rubbish in the passenger side footwell. McDonalds boxes, chocolate wrappers, and empty coke bottles battle it out for contention.

'Bloody DS Cartwright!' Frank bellows, making Prisha jump. 'I'll have his balls in a sling. I've warned him about this on numerous occasions. He's going to cop it this time. He's a bloody liability!'

Prisha is seeing a different Frank today compared to the usual easy-going and jovial man of the last couple of days.

Frank navigates the car down Falcon Lane until he comes to a T-junction, which is signposted to the Saltwick Bay Holiday Park. He pulls up at the side of the road and turns to Prisha.

'Get out,' he orders.

'What?'

'You heard, sergeant. Get out.'

'Can I ask why?'

'The experiment. This is where Dudley Fox was walking his dog. As he came to this junction, he looked left and said he noticed a Kombi van parked about a hundred yards up that laneway which leads to the holiday park.'

They both stare down the single vehicle lane.

'He's already either told a lie or got a terrible memory,' Frank adds thoughtfully.

'Why's that?' Prisha asks as she unfastens her seatbelt and alights from the vehicle.

'Dudley said the van was parked hard up against a stone wall. There is no stone wall, just a wire fence and overgrown shrubs. Right, I'll drive about a hundred yards down the track and park up. Have your phone handy. I'll call you.'

As Frank drives away, Prisha folds her arms and takes in the serenity. The car rounds a bend and disappears from sight. Her phone rings.

'Yes, boss?'

'Can you see any of the car?'

'No.'

'Okay, keep on the line and I'll find somewhere to turn around.'

A few seconds pass until the bonnet of the car edges back into Prisha's line of sight.

'I can see you now, boss.'

'Okay, that's more like fifty yards, not a hundred, but I'll give him the benefit of the doubt. Prisha, if you'd never set eyes on this car before, can you see enough of either of the side doors to determine its colour?'

'No, sir.'

'I'll drive forward slowly. Shout stop when you can see the colour of the doors.'

The car edges slowly forward.

'Okay, stop. Just as you came around the last bend, I could make out the colour on the passenger side. Is it white, sir?'

'Very funny, Prisha. Don't give up the day job.'

Frank pulls up at the junction and gets out.

'There's no stone wall. The lane is not wide enough for anyone to park without blocking the road. There is a passing point around the corner, but it's not visible from the main road. All in all, his story has more holes in it than a slice of Swiss cheese.'

'Maybe he's confused, sir.'

'Hmm... he said his medication can make him a little foggy headed. But this is more than muddled thinking.'

'What if he actually walked up the lane instead of bypassing it? Then maybe he could have seen a van parked at the passing point?'

'And the stone wall?'

Prisha glances down Falcon Lane. 'There is a stone wall along this main road boss,' she says nodding towards a thigh high structure in need of repair.

Frank stares at her and grins.

'What's so amusing?' she asks.

'You've gone from accusing Dudley of being a murderer and kidnapper to now being his duty solicitor.'

'Simply playing devil's advocate, boss.'

Frank arches his back and groans. 'Let's look at it from a different point of view. If he made the whole thing up, what could he possibly hope to gain from it?'

'As I said earlier, he could send us on a wild goose chase to buy some time. Which, if true, would implicate him in some way to the disappearance of the girls.'

'But why bring himself to our attention in the first place when there was no need to? He knows how tenacious the police can be after what he's been through. He'd be well aware we wouldn't take his word as gospel and would check out his story.'

'I've got an overwhelming feeling of déjà vu, Frank,' Prisha mutters.

'Why?'

'Once again, Dudley Fox gives us information which is impossible to prove or disprove.'

Prisha scans the horizon, admiring the beauty and wildness of the place. It's a moment's reprieve from the cloying feeling developing in the pit of her stomach.

'You don't think he's one of those types who likes to play games, do you, Frank? Some people get off on that.'

Frank rubs at the back of his neck.

Have I been wrong about Dudley all along? Surely not...

29

The drive to interview Alfred Bramwell, five miles west of Whitby, is a revelation to Prisha. Impossibly narrow lanes are flanked by dense hedgerows of hawthorn, hazel, primrose, blackthorn, elder, and blackberry bushes. Verdant greenery is sprinkled with flashes of rich yellow flowers, red, and purple berries, and white petals defended by vicious thorns. Sweet delicate scents and rich, earthy aromas drift through the open window and delight her senses.

On three occasions, she has to stop and reverse the car until she finds a passing point or the entrance to a field. It's a million miles from inner-city Birmingham. However, the irony of the situation is not lost on her—driving through a garden of Eden in a blissful reverie to interview a paedophile.

With the aid of the sat-nav on her phone, she finally pulls up outside Alfred Bramwell's address on the outskirts of the quaint, sleepy village of Rusholme. She's pleasantly surprised at the neat front garden bedecked with blossoming roses to the backdrop of a well-manicured lawn. The stone bungalow appears in immaculate condition. She takes a moment to ponder the discrepancies between her own imagination and reality.

She'd visualised a paedophile to be living in some squalid rundown shack at the end of a dark, hateful lane. Even the name Alfred Bramwell conjured up images of an ageing stick insect, bent double with stubble on his chin and food stains splattered over his moth-eaten cardigan. The inside of the house would be dirty, with mould on the walls and a washing-up bowl piled up with grimy crockery amidst a slimy pool of grungy water. Old, well-thumbed porno mags poking out from under a broken down settee.

She walks up the paved pathway and raps on the front door, which is decorated in a leadlight depiction of birds in a tree. The buzz of insects and the warble of birds only add to her sense of surrealism. A blurred figure ambles towards the door and pulls it open.

'Mr Alfred Bramwell?' she asks expectantly as she studies the man.

'Yes. Please, do come in. I've been expecting you,' he replies with a sincere, wistful smile as he extends his arm and steps aside.

Surprised by his reaction, Prisha quickly pulls her warrant card out and flashes it at him.

'Inspector Kumar, North Yorkshire Police.'

He's elderly, but certainly not decrepit by any means. Tall and with a wide frame, a shock of neat grey hair resides above twinkling blue eyes. He's wearing a pair of stylish moccasins, which match his fawn coloured chinos. A crisp white shirt is set off against a deep brown waistcoat with all the buttons neatly done up. A gentle whiff of fragrance, fresh and clean, percolates from him.

He closes the door and leads the way down a hallway to a modern kitchen-cum-dining room.

'I assume it's about the missing girls, Zoe, and Emma?'

'Yes... yes, it is. I need to ask you a few questions.'

'Of course you do. Would you care for a drink, Inspector Kumar? I've just made a fresh brew of plunger coffee.'

It smells damned good, and she could do with a little boost. She has a quick scan of the kitchen, which is as spotless and clean as the rest of the house.

'Yes, thank you, Mr Bramwell. Black, no sugar, and a drop of cold.'

A feeling of unease washes over her.

He's a paedophile. He took pictures of young girls coming down a slide. I should hate the bastard, but he's so disarming and, well... nice.

'You said you were expecting us—the police?'

'Yes. You wouldn't be doing your job otherwise,' he replies softly as he focuses on dispensing the coffee into two bone-white cups.

He places the drink in front of Prisha and positions himself on a high stool at the kitchen counter. Prisha follows suit as she pulls out her notepad and pen, then takes a genteel sip from her cup.

'Mr Bramwell, can you tell me where you were on Monday 17th August between the times of 10:30 and 11:30 am?'

'Yes, I can. I was doing some gardening work at Rusholme Church. You may have spotted it on the fringes of the village. Gardening is one of my pleasures. I find it relaxing and you reap a reward for your efforts.'

'And what time was this?'

'Oh, I probably arrived a little after nine, and packed away about one, one-thirty.'

'And can anyone corroborate those times?'

He runs a hand through his stylish, slicked back hair.

'Yes, a few people. I saw the vicar around an hour after I arrived. He had some work to do inside the church, but I had a quick chat with him when he left at midday. Mrs Clitheroe, the cleaning lady, turned up not long after the vicar. She departed at around one. And Mrs Brown, who lives next-door to the church, brought me tea and biscuits about eleven thirty.'

'You seem to be very sure of the times?'

'The church has a very large, and noticeable timepiece, inspector.'

Prisha feels her cheeks flush. 'Yes. Of course, the clock.'

He reaches for a small address book and flicks through the pages, then carefully writes on a piece of paper.

'Here are the names, addresses, and telephone numbers of my witnesses. It will save you a lot of time,' he explains as he pushes the note towards her.

Prisha studies the names for a moment. 'You have excellent handwriting, Mr Bramwell. That's a lost art these days.'

'Indeed. It was one of my specialities.'

'Specialities?'

'Yes. I taught English and English literature mainly, but I also ran an after-school class twice a week for students who wished to learn the dying art of calligraphy. It wasn't part of the school curriculum, of course. It was something I did voluntarily.'

Prisha's senses twitch. 'I didn't realise you were a schoolteacher?' she says, cursing herself for not reading Alfred Bramwell's case file more closely.

'Yes.'

'Whereabouts did you teach?'

'My career finished, rather abruptly you'd understand, at Fulford Grange, a special school just outside of York. Before then, I taught at Carston Hall for over twenty years.'

Prisha swallows hard as she scrutinises his eyes. 'Carston Hall is where our missing girls go to school.'

'Yes, inspector. I am aware of that.'

'Have you had contact with anyone from Carston Hall lately?'

He emits a deprecating chuckle. 'No. I would assume I'm a persona non grata in their eyes. You'd be aware I was released from prison on licence, which means I have certain conditions to adhere to. One of which is I am to have no contact with children.'

Feeling uncomfortable, Prisha takes a large gulp of coffee.

'Thanks for your time, Mr Bramwell, and the coffee. It was very nice,' she says standing up.

He follows her to the door. 'It was an aberration, inspector... the photographs,' he says, softly.

Prisha stops dead in her tracks. She doesn't want to hear this.

'That's a rather fancy word for the acts you committed.'

'My wife had passed away six months earlier. I was lonely, grief-stricken. With the benefit of hindsight, I can now see I was undergoing some sort of mental and emotional breakdown. While you're living through it, it's hard to detect.

In no way does that exonerate me from my actions on that day. But it was a one-off. Nothing before and nothing since. I paid my dues to society. My penance under the eyes of God will go on for eternity. Although they were only photographs, I am glad I was caught. These things need to be nipped in the bud before they blossom into some grotesque monster.'

He pauses briefly, deep in thought.

'I apologise. That was a rather poorly worded sentence, especially considering my background. When I said—they were only photographs—I didn't mean to trivialise my actions. It was wrong, vile, immoral. I won't use the word evil because I don't believe I am.'

She stares at him. His twinkling blue eyes are diminished by his recollections, his broad shoulders drooped.

Damn you! I don't want to feel sympathy towards you. I don't want to like you. Why couldn't you have been a filthy old lech with halitosis, BO, and rampant dandruff?

'I'll be in touch if I require any further information, Mr Bramwell.'

She steps out into the English country garden, which seems so incongruous to the conversation she's just had.

'I sincerely hope and pray you find the girls, inspector. As an aside, no one in the village knows of my past. But you must do what you think is best.'

She offers him a weak smile as she slips into the driver's seat and slams the door shut.

30

The drive from Rusholme village to Frodsham Spa, to corroborate Tiffany Butler's alibi, is less than fifteen minutes. Prisha is hoping it will be another person of interest she can tick off the list.

Alfred Bramwell's alibi stood up to scrutiny. She spoke with the vicar, the cleaning lady, and the woman who lives next to the church. All confirmed Alfred's whereabouts. Naturally, they were intrigued to know why Alfred had been questioned by the police regarding the missing children. Prisha told them it was routine. All teachers from Carston Hall, past and present, were being interviewed to eliminate them from the investigation. The two women appeared convinced at this explanation. The vicar—a little less so.

She wished Alfred no harm, and yes, she had to admit she felt sorry for him. He hadn't actually harmed any children; in fact, the children were blissfully unaware of his actions. It had been an eagle-eyed mother who found his behaviour odd and called the police. After seizing his camera at the park, they went through his computers, mobile phones, and internet usage at his home and work with a certain dedicated zeal and found nothing untoward.

The only evidence of predatory behaviour was a handful of photos on his digital camera, which he'd secretly used at the playground. It appeared it was a one-off, an aberration, as he termed it. But she also realised that all too often aberrations can become more frequent and escalate quickly. That's why he said he was glad he was caught.

Frodsham Health Spa is situated on twenty acres of pristine, undulating gardens and parkland. It looks more like Hampton Court than a state-of-the-art health resort. Another Georgian era building of exquisite design and grandeur.

'I'm in the wrong bloody job,' Prisha moans to herself as she climbs the ostentatious steps that lead to the reception.

She introduces herself to the receptionist and briefly explains her visit. The receptionist is polite and keen to assist in any way she can.

'It's purely routine,' Prisha explains, using the well-worn phrase that can hide a multitude of sins. 'I believe Miss Tiffany Butler visits your spa three to four times a year.'

'Yes, Miss Butler is a member. She was only here a couple of days ago... Monday, I think.'

'Can you confirm her arrival and departure time?'

The woman turns her attention to a computer screen. 'Give me a moment.'

'Sure.'

While the receptionist types at the keyboard, Prisha surveys the palatial surroundings. 'How much does it cost to come here?' she asks, almost absentmindedly.

The woman laughs. 'That's like asking how long a piece of string is. It depends on what you want; facial, massage, manicure, pedicure, hot tub, salt bath, flotation tank, waxing, aromatherapy. Ah, here it is. Yes, Miss Butler swiped in on Monday at 10:03 am and left at 2:05 pm.'

'Did you see her leave?'

'No. My shift was from eight until twelve-thirty.'

'But you definitely saw her come in?'

'Yes. We had a quick chat.'

'So how do you know she left at two?'

'We ask all clients to swipe in and out. It's part of our emergency response procedures. If there were a major incident, such as a fire, we need to tell rescue services how many people are still in the building.'

Prisha nods thoughtfully. 'Can you tell me what treatments she had?'

'Is this confidential?' she asks, concerned at handing over client information.

'Of course.'

'Let me see... she had a thirty minute massage, followed by two hours in the floatation tank, followed by a fully body waxing and finished with a pedicure and manicure.'

'Christ! How much did that little lot set her back?'

'Three-hundred-and sixty pounds.'

'Do you mind if I have a quick look at your flotation tank? I'm intrigued.'

The receptionist leads the way down a long corridor to a room at the back of the building with glorious views of the rolling countryside. In the centre is what can only be described as an alien pod. In shimmering white, with the lid open, it resembles the gaping chasm of a whale's mouth ready to devour its lunch. Pale blue waters reside in the body of the capsule.

Prisha giggles. 'Well, I never. So Miss Butler was in the tank for two hours?'

'Yes.'

'Is that normal?'

'Most people do an hour, but Miss Butler always does two.'

'Doesn't it make your skin wrinkly?'

'We use Epsom Salts. They're rich in magnesium, which is known to cure aches and pains and it has an emollient effect—so no, your skin doesn't wrinkle. You can close the lid to create sensory deprivation.'

'Sounds like torture.'

'On the contrary, the removal of external stimuli has been proven to aid relaxation and meditation, thereby helping the mind and body to recover.'

Prisha scoffs. 'Proven by who—the manufacturer of the flotation tank?'

The receptionist purses her lips. 'Is there anything else, inspector? I need to get back to my desk.'

'No thanks. You've been very helpful.'

Prisha takes one last glance around the room and outside at the magnificent vista of the North Yorkshire Moors. As she follows the woman back to the reception, a thought niggles away at her.

'You said Miss Butler had a full body wax?'

'That's correct.'

'When you say—full—do you mean head to toe?'

'Yes.'

'And everything in between?'

The receptionist halts and turns to her, bemused. 'Yes. Everything.'

'Even the old fandango?'

'Fandango?'

'Yes. The front bottom,' she adds as she discreetly points a finger downwards.

The woman frowns. 'If you're referring to the vagina, then yes, that as well.'

'Ouch!'

'Maybe you should try it some day?'

'No, thank you. I like mine the way God intended.'

31

The Ford Focus pulls off the main road and into a layby. Prisha stabs at her phone.

'Prisha, hope you're having a better morning than me?' Zac answers, his muffled tone clearly indicating he's feeding his face.

'Why, what's happened?' she asks, concerned.

'Nothing, that's the bloody point. Frank's been stuck in his office with the superintendent for the last two hours, which doesn't bode well. Most of my team are out on house to house grunt work with no new leads. We've got a list of twelve Kombi vans registered locally, which I need to get on to. The patrol I sent out this morning has spoken to the owners of eight other Kombis scattered around various campsites and fields—none of which have a rogue orange door. And to make matters worse, the sausage has just fallen out of my hot dog and onto the carpet.'

Prisha chuckles. 'Hell, you're as bad as Cartwright. I hope you didn't pick it up and eat it?'

'You're joking, although Cartwright would have. Have you seen the state of the carpet in the incident room? It can't have been steam-cleaned for a decade.'

'Budget cutbacks.'

'Yeah. Oh, and forensics have finally finished analysing the girls' phones.'

'And?'

'Nothing suspicious apart from a slight peculiarity.'

'Which is?'

'Have you heard of MiI?'

'No, but I can hazard a guess.'

'It's a real-time tracking device to keep tabs on your kids... or your missus,' he adds with a chuckle.

'Or husband!'

'Touché. Anyway, MiI was installed on Zoe's phone.'

'Parents tracking her?'

'No. Sarah and John Clark didn't even know what the app was.'

'Maybe the girls use it to see where each other are, you know, if they've arranged to meet each other somewhere?'

'That's the strange thing; it's only on Zoe's phone—not Emma's.'

'That is odd.'

'Anyway, what about you? How did you go?'

'Alfred Bramwell has a watertight alibi. He's definitely off the list. I felt sorry for him in a way. He's a lost soul and not anything like I was expecting. He was respectable, well-groomed, personable.'

'Do you think all paedos walk around with two heads, drooling from the mouth whilst playing with their dicks?'

'No. I was just expecting someone more... sinister, creepy. He was... normal. Eh, one spooky thing, though.'

'What?'

'He used to be a teacher at Carston Hall.'

'You're shitting me!'

'I shit you, not. It was a long time ago, though.'

'And you're certain about his alibis?'

'Yep, one hundred per cent. Just one of those weird coincidences that crop up from time to time.'

'You know what coppers think about coincidences?'

'Yeah... that they don't exist. That's a load of tosh. I also checked Tiffany Butler's alibi. She arrived at Frodsham Health Spa at ten on Monday and left at two—all verified, so we can scrub her from the list. Have you ever been there?'

'Where—Frodsham Spa?'

'Yeah.'

'No. I've passed it plenty of times. It's an impressive building. I once bought the missus a massage gift card for her birthday to use there. She was mightily impressed.'

'With you or with the spa?'

'Ha, ha, not sure. Where are you now?'

'I'm heading back to the station.'

'Okay, I'll see you soon.'

'Wait. Zac, would you be miffed if I called in and had a word with the Clarks and Tolhursts?'

There's a definite pause. 'Christ, Prisha! Frank was right about you; you're like a dog with a bone. Sarah Clark has been interviewed three times now. Once on the beach by the special constable, once by the Family Liaison Officer, and once by me. She'll be filing a complaint if we keep prodding her.'

'I still think we're missing something. She's had time to think. Maybe she's remembered some little detail that could be important. I wanted to be upfront with you. If we're going to be working together, then we need to trust one another.'

'And you obviously don't trust my interviewing technique, otherwise you wouldn't want to revisit the parents.'

'Don't get the hump on. A fresh pair of eyes, that's all.'

'You don't need my permission, inspector. Go for it, but you're wasting valuable time.'

'Come on Zac, don't be a jerk.'

Another pause. 'I don't mind, honest,' his voice softens. 'I hope you do bloody come up with something new.'

'Cheers. By the way, don't mention it to Frank.'

'Fair enough. See you soon.'

The visit to the Tolhurst home revealed nothing new. All it did was throw Prisha into the middle of an emotional cauldron. She felt like an intruder at a wake. Lenny and Rachel Tolhurst were pragmatists by nature and even though they put on a veneer of positivity, they'd just about resigned themselves to the worst fate in the world; that of grieving parents.

As she knocks on the Clark's front door, she hopes for a better outcome. Net curtains twitch in her peripheral vision. She waits, then knocks again.

Odd?

She stoops over, pushes open the letter box and calls out.

'Mrs Clark! Sarah, John, it's Inspector Kumar. I'd like a quick word, please!'

A few seconds pass until the unmistakable clank of a bolt being pulled back and the click of a key turning in its lock has the door opening a crack. Sarah Clark's worried frown greets Prisha.

'Sarah, can I come in? I'd like a few minutes of your time.'

The door opens an inch further.

'I'm sorry, I'm on my way out.'

'It won't take long, I promise.'

'What is it you want?' she snaps.

Prisha realises she will not be welcomed in.

'I'd like to go over events on the day of Zoe's and Emma's disappearance.'

'For Christ's sake! I've been quizzed three times. There's nothing further I can add. If I knew anything else, I'd have let you know.'

Appreciating Sarah Clark will not budge on the matter, she tries a different tack.

'I can see you're having a bad day. Would it be possible to speak with your husband, John, instead?'

'He's not here.'

'Do you know when he'll be back?'

'Not sure.'

'Can you tell me where he is?'

'London.'

'London?'

'Yes. A family emergency. His brother.'

'Oh... I see.'

'Really, if you don't mind, I'm running late.'

She rudely slams the door in Prisha's face.

'Well... that put me back in my box,' she mumbles as she turns to leave.

32

Frank is trying to eat a pot noddle as politely as one can eat a pot noodle. He undoes the top button on his shirt and yanks at his tie as Prisha and Zac share a smirk with one another.

'I told my wife I'd get a pre-made pasta salad from the supermarket for my dinner. If she knew I was eating this salt-laden crap, her hair would fall out. Two and a half wasted bloody hours under the grill with the superintendent. She wants me to make a breakthrough and yet wastes my time by getting me to go over the minutiae of the case! She should be counting beans and measuring KPIs instead of getting under my feet. Right, run by me what you've got. Prisha, you first.'

Each officer brings Frank up to speed with developments, most notably, two alibis verified, out of town Kombis checked and eliminated, and the news about Zoe's tracking app on her phone.

'Hmm... it's progress, of sorts at least,' Frank says as he throws the empty pot noodle into the waste bin and dabs his lips with a serviette.

'Did anything come from the bulletin about two girls hitchhiking on the A171?' he says, eyeballing Zac.

'No. A couple of time-wasters. One said he'd picked up a woman in her late twenties as he came through Hawsker, heading north. Another rang in to say he'd passed two young lads riding bicycles without helmets on Guisborough Road. I explained it wasn't a legal requirement, but he still banged on about it for ten minutes.'

'Give me strength!'

'I'm about to start checking these out, boss,' he says as he waggles a sheet of paper in front of him containing the twelve locally registered Kombi vans.

Frank sucks at his teeth. 'Fine. But be quick about it. I don't want us to waste too much time on the mysterious orange door. The information is not reliable in my mind. I'm not sure Dudley Fox is on planet earth at the moment. Who's on the list, any known reprobates?'

'Let me see,' Zac replies as he stretches and reads from the list of names. 'Okay, we have a Steve Watson, David Brewer, Jed Loveday, Katrina Hardcastle, Carly Sanderson...'

He freezes.

'What?' Frank asks.

'And a Mark Bridges...' he says in a whisper.

'The caretaker at Carston Hall,' Prisha murmurs.

'Did you get his home address, Prisha?' Frank asks, suddenly perking up.

'No.'

'Have you checked his alibi that he saw two girls saddling up about eleven thirty?'

'Not yet. I was about to head over there after this debrief, boss?'

'Okay, let's not get too excited for the moment. It could be a different Mark Bridges. Right, you two get your arses over to the school right now. Take it easy, you know what to do. Don't go in with all guns blazing. Let's see if our caretaker owns a Kombi with an orange door. And even if he does, it doesn't make him guilty of anything... yet. Prisha, before you go, get two of your team to check out the other names on the list and let's put this Kombi illusion to bed.'

'Yes, Frank,' Prisha agrees, feeling a shard of excitement stab at her chest. 'Supposing Bridges' Kombi has an orange door. What do you want us to do?'

'Bring him in, of course!' he bellows. 'Ask him to come voluntarily to answer a few questions and if he refuses, then arrest him on suspicion. Do I have to do my job as well as yours?'

'No, boss.'

33

The white Ford Focus pulls into the palatial grounds of Carston Hall Private Girls School.

'Hell,' Zac murmurs.

'Never been here before?' Prisha asks.

'No. I've heard about it. I knew it was flash, but didn't imagine it would be like this. It's like a mansion house from a period drama. I'm half-expecting Mr Darcy to come swanning down the steps to greet us.'

The ethereal cry of a distant peacock makes them both chuckle.

'Different world, isn't it?' Prisha says.

'Yep. Out of my league. My lads won't be coming here on my wage.'

'Probably not, considering it's an all-girls' school.'

'Oh, yeah. So, what's your gut instincts about this?'

Prisha shrugs. 'Not sure. When you first mentioned Mark Bridges' name back in the office, I got butterflies. You know, like when you're working a case and it's a dead-end then you suddenly get a breakthrough.'

'Yeah... it's a good feeling.'

'But now, driving down here, I'm not so sure.'

'Why?'

'Bridges came across as a regular guy. To work here, you need a police and working with children check. He has no previous. Seemed legit. In fact, out of all the people I've questioned, there's only two who gave me cause for concern, and for completely different reasons.'

'Who?'

'Charles Murray, who was more worried about the reputation of his precious school than the missing girls; and Tiffany Butler, who was a bit...'

'Spit it out.'

'... up herself. Slightly too self-assured. Like she was looking down her nose at me. Plus, she's extremely pretty and does very nicely, thank you very much. Her house must be worth upwards of four hundred grand.'

'She'll be in the same boat as the rest of us; mortgaged up to the hilt and chained to the bank for the next thirty years.'

'And another thing about Bridges, in my experience people with no criminal record don't jump in at the deep end by abducting two girls. There's usually escalation.'

'And in my experience, criminals who have not been caught don't have a record.'

She laughs. 'Fair point.'

Prisha parks the car outside the main entrance.

'So, what's the go?' Zac asks as he steps from the vehicle.

'I'll find Bridges. You go to the boarding house and question the two girls who were at the stables on Monday.'

'Will do.'

'Oh, and you better speak with Charles Murray. Tell him we have some routine questions to ask his caretaker and the boarders, keep it vague. Also ask him if he saw Bridges on Monday, and if so at what time, then ask where Bridges keeps his Kombi van, and take a snoop around.'

'No problem, boss. Would you like me to stick a broom handle up my arse and sweep the floor at the same time?' he adds with a chuckle.

Prisha stretches as she gets out of the car and wrinkles her nose up.

'Whatever turns you on, sicko.'

'Ah, I see you're not yet accustomed to the Yorkshire self-deprecating sense of humour.'

'I am aware of it, but I'm not sure I'll ever become accustomed. I find it rather crude, vulgar, and it paints a rather vivid picture in the imagination,' she replies with a hint of a smile. 'Anyway, you're Scottish.'

Zac puts one hand under his chin and one on top of his head and performs a violent jerk, which ends with a satisfying crack. Prisha cringes.

'Ah, that's better. There's not much difference between the Yorkies and the Scots, except they're way tighter with their brass.'

'Really?'

'Aye. They hide it under their soap.'

'I don't even know what that means.'

'Think about it.'

'Oh, I see. You're inferring they're tight but also unclean.'

'Elementary, my dear Watson.'

As Zac skips up the old stone steps to the main entrance in search of the deputy principal, Prisha sets off along the path which leads to the rear of the school.

She stands at the top of the stairs leading down to the cellar. The panelled wooden door is shut.

'Mr Bridges!' she calls out. 'Mr Bridges, are you down there? It's Inspector Kumar. I'm here to ask you a couple more questions.'

The only sounds are the gentle swish of leafy tree branches massaged by a languid breeze and the occasional mournful cry of a peacock. Prisha walks down the steps and raps on the door.

'Mr Bridges! It's Inspector Kumar.'

She notices the padlock is undone and flicks up the ring gate latch. Inside, it's gloomy. The only light comes from a distant, solitary light bulb. There's the distant hum of electrics and the atmosphere is humid and dusty with an earthy smell.

'Mr Bridges, are you down there! It's Inspector Kumar from CID!'

She wanders in further, her eyes slowly adjusting to the murkiness. As she takes in her surroundings, she's once again impressed with how neat and tidy everything is. It would be a depressing place to spend a lot of your time, but Bridges has made the best of a bad workplace.

A kettle and coffee maker are sitting on a wooden bench next to an old Belfast sink. Above it, neat shelves stacked with teabags, coffee, sugar, and a couple of mugs. Below the bench is a small fridge. She pulls open the door; it's spotless inside—and rather empty, apart from a carton of milk and a sandwich wrapped in plastic film.

Prisha is hoping Bridges is not involved. He's an attractive man, similar age to herself. Quiet, yet self-assured. Neat, clean, handy to have around the house fixing all those annoying little jobs she's so useless at.

Moving towards the distant glow of the light, she calls out again.

'Mr Bridges, are you down here?'

She ambles over to an office desk with a metal filing cabinet standing alongside. The desk is old and well-worn, but functional and polished.

She grabs the handle of the cabinet and is about to pull it open and have a little snoop inside when an almighty bang makes her physically jump backwards, bumping into someone. She spins around and stares into the eyes of Bridges who is smiling. He lifts his palm from the top of the filing cabinet.

'Sorry, inspector. Didn't mean to spook you,' he says, staring intently into her eyes.

Prisha's heart rate subsides. He takes a step closer. She averts her eyes downwards, noticing a long screwdriver in his left hand. Swallowing hard, she takes a step back, trying to regain her professional composure and put thoughts of a baser nature to the back of her mind.

'Mr Bridges, you nearly gave me a heart attack. I did call out; didn't you hear me?'

He holds up headphone pods which rest around his shoulders.

'It's Mark, remember? I was listening to a podcast at the back of the cellar whilst putting a new jubilee clip on a dodgy bit of piping. Tea, coffee?' he offers politely.

'Ahem, no thanks. I have a couple of questions I'd like to ask you regarding the disappearance of Zoe Clark and Emma Tolhurst.'

He smiles, moves towards the kettle, and flicks it on.

'Still not turned up yet?'

'No. Unfortunately, not.'

'That's no good.'

'No, it's not.'

'Am I a suspect? Or how do you phrase it these days—a person of interest?'

He turns to her and folds his arms. She can't tell if it's a defensive gesture or the sign of someone relaxing.

'Everyone is a person of interest until we've eliminated them from our enquiry. It's nothing personal.'

He relaxes. 'You said you had questions; if I can help, then fire away.'

'Where were you on Monday, 17th of August between 10:30 and 11:30 am?'

'You asked me the same question yesterday. Nothing has changed. I was here all day.'

'And you definitely didn't leave the school for any reason?'

'No, once again for the record—I was here all day.'

His arms fold tighter as he leans back against the filing cabinet and crosses his feet, mild puzzlement flits across his face. His stance does not go unnoticed by Prisha.

'Inspector, I'm not telling you how to do your job, but why are you asking me the same questions? Something must have cropped up?'

Prisha wants to make one hundred per cent certain he can't turn around later and use the—oh, now I remember, actually...

'Mark, do you own a Kombi van with the registration plate SYO 724F?'

'Yes. She's my dream machine. A 1968 model and in mint condition. Why?'

'What colour is it?'

'Bottom half is blue, top half white.'

'Pale blue?'

'No, royal blue, like the Mediterranean in July.'

'Any other distinguishing features?'

'No. Look what's this about?' he says, for the first time sounding slightly defensive.

'It's just a line of inquiry. We're checking out all the Kombi vans in the area.'

'Which means you must think it had something to do with the girls' disappearance. Do you have a number plate, a colour scheme, how old it is?'

'Details are vague.'

The kettle beeps twice. He busies himself with making a brew while chuckling.

'Sorry to laugh, but Kombi's are a popular van and if you hadn't noticed, it's the school summer holidays, and Whitby is a big draw card. I bet there're at least a few dozen in the area. Maybe you should check out surfers. A Kombi van is their favourite mode of transport.'

'Is your van on the school grounds at the moment?'

'No. A mate of mine borrowed it from me for the day. He dropped me at school this morning. He's into his surf fishing. The van's good for carrying his rods and tackle.'

'I see.'

She changes her disposition and smiles. It's time to put him at ease.

'Are you in a relationship at the moment?' she asks in a soft tone.

He swirls the tea bag around in the cup and tilts his head.

'Is that a police question or a personal one?' he says with an impish grin, detecting a change in mood.

Prisha drags a finger along the top of his desk. 'Bit of both,' she replies coyly.

'I'm a free agent... at the moment. You?'

'Likewise.'

'Interesting.' He drops the tea bag into a bin and pulls milk from the fridge. 'Maybe we could go for a drink sometime?'

'Maybe we could, once things are a little less hectic.'

'Of course. I fully understand. Was this your real reason for dropping in?'

She raises her eyebrows and smiles.

'Inspector Kumar!' Zac's voice calls out.

'Down here sarge!' she yells back.

'You came with back up.'

She laughs. 'Sergeant Stoker had a few clear-up questions to ask the deputy principal.'

Zac appears in the cellar's gloom, panting slightly.

'Quick word, boss,' he says.

Prisha saunters over to him. He leans into her and whispers.

'Found his van. Blue and white... with an orange door.'

34

Prisha takes a quick glance over her shoulder at Bridges, who is returning the milk to the fridge. She puts a finger to her lips.

'Play along,' she murmurs.

Zac is puzzled, but nods his agreement.

'Thank you for your time, Mr Bridges,' she declares, resuming her officious police manner. 'We're all done here.'

'New lead?' Bridges quizzes.

'Possibly,' she says, turning and scampering up the stone steps with Zac in her shadow.

They march quickly around the building.

'What the hell are you playing at, Prisha?' Zac hisses.

'Shush. Not a word until we're in the car and out of the grounds.'

They jump into the car.

'Put your foot down,' Prisha commands.

'Why?'

'Make it look like we're in a rush.'

Without fully understanding, he obeys her command. Prisha checks the wing mirror, catching the sight of Bridges, who is hugging tightly to the side of the school building, trying to be invisible.

The car heads out onto the main road.

'Pull over here,' Prisha says, pointing at a farm gate.

The car comes to a stop and the engine dies.

'Right, do you mind telling me what's going on?'

'You first.'

'Charles Murray recalls seeing Bridges about nine o'clock in the morning, and again about three in the afternoon. Definitely at no other point. He told me Bridges keeps his Kombi in an old barn behind the stables. Also, something you forgot to check on your first visit...'

'What?'

'CCTV.'

'Damn!' Prisha moans.

'I asked Murray if he had footage from Monday, and guess what? Miraculously, it was off all day. It stores the video to the Cloud, but if there's a brief power outage, the server drops out and doesn't automatically reconnect, it needs to be reset manually. The only one who knows how to reset it when the IT guy is away is guess who?'

'Bridges.'

'Correct. I spoke with the two boarders who were saddling up in the barn. They saw Bridges, but they both agreed it was definitely more like two thirty, not eleven thirty, when they went horse riding. And for a nice trifecta, his Kombi van has one orange door, front passenger side.'

'The lying little toe-rag.'

'He must have pranged it at some point and got a replacement from the scrap yard. Obviously not got around to getting it spray painted yet. The rest of it was a vivid blue colour and white. It's in tip-top condition mind. Now, your turn; why haven't we brought him in?'

'He doesn't suspect we know anything. After a few questions, I put him at ease.'

'How?'

'By giving him the come on.'

'You crafty git.'

'And he was watching us as we sped away. He'll think we've got a breakthrough.'

'You heard what Frank said—bring him in.'

'I know, but I don't agree. If we took him to the station, what do you think he'd do? He'd call for a duty solicitor and shut up shop. Even if we could get some real evidence against him and lay charges, it would be months before his trial.'

'So, at least we'd have our man.'

'And what about the girls?'

Zac falls silent as he stares at the passing traffic.

'So, what's next?'

'I want to get surveillance on him. If he is our man, then there's a good chance he could lead us to where Zoe and Emma are being held captive.'

'And what if they're already dead?'

Now it's Prisha's turn to go quiet as she contemplates the unthinkable.

'Then bringing him in would have served no purpose. Even if they are... dead, then you know what some killers are like; they go back to the site of the body to make sure they haven't left any clues. If they are still alive, then this is our only chance to save them.'

Zac brushes a hand through his long, tousled hair and exhales.

'Christ Prisha! Frank will do his bloody nut.'

'Are you with me on this?'

He purses his lips. 'Okay, I'll back you up. But you can be the one to tell Frank.'

35

The rumble of Frank's voice is so loud it makes the window in his office rattle.

'You did what!'

'We... I... didn't bring him in, sir,' Prisha says, trying to sound defiant as Zac stares at the carpet.

Frank kicks at his chair, sending it crashing to the floor.

'He's a bloody liar! He lied about the van not being there; he lied about what time he saw the girls in the stable; he lied about the van not having any distinguishable features. He's the only one who knows how to reset the bloody CCTV!'

'If you'd let me explain...'

Frank glares furiously out of the window into the car park, hands on hips.

'Right now he could be destroying evidence—evidence that could put him away. All he's got to do is drive to a remote field and torch the Kombi then report it stolen. If those girls were in that van, then forensics would have found *some* evidence. What in blue blazes possessed you, sergeant!'

'Inspector... actually, sir.'

He rounds on her. 'I could drop you back down to constable in an instant and have you doing crossing duty outside an old people's home by three o'clock,' he whispers menacingly.

'Sir, we've got surveillance on him,' Zac enters the fray, hoping to calm the situation. 'DC Hill is outside the school right now. We waited until he arrived, so we know Bridges hasn't left yet. I worked with DC Hill last year on that heroin job—he's one of the best when it comes to surveillance work.'

Frank straightens and shakes his head. 'I don't remember you coming to me to request surveillance.'

'Well, under the...'

Prisha cuts her colleague off. 'Under the circumstances, I thought it wise to get someone onto it immediately.'

'I see. Disobeying orders, overriding the chain of command—any other misdemeanours you'd like to confess to?' He receives no response. 'I should bang your bloody heads together. Well, you can both get back in your car and bring Bridges into the station, right now.'

'Sir, you're not listening. I'm not some wet behind the ears cadet. I've been on the force for eight years, DS for three. I had a hunch and made a decision,' Prisha pleads.

'Guess what, I've been on the force for thirty-eight bloody years! And with all due respect, *acting inspector,* your hunch, as you call it, could have jeopardised the entire operation!'

His voice reverberates around the room as his large head bulges with blue throbbing veins.

Prisha can contain her frustration no longer. 'And with slightly less respect, chief inspector, this could be our last chance to get Zoe and Emma back alive!' she yells. 'If we'd brought him in and he went down the—no comment—route, then we may never have found the girls! Oh, yes, we may have gathered enough evidence to get a conviction. That way you could stand in front of the TV cameras with a grave expression on your face telling the world how sorry you are for the loss of two young girls, but at least you've put a killer behind bars. Big Frank Finnegan always gets his man!'

'How dare you!'

The door is thrown open as Chief Superintendent Banks storms in.

'What the hell is going on Frank? I can hear your voice at the end of the corridor.'

Frank breathes heavily as he smooths down his hair and fastens the top button on his shirt.

He coughs. 'Sorry, ma'am. A minor disagreement on procedure, that's all. I apologise. It got a little out of hand. It won't happen again.'

The Super eyes everyone suspiciously.

'Hmm... well, make sure it doesn't. You're not in the Houses of Parliament now.'

She closes the door and strides away.

'Sorry, Frank,' Prisha murmurs, contrite in the extreme.

Frank nods. 'Apology accepted.' He glances at the wall clock. 'What time does Bridges usually start work at the school?'

'8 am, sir.'

'Right, I'll authorise surveillance until he drives through the school gates tomorrow. Let's hope he leads us somewhere between now and then. If he doesn't we bring him in—agreed?'

'Yes, boss,' Prisha and Zac say enthusiastically.

'Get warrants to search the school, Bridges' home and one for his arrest. We may as well use the time to our advantage,' he says as he rights his chair and drops into it.

They turn to leave.

'By the way, Prisha, there's not a minute of the day goes by when I don't think about those girls. They're even in my dreams,' he adds, large glassy eyes stained with sorrow.

Prisha wishes the ground would open up and swallow her alive.

'Frank, I didn't mean...'

'I know you didn't. Before you go... do you really think Bridges is our man?'

'Yes, boss. We've eliminated any other possible suspects. I know it's him.'

'Okay. I'm backing you on this. Go on, get on with your work. There's been enough words for one afternoon.'

36

Frank carefully pulls at the ripened tomatoes and drops them into a plastic bag.

'They're little beauties,' he murmurs to himself before popping one in his mouth.

The cherry tomato bursts releasing a sweet explosion of blissful flavours that carries him back to his childhood. He gazes out to the abbey.

'You'll have seen some things in your time. The good, the bad, and the ugly. Humanity in all its shining glory. Humanity in all its squalid, corrupt ruination. And yet the world keeps turning, the tides ebb and flow, daylight follows darkness.'

He collects his assortment of vegetables, locks up his shed, and saunters down the allotment path towards the gate.

Prisha sprints the last two hundred metres along Whitby beach puffing hard. Clambering the steps to Battery Parade, she sidesteps the throng of tourists who are out in force on the warm summer evening. She buys herself a black coffee and a cinnamon donut from the café and wanders towards the west pier. A local jazz band are playing in the bandstand.

For a few brief minutes, the stress lifts from her shoulders. The caffeine hit, the endorphins from her run, the moist comforting syrupiness of the donut, the spectacular scenery all mask her anxiety. The jumble of musical notes dance towards her, enticing, cajoling.

Two young girls, of similar age to Zoe and Emma, walk past, sharing a joke amidst howls of laughter. Prisha remembers what it was like to be that age, it's not so long ago. Excitement, new adventures, fun, the first kiss. Frank is right—childhood is precious.

She finishes her coffee, drops the cup in a nearby bin and jogs off home.

<hr />

As Zac enters the house, his two sons run up to him shouting and squealing their delight.

'Dad, come and have a kick of the footy with us in the back garden,' Sam yells.

He picks him up and swings him around.

'Okay, okay! Just give me a minute to have a word with your mum.'

The two boys scamper out of the patio doors, collecting a football on their way, heading towards the miniature goalposts in the back garden.

Zac walks into the kitchen and puts his arms around his wife and rests his head on her shoulder.

'It's not bad news, is it?' she says, concerned.

'No,' he replies wearily. 'But it's not good news either. Still no sign of them.'

She kisses him tenderly on the lips and strokes his cheek.

'Listen, you go have a play with the boys. I've got tea sorted.'

'What's on the menu?' he asks, pulling away.

'Your favourite; homemade burgers with chips and salad.'

'You make it all worthwhile,' he says with a wistful smile.

He jogs into the garden. 'Right, who's going in goals?' he yells.

His wife watches him from the window as her mind flits back to the missing girls.

37

Thursday 20th August

Prisha arrives at the incident room just after seven-thirty and makes her way directly to Frank's office, where she finds Frank and Zac sitting quietly sipping on coffee.

'Any news?' she asks.

The downcast expressions of her colleagues tell her the answer.

'No,' Frank replies in a deep baritone. 'DC Hill clocked Bridges at five-fifteen yesterday evening leaving the school. He followed him back to Whitby, where Bridges stopped at the Malting Pot for fifteen minutes for a pint in the beer garden. From there, he tailed him back to his house on St Michaels Close. And there he remained. DS Cartwright took over the surveillance at ten last night. He's just called in to say Bridges is on the move. He's on the A171 heading towards Carston Hall.'

Prisha lowers herself into a chair and cups her face in her hands.

'I was wrong,' she gasps, dispirited and feeling foolish.

'It was worth a try,' Frank offers in a sympathetic tone.

'Sorry Frank. You were right. If we'd brought him in yesterday afternoon who knows what may have unfolded. He might have cracked under pressure and told us where Zoe and Emma are. They could have spent the night in their own beds.'

Frank and Zac swap embarrassed glances.

'The thing is Prisha, we're now into day four since their disappearance... and you know what that means,' Frank says softly.

'Every hour that ticks by, there's less chance of...' Zac says as he places a hand on Prisha's shoulder.

'Don't say it. You don't need to spell it out. Christ, we don't even really know if it is Bridges. We could be barking up the wrong tree.'

'Don't start doubting yourself,' Frank says as he stands up and pulls his jacket on. 'Now is not the time for self-recrimination. Today we find out what happened to those two girls—one way or another. Come on, look lively, chop, chop!'

Zac and Prisha jump to their feet.

'What's the plan of attack, boss?' Zac asks.

'Prisha, you take a uniformed officer with you and arrest Bridges on suspicion and bring him in. No doubt he'll want a duty solicitor. While that's being arranged, pay a visit to Dudley Fox and get a written statement from him about his sighting of the Kombi van on Monday. What he told me the other day was off the record. I know it's circumstantial evidence. His van being in the area doesn't mean he took the girls, nevertheless, it's time we started pulling all the pieces together to build a compelling case against Bridges.'

'Yes, sir.'

'Zac, you put a team together and follow Prisha to the school and search the place from top to bottom, starting with his workshop. It's not a crime scene, so no need for forensics, but make sure you put overalls and gloves on. We don't want to foul up any evidence.'

'Frank.'

'Any little thing you find, I want it bagged, and brought to the station. Keep me updated by phone. If I don't answer, text me as I may be in the interview room. It's a dynamic situation but anything I can throw at Bridges may help. Does everyone understand what they've got to do?'

'Yes, Frank.'

38

Prisha parks up outside Dudley Fox's house and knocks on the door. A few seconds pass before it's gently pulled open.

'Mr Fox, I'm DI Kumar. DCI Finnegan asked me to call around and get a written statement from you regarding your sighting of the Kombi van on Monday. Do you mind if I come in?'

'No, of course not.'

She takes a step into the hallways as a boxer dog appears and sticks its snout between her legs.

'Tyson!' Dudley yells, as he yanks at the dog's collar. 'I do apologise inspector. Tyson's introductions are a little crude.'

Prisha chuckles. 'Don't worry about it. I'd have been more surprised if he'd offered to shake my hand.'

She follows him to a well-kept and comfortable living room, which has a magnificent vista of Whitby Abbey in the distance.

'Stunning view,' she comments.

'Yes, it is. It's the reason Shirley and I bought the place. A nice quiet crescent, glorious panorama, plenty of open spaces.'

He hesitates as though contemplating his thoughts.

'Am I right in assuming you've found the owner of the Kombi?'

'Yes, we have him in custody now, thanks to your information. It was extremely useful.'

'And do you think he's involved in the disappearance of Zoe and Emma?'

'Time will tell. We've yet to interview him. He's awaiting a solicitor.'

'Is he connected with the school?'

'I'm not at liberty to say.'

'Of course not. I once had a connection with Carston Hall myself,' he says, staring off into the distance.

'Really?'

'Yes. I'd occasionally conduct field trips on the moors. The school had a place up there. Apart from being a bio scientist, I'm also a qualified botanist. I'd take some of the older children out onto the moors and point out the different flora and fauna. It was purely voluntary, of course.'

'When was this?'

'It would be going back maybe ten years or so. Before I got the position at Menwith Hill. It was Charles who first mooted the idea.'

'Charles?'

'Yes, Charles Murray, deputy principal. I'm sure you must have met him at the school?'

'Yes. He was very helpful.'

'That's Charles. We occasionally bump into each other and have chinwag about the old days.'

He pauses as though lost in a reverie. Prisha coughs.

'Oh, sorry inspector. Can I offer you a tea or coffee? I was just about to make one for myself.'

Prisha realises she's been on the go for two hours and hasn't yet had her caffeine fix.

'Thank you. A strong black coffee would do wonders.'

Dudley leaves the room as Prisha takes in her surroundings. Nothing is out of keeping with what a well-off, middle-aged, doting couple would have in their main room. A large flat-screen TV positioned in a corner. Newish dark brown carpet. Comfortable lounge suite. A chair opposite the TV with an accompanying coffee table. Magazines stacked neatly on its polished surface alongside a plugged in mobile phone and a single white rose in a delicate glass vase. A framed photograph of Shirley Fox in her younger days stands centre-stage, like a shrine. In the corner opposite the door is a set of bookshelves, below them a drinks cabinet. A tasteful wooden fire surround envelops a fake, coal fireplace. It's peaceful, serene.

Something catches her eye on the top of the fireplace. She examines the packet of tablets.

Lexapro? Maybe sedatives or antidepressants. Prescription.

She picks up a small, purple coloured bottle nestled between the tablets and an empty tumbler.

Lithium drops. I didn't know you could buy this over-the-counter?

Sticking her nose over the tumbler, she sniffs.

Whisky, or maybe brandy.

Inspecting the drinks cabinet, she notices a near empty bottle of whisky and a new unopened one next to it.

Poor old bugger. Drinking away his sorrows.

Pulling her phone out, she quickly takes a handful of photos of the medication before Dudley returns carrying a tray and a plate of chocolate digestives.

———◦———

Prisha washes the biscuit down with a hearty slug of exquisitely strong coffee. Her heart rate has already bumped up a few notches as the stimulant sets to work. She prepares her notebook and phone.

'Mr Fox, if you could begin slowly and recount the details of Monday when you went for a walk. Just keep to the relevant points; approximation of time, location, what you saw. I'll take notes but also record it on my phone. We'll get it typed up at the station then get you to come in and sign it. Are there any questions before we start?'

Dudley finishes his drink and stares mournfully at the white rose.

'It's what I used to call her?'

'Sorry?'

'My Yorkshire Rose. It was my nickname for Shirley.'

'Oh, I see. That's very touching.'

'Of course, the red rose symbolises everlasting love, so that would have been more appropriate. But as we are both Yorkshire born and bred, it always had to be a white rose.'

Prisha has things to do, and time is ticking by, but she's also compelled to show patience and empathy.

'It must be a very difficult time for you,' she offers, almost embarrassed at her glib reply.

He shows her a warm half-smile but says nothing.

'Ahem, back to the statement...'

'Would my evidence help convict your suspect?'

'Well, no, not on its own. It's not a smoking gun, it's circumstantial. But every little bit can help to convince a jury.'

'I see. Then I'm afraid I can't.'

Prisha is confused and losing patience fast.

'You can't what?'

'I can't give you a statement about the van.'

'Why not?'

'Because I never saw it.'

Prisha goes deaf for a moment as a shrill ringing in her ears throws her completely.

'Are you all right, inspector?'

'Yes. I'm fine. Mr Fox, you told DCI Finnegan you had witnessed a Kombi van parked near to Saltwick Bay holiday park on Monday at about eleven. Your description of the van, although vague, had one noticeable detail: the Kombi had an orange passenger door out of keeping with the rest of the colour scheme—is that correct?'

'Yes. That's what I told Frank.'

'Then why have you just told me you didn't see it?'

'Because I didn't. I had to make something up that you'd believe. If I'd told you the truth, you'd have thought I'd lost my mind.'

'I'm sorry, Mr Fox, but you're not making sense. If you didn't see the van, then how come we've located a van matching your description?'

'I'm glad you have. I truly am. The information was given to me.'

A small wave of panic floods through Prisha's body. If the sighting was false, then there really is no case against Bridges. She rubs at her temple in an agitated manner.

'The information was given to you?'

'Yes, via a text message.'

'By whom?'

'By Shirley... my wife.'

39

Frank is behind his desk scribbling notes with one hand as he feeds a bacon and egg roll into his mouth with the other. A tap on the door and Prisha walks in. He barely looks up.

'Ah, Prisha, take a seat. Bridges' solicitor will be here in twenty minutes, so I'm jotting down some bullet points on our line of questioning. Did you get Dudley's statement?'

Prisha is still trying to make sense of her visit to Dudley Fox. Frank drops his pen, takes a slurp on hot sugary tea, then takes another bite of his roll. He looks up at his inspector.

'Prisha, you're white as a sheet,' he mumbles through a mouthful of food. 'You look like you've seen a ghost. Are you feeling all right?'

'Yes, fine. Dudley's sighting of the Kombi van was false.'

'False?'

'Yes. A complete fabrication. He got a tip off about the van through a text message.'

Frank's expression exudes bewilderment. 'From?'

Prisha takes a seat. 'From his dead wife—Shirley Fox.'

As the pair make their way down the steps, heading towards the interview room, Frank throws instructions at his subordinate.

'As far as I'm concerned, I know nothing about Dudley's retraction and his fanciful tale about communicating with his dead wife... got it?'

'Yes, boss.'

'The Kombi van sighting was the fundamental basis for getting a warrant on "reasonable grounds". For the record, you can tell me about it later. Let's see how this first session goes with Bridges, although we've got bugger all now apart from him lying about his van not being at school yesterday and a couple of teenage girls disputing when they did or didn't see him when they were in the stables. Shit the bloody bed! This is turning into a clusterfuck of epic proportions. Let's hope Zac comes up with something, quickly.'

As they reach the bottom of the steps, Frank stops and shoves his leather document case under one arm as he fastens his top button and straightens his tie.

'Tell me about Bridges. What's he like, his disposition, his manner?'

'He's self-assured, relaxed.'

'Cocky?'

'Erm... no, I wouldn't say cocky, just confident. He's fastidious. His workshop is clean, tidy, functional. His Kombi is immaculate. He's organised, likes routine.'

'You definitely mentioned nothing about the orange door when questioning him about his van?'

'No, boss.'

'Good. Do you know the silence technique?'

'Yes. Leave long silences between questions and answers. It makes people uneasy, and they feel the need to add extra information and maybe blurt out something they didn't mean to.'

'Correct. When I place the fourth photo on the table in front of him, I want you to gauge his reaction.'

'Sir.'

They resume their walk to the interview room.

'Have you checked the custody record?'

'Yes, sir.'

'Everything tickety-boo? I don't want this going tits-up on a technicality.'

'Everything's correct, sir.'

'You cautioned him; let him know why he's been arrested? He was given the codes of practice and risk assessed for health and medication issues by the custody officer?'

'Yes.'

They stop outside the interview room as Frank holds his fist out.

'Okay, inspector. Let's do this. Our first interview together.' They bump fists. 'By the way, the duty solicitor is Ms Temple, a real laugh a minute.'

40

As they walk into the interview room, Frank Finnegan offers Bridges a broad smile.

'Ah, Mr Bridges, I'm DCI Finnegan and you're already acquainted with DI Kumar.'

Bridges nods at them.

Prisha spends the next five minutes explaining the interview process and what rights he has, and how everything is being recorded on audio and video. She finally ends with the caution.

'You do not have to say anything. But it may harm your defence if you do not mention when questioned something which you later rely on in court. Anything you do say may be given in evidence. Do you understand the caution, Mr Bridges?'

He nods impassively. 'Yes.'

'DCI Finnegan,' begins the duty solicitor, 'my client informs me he was more than willing to come to the station voluntarily and answer your questions. I really think this is overkill.'

Frank pulls his chair up close to the table. 'We believe Mr Bridges may be involved in the disappearance of two thirteen-year-old girls. These are very serious allegations and I like to make sure we follow the letter of the law. Now, if I may continue.'

The solicitor adjusts her spectacles and readies her pen and notepad.

'Mr Bridges, or do you prefer Mark?'

'Mark.'

'Okay, Mark. Can you tell me where you were on Monday 17th August between the times of 10:30 and 11:30 am?'

'I was at work. At the school—Carston Hall.'

'And do you have any eyewitnesses who could testify to that?'

'I don't know. The school is closed for the summer holidays, so there's only a handful of people around.'

Prisha leans forward. 'We've questioned everyone who was at the school last Monday, and no one can verify they saw you between those times.'

Bridges shrugs. 'So what? That doesn't mean I wasn't there.'

The room falls silent as both officers stare at Bridges then down at their notes.

'Look, I want those two girls to turn up safe and sound as much as anyone,' Bridges says.

'Hmm...' Frank mutters as he does a few neck exercises.

'They're good kids. I'm sure they just went off on an adventure or something.'

Prisha stares at him. 'Good kids?'

'Sorry?'

'You said they were good kids.'

'Yes.'

'When I questioned you on Tuesday, you said you didn't know them personally, but you recognised their faces from the newspaper. So how would you know if they were good kids or not if you didn't know them?'

'What I meant was, most of the girls at the school are good kids. Their parents spend a lot of money to send them to Carston. We don't get riff raff.'

Stillness pervades the sterile room as Frank eventually finishes his neck manoeuvres.

'Mark, how long have you been caretaker at Carston Hall?'

'My title is site manager,' Bridges corrects, with a slight smirk.

Frank laughs. 'Why have they got to change the bloody names for everything these days? A site manager could mean anything, whereas you know where you stand with a caretaker. Although, I think our American cousins use the term janitor. So, how long have you been site manager?'

'Six years,' Bridges answers.

'Do you enjoy your job?'

'Yes. It's a cushy number... erm, I don't mean I toss it off or anything, what I mean is the work's varied, I'm treated well, the pay's not bad and I'm sort of my own boss.'

Frank pulls an expression as though he's deep in thought as the second's tick by. 'And very pleasant surroundings, from what I hear?'

'Yes. It's a nice old building on great grounds.'

'I didn't mean that. I meant being surrounded by hundreds of young girls.'

Bridges' eyes narrow, but he doesn't answer.

'What's the age range?' Frank continues.

'Twelve to eighteen.'

'Are you currently in a relationship, Mark?'

'No. I'm not in a relationship. But you never know what's around the corner.'

He clasps his hands together and peers at Prisha. Frank pushes back dramatically in his chair.

'Really? I find that hard to believe. You're a handsome young man. You hold a steady, well-paid job. You've no criminal record and by the looks of you, you obviously work out, keep yourself fit.'

'If you're implying I have something dodgy going on with the girls at Carston, then you're wrong, inspector.'

'It never crossed my mind. I'm merely pointing out the fact you're a young virile man and it must be distracting being surrounded by pretty girls every day. I'm sure some of them must come on to you.'

Bridges clears his throat. 'Occasionally, some do, more in jest than anything else.'

'And how do you handle that?'

'I laugh it off and tell them to come back in ten years.'

As Bridges' final syllable is barely out of his mouth, Frank hits him hard with another direct question.

'On Monday, what time did you arrive at Carston Hall?'

'Just before eight.'

'And what time did you leave?'

'About four-thirty.'

'Did you leave the school grounds for any reason during the day?'

'No.'

'Did you drive to work in your Kombi Van?'

'Yes.'

'So, your van was parked at Carston Hall all day on Monday?'

'Yes.'

'You didn't lend it out to anyone?'

'No.'

'Are you definite?'

'Yes.'

'Hmm... I see,' Frank eases the words out slowly as he meticulously jots something down onto his notepad.

Prisha takes the reins. 'When I spoke to you yesterday, you said you'd lent your van to a mate to go fishing.'

He shrugs. 'Yeah, so? Yesterday was Wednesday.'

'But my colleague, DS Stoker, spotted your van in a shed. He got photos of it.'

'My mate dropped it back. He didn't tell me, that's all.'

'And what's your friend's name?'

Bridges readjusts himself in his chair. 'Ben.'

'Last name?'

'I don't know. I just know him as Ben.'

'Do you have a phone number or address for this, Ben?'

'No. He's just a guy I know from the local pub.'

Prisha and Frank swap doubtful glances.

'So, a random guy from your local asks to borrow your Kombi van to go surf fishing. You agree. He drops you at school in the morning, then he returns the van some time yesterday, but doesn't tell you he's returned it?'

'Yeah.'

'Come off it, Mark! That's bullshit.'

'It's the truth,' he replies calmly.

A yawning silence ensues for a good thirty seconds before Bridges feels the need to talk.

'Chief inspector, from what Inspector Kumar told me, the description of the Kombi van was extremely vague. No licence number, no colour scheme was mentioned or what condition it was in. As I said yesterday, it's the summer holidays, we're in Whitby, the place is crawling with holidaymakers, there'd be at least two dozen Kombi's in the area. Any one of them could have been at Saltwick Bay on Monday.'

An alarm bell pings in Prisha's head as adrenalin surges through her body. She leans forward, resting her arms on the hard, white table.

'Who mentioned a Kombi van at Saltwick Bay?'

Bridges appears taken aback. 'You did. Yesterday afternoon. You said one had been seen near Saltwick Bay around the time the girls disappeared.'

'No, I didn't. I chose my words very carefully. I asked if you were the owner of a Kombi van with the registration plate SYO 724F. I mentioned nothing about one being seen around Saltwick Bay the time the girls went missing.'

'Are you sure?'

'Positive.'

He tries to laugh. 'I'm sure you did, but if you didn't, then I'm just joining the dots in my head.'

Both detectives sense a breakthrough.

Frank slowly unzips his document case. 'You're right, Mark. A Kombi van was seen near Saltwick Bay at the time of Zoe's and Emma's disappearance. You joined the dots correctly. But it couldn't have been yours, could it? Because yours was at school all day.'

'That's right.'

'And you're also correct about the description—it was a little vague.'

Frank pulls three photos from the briefcase and places them on the table facing Bridges.

'Can you confirm this is your vehicle?'

'Yes.'

'Grand looking motor. What type of blue is that?'

'Royal blue.'

'Hmm... royal blue... I see.' Frank stares at the photos then fixes his gaze on Bridges. 'The sighting of the Kombi van at Saltwick Bay on Monday—the day your van didn't leave the school grounds—had one particular, noticeable feature.'

Frank places the last photo down in front of Bridges.

'The front passenger door was orange, which made it stand out like the proverbial dog's nuts.'

41

Frank's hand slams down on the bar of the red emergency exit door. He strides out into the blinding sunshine trying not to spill his cup of tea. Prisha follows closely behind clutching a bottle of water.

'That's a promising start,' she says unscrewing the cap and taking a brisk swig.

'Bloody oath! We were barely in there ten minutes before he wanted a toilet break and a chat with his solicitor. Did you see the look on his face when I revealed the last photo?' Frank says, followed by a cynical chuckle.

'Pure gold. I thought his eyes were going to pop out.'

'He's acting all nonchalant and helpful, but I dare say his solicitor will advise him to go down the—no comment—route. I thought he'd be harder to rile, actually. He's no hardened criminal and if we can frighten him, he may spill the beans.'

'If it is him, do you think it's sexual?'

'I hate to admit it, but what else could it be?' A vibrating sound distracts him as he pulls his phone from his pocket. 'Ah, Zac, what have you got?' he says as he puts him on speaker.

'Had a win for a change, boss.'

'Go on.'

'First up, we found a bobble under the back seat of the Kombi van.'

'A what?'

Prisha leans in. 'It's a hair tie, sir, that girls use to hold a ponytail in place. Zoe Clark was wearing one according to her mother—a black one.'

Frank nods at her. 'I see.'

'Yep, this one's black as well, and more importantly, it has a few strands of hair knotted around it,' Zac continues. 'We also found a roll of porno mags stashed at the back of the cellar behind a water pipe.'

'Unsavoury, but not illegal.'

'These are sir, it's kiddie porn.'

'Sweet merciful crap,' Frank murmurs, shaking his head. 'How bad?'

'No kiddie porn is good, boss, but on a scale of one to ten, I'd say they were a three. No penetration, no adults in the photos, just pictures of girls aged between about eight and twelve with their clothes off, some with make-up on. And the mags are old, very old, maybe nineteen eighties or even seventies.'

'I suppose we should be thankful for small mercies.'

'And here's another thing which will make your hair drop out, boss.'

'I hope not, I haven't much left.'

'A filing cabinet jam-packed with cigarettes and tobacco pouches.'

'Well, well, well! Mr Bridges does like to keep himself busy.'

'We're getting fingerprints off them right now.'

'Excellent work, Zac!'

'Wait, boss, one more thing.'

Frank shoots Prisha a dry smile. 'The man who keeps on giving,' he murmurs.

'The deputy principal pulled me to one side, didn't want it on the record but...'

'But?'

'Just a rumour, but he overheard in the staff room that Bridges was having an affair with one of the teachers. A Miss Tiffany Butler.'

'The girls' form teacher, sir,' Prisha confirms.

'That's right,' echoes Zac. 'You interviewed her at her home, didn't you, Prisha?'

'Yes. She appeared concerned about the girls going missing... but the thing was,' she pauses as she recollects. '... the thing was, when I interviewed the girls from her class, most were reticent about commenting on Miss Butler, as if they were scared. But there were maybe four or five who said Tiffany Butler was a psycho bitch with a split personality.'

'Explain?' Frank demands.

'They said when she's around other teachers or parents, she comes across as this wonderful, caring individual. But in the classroom, behind closed doors, she was anything but that.'

'In what way?' Frank asks.

'Old school, authoritarian, her way, or the highway sort of thing.'

'Any physical violence, hitting, smacking, slapping?'

'Not that any of them admitted to. Just verbally and psychologically intimidating, scary, threatening.'

'Hmm... that could be disgruntled teenage girls having a dig. I've heard they can be rather...'

'Bitchy?' Zac chimes in.

'I was going to say spiteful, snidey. Okay, anything else, Zac?'

'No. That's all, sir.'

'Good work and keep at it. Get the hair tie to forensics asap. They already have samples of both girls' hair. If we get a match, then we've got our man.'

'Righto, boss.'

'Hell, do you think he's half of the armed robbery gang?' Prisha asks.

'Could be, or maybe a fence.'

'Or a secret smoker,' Prisha says with a chuckle.

Frank checks his watch. 'Let's get back in there and really turn the screw—nice and slow. That's three things we've got on him. We'll drop them in one by one, give him the slow burn.'

42

Frank and Prisha take seats opposite Bridges and his solicitor.

'You will have probably guessed we have a search warrant for the school and your home address,' Prisha says as the interview resumes.

'No comment.'

'We have specialist teams there right now, going over everything.'

'No comment.'

'I didn't ask a question.' Prisha grins.

'No comment.'

'Can you explain why your van was seen near Saltwick Bay on Monday?'

Bridges throws his solicitor a quick glance. 'I was up there, Sunday.'

'That's a little obtuse. Care to elaborate?'

He shuffles in his seat. 'There's a secret fishing spot about two miles down from the bay. There's a deep hole not far from the rocks which attract a lot of fish; mackerel, cod, haddock. The quickest way to get there is to park up on Falcon Lane and walk across the fields. Bit of a faff, but worth it.'

'And you went there Sunday?'

'Yes.'

'What time?'

'Early. Probably parked up around six and left about midday.'

'How come you've only mentioned this now?'

'Because you were asking about Monday. Obviously, someone saw the Kombi on Sunday and got confused about the day.'

'Obviously,' Prisha says as her eyes flit across to Frank.

Frank rolls his shoulders, creating a painful stretch. He decides that now is a suitable time to put the wind up him.

'Mark, all we want is to find the bodies of Zoe and Emma.'

Bridges is startled. 'Bodies? What are you talking about?'

'It's now over seventy-six hours since they disappeared, and no one's seen them. We have to fear the worst,' Prisha adds.

'Abduction is one thing, murder another,' Frank says as he plays tag with Prisha.

'What's the usual sentence for abduction, boss?'

'Depends on several factors; how cooperative the accused was; if the abductees have been sexually abused or maltreated in any way; even comes down to the judge and what sort of mood they're in on the day. But... I guess you'd be looking at a ten to fourteen stretch.

Of course, if the accused pleaded guilty, told the police where his captives were located, then it could be an eight to ten spell. Good behaviour, parole after maybe five years.'

'Five years? I'd take that every day of the week,' Prisha says.

Frank shuffles his papers. 'Of course, murder would be a different ball game, especially of two young girls. You know how the public, media, and politicians react to something like that, and quite rightly.'

'Yeah, a minimum life sentence to start with. That's twenty years gone. But there's a lot of emotion around those sorts of cases.'

'That's right. Reminds me of a similar case about fifteen-years ago in London. Two young girls—murdered. Can't remember the killer's name now... anyway, he got a minimum of forty years before he was even eligible for parole,' Frank states with a weary, reflective tone.

Prisha places her hands on the table. 'Imagine that Mark, coming out of prison when you're sixty-eight. Your whole life gone, nothing but old age to look forward to.'

'A lot of them never make it out of prison. It's not a good place to be for a child killer. Constant physical assaults, mental and verbal abuse. God knows what sort of filth they'd put in your food. Turns my stomach to think of it.'

Bridges' leg twitches up and down at ten to the dozen.

Frank continues in a relaxed manner. 'I've spoken with one of my sergeants who's at the school, Mark. He found some magazines stuffed behind a pipe in your workshop.'

'What magazines?'

'Kidde porn?'

Bridges jumps to his feet and leans across the table. 'Bullshit!'

'Sit down, Mark,' Prisha orders as he drops to his seat.

'I'm not into that sort of crap! You've planted it there to fit me up.'

'In that case, your fingerprints won't be on them, will they?'

'No, they won't! I'm telling you; they are not mine. They must belong to the guy who was there last.'

'Possibly,' Frank says, calmly.

'What about the hair bobble we found under the back seat in your Kombi?' Prisha says, taking the lead.

'What?'

'A hair tie, matching the description of the one worn by Zoe Clark on Monday. How did it get there, Mark?'

'I've no idea, unless one of you lot put it there.'

Prisha laughs sarcastically. 'Oh, come off it Mark. Is this going to be the sum of your defence? Duh, the police put it there, your honour,' she adds in a dumbed-down voice. 'That sort of rubbish never works well with a jury. The dog ate my homework, miss.'

Bridges is now tapping the tabletop with one fingertip as a silence pervades the bare room.

'It's times like this I could really do with a smoke,' Frank says looking at Prisha. 'Forty years a smoker. From the age of fifteen until I gave up three years ago, thanks to my wife's insistence. It's still difficult though, always hankering after one. To be honest, I do occasionally sneak the odd one in. I have a packet hidden in my shed at my allotment. I think of it as a little treat once in a while for giving up, if you'll pardon the contradiction. Do you smoke, Mark?'

He shakes his head.

'That's odd, because we found enough cigarettes and tobacco products in your workshop to sink a battleship.'

'Maybe we planted them too, boss,' Prisha says, grinning.

'Ah, yes. Silly me. But there's always fingerprints and DNA analysis to rule that out, isn't there? Like the hair strands still attached to the bobble found in Mark's van. That shouldn't take long for forensics to get a match on. Maybe a few hours, max. And if it belongs to Zoe Clark, then it means she's been in Mark's Kombi with the odd coloured orange passenger door seen near Saltwick Bay the day the girls went missing.'

'Mark, you're a local, so I'm sure you're aware of the spate of robberies that have occurred over the last eighteen months on petrol stations?' Prisha says.

'No comment.'

Prisha folds her hands together. 'Those sentences are going to add up. Abduction, murder, rape, plus another charge for a spate of armed robberies. Hell, Mark, you won't even get to enjoy your old age at this rate.'

Frank takes over. 'Compare that with helping to locate Zoe and Emma—you may be out in five. You'd only be thirty three. You'd have your whole life ahead of you. You could resettle, get married, even have children of your own and put all this behind you, like a bad nightmare. What do you say, Mark? Are you willing to work with us? We're not the bad guys here—we're the cavalry and all we want is to find the two little girls who had their whole lives ahead of them.'

'You're not a bad man,' Prisha adds. 'You've just done some bad things. There is a difference. Yes, you'll have to serve time for those crimes, but think of those girls and what they're going through right now... if they're still alive. Think of the anguish of the parents. Come on, make it easy on yourself, the girls. What do you say, Mark?'

Bridges rubs nervously at his cheek. 'I want another word with my solicitor.'

43

With everyone seated, Bridges' lawyer leans forward to read a statement from a sheet of paper.

'My client has advised me to inform you he is willing to cooperate with the police in any way he can. His utmost concern is for the welfare of the missing schoolgirls, Zoe Clark, and Emma Tolhurst. He is doing this for the sincerest of motives and not for any favourable benefit to himself. Having said that, I would like to put it on notice that his full cooperation and concern for the girls' welfare be noted by the attending officers.'

'Duly noted,' Frank says with an appreciative nod towards Bridges. 'First and most important question, Mark; where are Zoe and Emma?'

'I don't know,' he pleads.

Thwarted, Frank loses patience. 'For God's sake, man! Your solicitor has just read a statement making you out to be St Francis of Assisi, and the first question I ask—you block me. Now, where are the girls?'

'I swear to God, I don't know. I took them. But I don't know where they are now.'

'What does that mean? Have they escaped? Have you misplaced them like a set of car keys? Start talking, man!'

'I'm telling the truth! I don't know where they are. None of this was my idea. It was hers. Everything. The detailed months of planning, the dry runs. Everything was her idea. I had my part to play—taking the girls—but that was all. She said it would run like clockwork and no one would get hurt. We could start a new life together. My God, what have I done!'

Bridges is in danger of completely falling apart, which won't help the investigation. Prisha gives Frank a nod, to let her take over.

'Mark, take a deep breath, calm down then focus. We're here to help everyone get the best out of a bad situation. I understand it's difficult, so let's start again. Do you know where Zoe and Emma are?'

'No,' he sniffles fidgeting with his fingers.

'Did you ever know where they were?'

'No.'

'But you admit to taking them from Saltwick Bay on Monday?'

'Yes.'

'Are they still alive?'

'Yes... I... I don't know now. They should be. That's what she told me, that no one would get hurt.'

'You keep referring to she—as in a woman?'

'Yes.'

'Who's she?'

'Tiffany, Tiffany Butler.'

44

Frank gets another buzz to his phone and quickly checks it.

'Zac's back. See what else he's got and get him up to speed with proceedings. I'll carry on here.'

'Boss.'

'For the record, Detective Inspector Kumar is leaving the room.'

Prisha races upstairs, almost bumping into Zac as she enters the incident room.

'Hey, calm the farm, lady,' he says with a wide grin.

'Hell's bells Zac, it's snowballing. I've left Frank downstairs with Bridges. He's cracked wide open and confessed to taking the girls but doesn't know where they're being kept. He reckons Tiffany Butler is the mastermind behind it all.'

'Are thy still alive?'

'Maybe... he assumes so. But he reckons he hasn't had anything to do with them since he handed them over to Butler.'

'What's the motive?'

'Still not sure. How did you go?'

'The hair tie is with forensics now. They can get the results back to us within the hour. They've also confirmed the suspected dog hair found on Cleveland Way, near to the footprints, is in fact—dog hair—white dog hair. They haven't determined the breed yet, but it's definitely not a mongrel.'

'Which means it's a pedigree.'

'I suppose. As an educated guess, they think it might be a terrier of some sort. And it's a puppy or a young dog, because of the make-up of the protein molecules in the fibres. Got me beat.'

'Very interesting. Hey, do you want to hear something totally bizarre?'

'Don't tell me—Frank's joined the Hare Krishnas?'

'No. I saw Dudley Fox earlier to get a statement in relation to his Kombi van sighting.'

'So?'

'He never saw it. He made the story up.'

'You're shitting me?'

'Nope. His dead wife, Shirley, texted him the details of the van.'

Zac's eyes scrunch into a ball. 'He's lost the bloody plot!' he cries.

'He's on prescription medication which boosts serotonin levels—antidepressants, prescribed for chronic or general anxiety.'

'To be expected.'

'Except, he's supplementing it with over-the-counter lithium drops, another medication which boosts serotonin levels.'

'He should be happy as a sandboy, then.'

'Not really. It raises the lows, makes you more stable. I did some research online and found out that too much serotonin release can have an adverse effect, especially when mixed with alcohol. I think he's a big whisky drinker.'

'What sort of effects?'

'Hallucinations, especially hearing voices or seeing things.'

'You mean he's off his trolley?'

'Either that or he has a direct line to the afterlife.'

'But what about the Kombi and the orange door?'

'Not sure. All I can assume is he was out walking. In a stupor, he saw the van, and it stuck in his mind. Then later, he thinks his wife texted him the information.'

'Did you ask to look at his phone?'

Prisha rolls her eyes. 'As if! I'd be as bonkers as him if I had. And one last thing—he said he was going to ask Shirley if she knew where Zoe and Emma were being held.'

'You'd think the first thing he'd ask her is who her killer was. Does Frank know about this?'

'Yes.'

He laughs. 'Christ, I'd have loved to have been a fly on the wall when you told him. What did he say?'

'The phrase he used was—strike a light, shit the bed and shaft me sideways.'

'Actually, I might call by at Dudley's later and see if his dead wife can text me the winning lottery numbers for Saturday night's jackpot.'

'Yep, you're definitely a sicko,' she sniggers.

'I've told you—it's northern humour.'

'Can we get a live stream from the interview room up on a monitor?'

'Yes, there's a PC set up for that in Frank's office. Come on.'

They race across the room, which is deserted apart from a couple of civvies inputting data into computer consoles.

Zac stabs at the keyboard as a black and white view of the interview flickers onto the monitor. He fiddles with the volume control until Frank's voice can be heard clearly.

'I think you're playing games with me, Mark. You've told one lie after another since we first questioned you. Every time I present you with new evidence, your story changes. It's the sign of a bad liar. No one has time for this. I'll ask you again: do you know where the girls are?'

Bridges bangs his fists onto the table.

'You're not listening! No I don't. I took them and handed them over to Tiffany!'

'Frank's playing it wrong,' Prisha murmurs. 'Bridges has already caved in and admitted his wrongdoing. Now's the time for softly softly. Frank is getting him more upset and confused.'

'He's old school,' Zac concurs as the pair refocuses on the grainy vision.

'Okay, let's start from the beginning. Why did you abduct Zoe and Emma?' Frank says, resigned to a long, drawn out interview.

'I didn't abduct them. That makes me sound like a paedo, which I'm not. I hate that shit.'

'Did you take them against their will?'

Bridges wipes snot away on the back of his hand. 'Yeah, I suppose so. I drugged them with a very small and measured dose of Rohypnol in a fruit drink. Just enough to knock them out for twenty minutes and keep them drowsy for another twenty.'

'Okay, in your own words, if that's not abduction, what is it?'

'Kidnapping.'

'Kidnapping!' Prisha exclaims. 'This isn't sexually motivated... it's about money!'

'We took Zoe Clark to ransom her,' Bridges continues.

'And what about Emma Tolhurst?'

'Collateral damage. Those two are joined at the hip. I couldn't take one without the other.'

'Zoe's father—John Clark—is an accountant. He might be on a good crack, but he's hardly Rockefeller, is he?'

'Who?'

'Never mind. My point is he's not a billionaire.'

'No, he's not... but his brother Andrew is.'

Prisha mutes the sound as a thousand thoughts and computations flood her brain. She feels alive, energised, as her mind processes snippets of information, half-thoughts, and small clues like a supercomputer.

'Holy shit!' she exclaims to Zac.

'What?'

'Yesterday, I called around to quiz the Tolhursts and the Clarks to see if we'd missed something.'

'Yeah, I remember the conversation. And?'

'The Tolhursts were almost resigned to the knock on the door and bad news. But when I went to the Clarks, only Sarah was home. She wouldn't even let me in over the threshold. I assumed she was having a bad day. When I asked if I could speak to her husband, John, she said he'd gone down to London. A sudden family emergency involving his brother.'

'That's odd. What's more important; your missing kid or your brother? I know which I would choose, not that I don't love my brother.'

'Exactly what I thought. People can act weird when under enormous stress... but now it all makes sense. Pull up a search engine and type in—Andrew Clark rich man.'

Zac scowls. 'Get real.'

'Just do it. Those search engines are amazing these days. They can almost predict what you're going to type before you type it.'

Zac reluctantly obeys. The search pulls up a full page of hits on Sir Andrew Clark, along with a photo of a well-dressed, handsome, middle-aged man.

'He looks like his brother,' Prisha notes.

'Aye. They were both plucked from the same flowerbed, that's for sure.'

Zac clicks on the number one hit, a Forbes richest man article, and reads aloud.

'Net worth: £1.2 billion. Source of wealth: batteries, renewable energy, electronics. Andrew Clark was born into a modest family in the fishing and seaside resort of Whitby. At age twenty-five, he set up his first company, BlitzCharge. It was listed on the stock market in 2005 for £340 million. It is now valued at a hundred times that amount with shares hovering around the £150 mark.'

'I wonder if he's married,' Prisha says with a chuckle.

'Bit old for you, isn't he?'

'Who cares about age when he's got that sort of money?'

'You can be very mercenary.'

'If it is a ransom demand, there's a good chance the girls are still alive,' Prisha says.

'Unless it's already been paid, in which case the girls' survival chances diminish drastically.'

'Damn, you're right. I want you to get over to the Clark's house and bring Sarah in for questioning. If she refuses, threaten her with arrest.'

'On what grounds?'

Prisha is already heading out of the door. 'I don't know. Use your imagination. Perverting the course of justice... impeding a police investigation... whatever. And organise a warrant to search Butler's home. And pull the whole team in. There's no point in house to house anymore. We can better utilise their time.'

'And where are you going?' Zac shouts after her.

'To see a man about a dog!'

45

Tiffany's car is not in her driveway as Prisha parks the Skoda outside the next-door neighbour's house. She raps on the door as the sound of the yappy dog starts up. A few seconds pass until a small, grey-haired man appears. His left eye is bloodshot and swollen. She flashes her card at him and introduces herself.

'I'm wondering if I could have a quick word, Mr...'

'Mr Lee. Yes, please come inside. What's it about, inspector?' he asks with a concerned frown, closing the door behind him.

'It's about your dog.'

'Cooky? Oh dear, is it the neighbours? Have they complained about his barking? He is only a puppy and I'm still training him.'

She follows behind as he totters into the front room.

'It's not about his barking, Mr Lee. Could I see Cooky?'

The dog is still yelping from behind a closed door.

'Yes, of course. I've locked him in the kitchen. He doesn't care for strangers, I'm afraid.'

A moment later a tiny, white-haired terrier darts into the room, comes to an abrupt halt as it spies Prisha, then growls. Kneeling down, she holds the back of her hand out. The dog

259

tentatively inches forward and sniffs a few times. She tickles it on the head. It relaxes, then scurries off and chews on a rubber bone laid next to its bed.

'What breed is he?' Prisha enquires.

'A Westie.'

She scrunches her nose up, confused. 'A Westie?'

'Yes. A West Highland White Terrier.'

The dog drops the bone and has a good old scratch at its underbelly, shedding fur.

'Is he a pedigree?'

'Yes, he's purebred and wouldn't you know it. He thinks he rules the roost, and he's only five months old,' he says with a chuckle.

'He's adorable,' Prisha notes, not that she's a big dog fan. 'Mr Lee, were you at home on Monday just gone?'

'No. I had a medical appointment in York to have a cataract removed.'

'What time was that?'

'The appointment was at ten-thirty, but I had to set off at eight. I went by train. May I ask what this has got to do with Cooky?'

'What time did you return home?'

'About three.'

'That's a long time to leave a puppy alone.'

'Inspector, if you're implying I mistreat my dog, I can assure you that's not the case. I left Cooky with my next-door neighbour.'

'Miss Butler?'

'Yes, that's right.'

'So, you get on with her?'

'Yes, she's a lovely young woman. Very polite, neighbourly, not an ounce of trouble. She adores Cooky.'

'Mr Lee, could I bother you for a glass of water?'

'Certainly.'

He walks into the kitchen and out of sight. Pulling a snap lock bag from her pocket, she walks to the dog's bed, kneels, and scrapes a tuft of dog hair together with her fingernails. As she drops it into the bag, Cooky growls without any menace. Standing up, the noise of a car engine has her peering out of the window, as Tiffany Butler's Subaru Impreza rolls slowly into her driveway.

'Here you go,' Mr Lee says returning with the water.

Prisha takes a gulp. It's tepid and tastes a little tainted.

'Okay, that's all for now, Mr Lee,' she says as she hands the glass back.

'But I don't understand why you called?'

'To ascertain where your dog was on Monday—that's all. And since you've cleared the matter up, I won't take up any more of your time.'

'Oh, I see,' he replies, completely perplexed.

'I'll see myself out.'

———◦◦◦———

Prisha strolls next-door and knocks on Tiffany Butler's door.

'I'm going to enjoy this,' she murmurs with a sly smile. 'Bridges' story could be complete balderdash, but a little piece of schadenfreude in the afternoon always cheers me up.'

Tiffany Butler opens the door and peers down her pert little nose at Prisha.

'Oh, you again, inspector,' she says with barely hidden contempt as she swishes her perfect ponytail to one side.

'I was going to ask to come inside, but stuff it! I'll do it here out in the open for all the neighbours to see. Miss Tiffany Butler, I am arresting you in connection to the kidnapping of Zoe Clark and Emma Tolhurst. You do not have to say anything, but it may harm your defence if…'

46

Zac and Prisha hover outside the door to interview room two. There's a buzz of excitement that permeates the station as the rest of the incident team drift back in.

'How is Mrs Clark?' she asks.

'Nervous as a kitten. I feel sorry for her,' Zac says, wincing a little. 'Prisha, I think we should have questioned her at home. She's been through enough. She thought I was arresting her.'

'Did you put her at ease?'

'I tried. Said we had a new line of enquiry she may be able to help us with. It seemed to make her even more jittery.'

'I know it sounds cruel, Zac, but being in an interview room in a police station is more intimidatory than being in one's living room. I'm hoping it will clarify her thoughts. I take it John Clark has not returned from London yet?'

'No. Due back in a few hours. Where's Tiffany Butler?'

'In the holding cells. Supercilious bitch. I'll leave her there until Frank has finished with Bridges or takes a break. You better get a team together to ransack, oops sorry, I mean search Tiffany Butler's place.'

'Will do,' Zac nods as he turns to leave.

Prisha turns the handle and pushes open the door.

'Ah, Mrs Clark, I'm sorry to bring you into the station, and we certainly won't keep you long,' she says with the warmest smile she can muster.

'I can't tell you anything I haven't already told you before. And call me Sarah,' she replies as she rocks ever so slightly back and forth. 'Is there any news on Zoe and Emma?' she asks with desperation.

Prisha takes a seat opposite.

'I'm afraid not. But we have all our best officers on this case, and they are working their backsides off. I realise that isn't much comfort to you at the moment, but we must keep believing in a positive outcome.'

Sarah Clark is less than convinced.

'Sergeant Stoker said you had a new line of enquiry?'

'Yes, but that isn't unusual in case like this. You understand we have to investigate every little thing that comes to our attention.'

'Yes, of course.'

Prisha relaxes in her chair and fixes Sarah with a steady gaze, which she immediately avoids by staring at her clasped hands.

'We believe this could be a kidnapping and ransom situation.'

Sarah's head snaps upright as her eyes flick continuously between Prisha and the side wall.

'I realise it's not the news you'd want to hear, Sarah, but it could actually be a good thing.'

Damn! I could have phrased that better, Prisha, you dingbat!

'A good thing!' Sarah Clark yells. 'Kidnapping and ransom—a good thing!'

One palm slams hard onto the table.

'What I meant to say is—if it is ransom, there's a good chance the girls are still alive.'

'Meaning what? If it isn't ransom, then they're both dead?'

This isn't going as she intended. Sarah Clark is on the edge, and Prisha doesn't want to push her too hard, but she needs to find the truth. She cannot skirt around the issue with the clock ticking.

'Sarah, I'm going to be completely open and honest with you. In cases like this, when two young girls disappear without a trace it usually means one thing; they've been abducted, sexually abused, and killed within the first twenty-four hours.'

She'll know that already, but I needed to emphasise the obvious to focus her mind. Now to let her know—that I know.

'Your husband's brother is Sir Andrew Clark.'

She's startled by the statement. 'So, what of it?'

'How is he? You said he was unwell?'

'Oh, he's on the mend. John is on his way home. Bit of a false alarm.'

'He's a very rich man, your brother-in-law.'

'I don't see how this is going to help Sarah or...'

'Mrs Clark, I believe the kidnapper has already been in touch with you. Is that true?'

Her gaze falls onto the table.

'No, of course not,' she mumbles

'Because if they have, then you must tell us everything.'

'I said, no.'

'Sarah, if you're withholding vital evidence, it's not helping anyone, especially Zoe and Emma,' she reiterates gently.

'How long do you intend to keep me here?' she whispers.

'Not much longer. Do you have it with you—the ransom note?'

She blinks, on the verge of tears.

'Sarah! Every second wasted is a second we can never get back!' Prisha shouts at her.

Sarah quietly weeps as she pulls a folded envelope from her jacket pocket and slides it across the table.

'It was in the letterbox yesterday morning.'

'Who else has seen or knows about this?' Prisha says as she pulls on a pair of latex gloves and removes the paper from the envelope.

'No one. Just me and John. We were scared, terrified. We thought if we did as they said, we'd get Zoe back.'

Prisha studies the typed demand.

Transfer £20,000,000 into the account below before 2 pm Friday 21st August

If you do, Zoe and Emma will be released unharmed.

If you don't, you'll never see your daughter again.

If you go to the police, you'll never see your daughter again.

There will be no further contact.

037-822-795476_0017364

'Well done, Sarah. Believe me, this will take us a step closer to finding Zoe and Emma. You must call your husband immediately and tell him under no circumstances is he to allow his brother to deposit the money into that account, do you understand?' she says, forcibly.

Sarah stares at her through the tears. 'Why? What would happen if he did?'

'Once the kidnapper has the money, it's not unusual for them to dispose of their captives. They stand a better chance of success with no witnesses.'

She breaks down and sobs uncontrollably.

'Sarah, what is it?' Prisha asks as she takes Sarah's hands in her own.

'It's too late. It's already done,'.

47

The broiling sun hangs in the sky, bridling the holiday makers below into the shade or relative cool of the beach. The air in the office is tainted with the musk of three bodies. The whirring pedestal fan does little but redistribute the faint smell of sweat.

Frank pushes open a window. The air outside is languid, reluctant to offer any relief. He gazes at the dark clouds forming on the horizon to the north as muted carnival sounds from the arcades on the promenade drift aimlessly on tired thermals.

'It's a warm one,' he mutters. 'What was the top temperature today?'

'It nudged thirty-two degrees at four o'clock,' Zac replies as he slides his tie off and stuffs it into his jacket pocket hanging on the back of his chair.

'What's that in old money?'

'Ninety Fahrenheit.'

'Hellfire. I think we're in for a thunderstorm later. Excuse me,' Frank says as he pops the buttons on his shirt and disrobes. Zac suppresses a chuckle as Prisha rolls her eyes. He grabs a can of deodorant from the desk drawer and gives his armpits a quick blast, then pulls a fresh white shirt from the hat stand and slips into it.

Prisha notes the time. 'Five minutes until the next briefing, boss. What's going to be our primary focus?'

'We'll get everyone up to speed with developments, then take a break. When we reconvene, it will be all about the map. It's all we have at the moment.'

As everyone pulls chairs up in a semi-circle around the whiteboard, Chief Superintendent Anne Banks takes a seat at the back of the room, silent, watchful.

Frank wipes half of the whiteboard clean, then begins.

'Listen up everybody,' he declares as he turns to the assembled audience. 'It's been a long day. We're all tired. It's hot and humid and none of us want to be here. But you all need to focus for the next fifteen minutes. Then we'll take a thirty minute break. If you live nearby, go home, get a shower, and freshen up. Or go for a walk and take in some air, if there is any. Grab a bite to eat and keep those fluids up. We could be in for a long night. Prisha, can you summarise what we've got so far?'

'Yes, boss.'

She takes up a position in front of the board, like a headmaster about to address an assembly.

'Okay, most of you will know parts of the information I'm about to relay—but here's the official version. We have two suspects in custody: Mark Bridges—caretaker at Carston Hall, and Tiffany Butler, the form teacher of our missing girls, at the same school. According to Bridges, he and Miss Butler have been in a relationship with one another for about eighteen months.

This is a case of kidnapping and ransom.

I'll go through Mark Bridges' account first, followed by Tiffany Butler's version. Questions at the end, please.'

Frank draws a black line down the whiteboard and scribbles Bridges' name to the left and Butler's name to the right.

'What I'm about to say is based on the account of Mark Bridges, so don't take it as gospel.

Zoe and Emma started at Carston Hall last September—their first year at the school. At some stage, Tiffany Butler overheard Zoe Clark bragging to another classmate about how rich her uncle was. And it's true, Sir Andrew Clark, Zoe's uncle, is CEO of BlitzCharge, a company involved in renewables. He's seriously wealthy.

Tiffany Butler—according to Bridges, masterminded the kidnapping and ransom plan.

On Monday August 17, at approximately ten o'clock, Bridges was going about his duties at the school when he claims to have received a message from Tiffany saying Zoe had been at the abbey car park and was now walking along Cleveland Way towards Saltwick Bay Beach—a favourite of the Clark family at this time of the year because it's relatively unknown and not as busy as the other beaches in the area.

Tiffany told Bridges to enact the kidnapping and to stick to the plan they'd engineered so meticulously. She was going out and about, so she'd be seen in public—therefore, giving her an alibi.

She immediately sent another message telling him she was dog-sitting her next-door neighbour's puppy, and she'd leave it in the back garden, and he should collect it to use it as a lure for Zoe.

Mark Bridges left Carston Hall shortly after ten and drove to Whitby, following the back roads so avoiding the main A171 and the ANPR cameras. He collected the puppy from Tiffany's rear garden, which backs onto empty grasslands, before heading back to Saltwick Bay.

At around eleven-fifteen Bridges made contact with Zoe and Emma about a mile down the coast from Saltwick Bay Beach, on top of the cliff close to where we discovered the footprints of Zoe Clark, and also where we discovered white dog hair.

He admitted, as part of the kidnapping plan, he'd gained the girls' trust over the previous school year.

He told the girls the puppy had been abandoned on the school grounds, along with two other puppies. He said they were in his workshop at the school. Zoe and Emma asked if they could see them.

With the aid of the puppy, he coaxed the girls into his Kombi van, which was parked in a dilapidated hay barn about two hundred metres from the cliff top.

Inside the vehicle, he gave them each a carton of fruit juice laced with a mild dose of Rohypnol. Enough to put them to sleep for twenty minutes and make them very drowsy for another twenty minutes.

Once the girls were unconscious, he drove fifteen minutes west of Whitby to the village of Aislaby. Remember that point for later—as it's only a ten-minute drive from Frodsham Spa—which I'll get to.

About a mile outside Aislaby, he pulled off the main road and onto an old farm track which was obscured from the road by trees and bushes. The estimated time is now eleven-thirty-five.

This is where Tiffany Butler was waiting for him.

With the girls still unconscious, Bridges transferred them from his Kombi van and laid them on the grass at the side of Tiffany Butler's car—a Subaru Impreza—whilst she unfolded a heavy duty, green, plastic tarp to line the boot with. They were gagged and their hands and feet had been tied together.

After that, his story ends. He doesn't know where Tiffany took the girls, saying Tiffany insisted the kidnapping plot be split into two operations; one—the initial taking of the girls by Bridges; and two—the detainment of the girls by Butler. She said the less he knew, the better. That way he couldn't incriminate himself if interviewed by the police.

Now to Miss Tiffany Butler's version of events, which will be a lot briefer.

She denies any knowledge of what happened to the girls. She admits she began a physical relationship with Bridges about eighteen months ago. They kept it hush-hush as the school frowns upon fraternisation between its staff members. It has old-fashioned values.

She said she ended the affair about six months ago when Bridges bought her an outfit to wear in the bedroom—a schoolgirl outfit.'

'Dirty get!' someone mutters.

'She alleges she was horrified and sickened, immediately ending the relationship with Bridges. Apparently, he didn't take the break-up well. She claims he stalked her for a few weeks until she threatened to tell the principal of Carston Hall about his behaviour, which would have undoubtedly led to his dismissal. The stalking stopped. Since then, she says she only sees him at school, and the very thought of him now makes her skin crawl.

She also has a seemingly watertight alibi. She was at Frodsham Spa between ten and two on Monday. She's a member and has a swipe card, which electronically records her entry and exit. I checked the records and corroborated she was indeed there between those times.'

Prisha nods towards Zac, who steps forward and takes the lead.

'We have conducted an extensive search of the school, Bridges' house, and Butler's house. In Bridges' workshop we found a stash of very old kiddie porn magazines—mild compared to some of the stuff we see nowadays, but nevertheless. He denies any knowledge of them.

We also discovered over a thousand packets of cigarettes and pouch tobacco. He says he bought them off a random guy in a pub, hoping he could sell them online and make a small profit. Pigs might fly. We will interview him again in relation to the armed robberies on petrol stations.'

'That's right,' Frank breaks in. 'Mr Bridges won't be going anywhere soon. But we need to prioritise, and as bad as armed robberies are, finding two missing schoolgirls is our number one goal at the moment. Sorry Zac, please continue.'

'Boss. In Bridges' Kombi van, we located a black hair tie similar to the one Zoe Clark was wearing on Monday. The lab confirmed the hair attached to the tie is a perfect match to the hair from Zoe's hairbrush, which they took from her bedroom on Tuesday.

Searching Bridges' house, we found a pile of books in a wardrobe in his spare bedroom. I'll read out the list: How To Disappear and Start a New Life with a New Identity, Fundamentals of Offshore Banking, Understanding the International Monetary System, Banking Secrecy and Money Laundering, The world's Best Tax Havens—the list goes on, but you get the picture. Not my idea of a ripping yarn, but each to their own.'

A few chuckles go up around the room.

'Digital forensics are still analysing his laptop, but initial reports have found internet searches similar to his reading material. Thankfully, no kiddie porn sites—yet.

We also found a passport belonging to a Mark Cosgrove—the photo is of Bridges, i.e. a false passport.

Now to Miss Butler. We searched her house and found nothing of any note. Her laptop has nothing dubious on it. Her internet searches are innocuous; Mediterranean recipes, modern teaching techniques, latest movies, etcetera. Likewise, her laptop at school.

Forensics have gone over her car, specifically the boot and so far, have come up with nothing, although Bridges claimed it was lined with heavy duty plastic. All in all, she appears to be squeaky clean.'

Murmurs and mutterings stalk the room as Frank finishes jotting down the salient points in bullet form on the whiteboard. He puts the pen down and fronts his officers, who are bleary eyed and devoid of energy and enthusiasm.

He falters for a moment. 'Okay, time for a five-minute break. I want to see everyone around the water-cooler taking in liquid.'

48

The banter and occasional joke seem incongruous to the situation. A uniformed constable is relaying to DC Hill what happened on Eastenders the previous evening. Zac is chatting with his son on his mobile, explaining their planned fishing trip on Saturday may have to be cancelled. Prisha is sitting off to the side of the throng of bodies, subdued, thoughtful. Frank strides back into the incident room.

'Righto, you lot, let's get this finished.'

Everyone returns to their seats as an uneasy quiet falls over the room.

'Now to the ransom demand,' Frank says as he slowly paces back and forth in front of the whiteboard. 'At two-fifteen this afternoon, Andrew Clark transferred twenty million pounds into a bank located in the Cayman Islands.'

Muted gasps and a few indecipherable mumbles are uttered.

'Tracing international banking transactions is way above our pay grade. That part is now being investigated by the Serious Fraud Office, who are liaising with the National Crime Authority, Her Majesty's Revenue and Customs, and Interpol.

Two officers from the SFO are already interviewing Andrew Clark.

From the brief chat I had with the SFO, it's extremely difficult to follow a paper trail when dealing with overseas jurisdictions.

He said what often happens in money laundering cases is the money is split multiple times and moved around from one offshore bank account to another at regular intervals, so muddying the waters. By the time the investigating team has all the paperwork ticked off, and the bank's authority to examine accounts, the money is long gone.

The SFO also said setting up offshore accounts and transferring money internationally was not for the faint-hearted. It's complex and one needs a deep understanding of banking systems and each country's banking laws.

Of course, this is not a money laundering case, but the intent is the same—hiding dirty money. Righto, questions?'

A flurry of arms are raised.

'Yes, DC Hill?' Frank says with a nod of the head.

'How did Tiffany Butler or Bridges know Zoe was heading towards the beach at Saltwick Bay?'

'A tracking device. According to Bridges, at the start of the second school term, Tiffany Butler confiscated Zoe's mobile phone when she brought it into the classroom with her. All the kids are supposed to leave any technology in their lockers until the end of the school day.

Tiffany then went down to Bridges' workshop in the cellar under the pretext of getting him to fix a broken desk. She installed a tracking app on Zoe's phone and linked it to her own and Bridges' phone. I forget the name of the app...'

Zac steps forward. 'My I, spelt MiI, boss. I have it on my son's phone. It uses GPS so you can monitor where your kid is.'

'Thanks, Zac,' Frank says. 'Bridges said he and Miss Butler both had second phones, pay-as-you-go—or burner phones as they've come to be known. They communicated via these phones using another app called Wickr—over to you again, Zac.'

'Wickr is a secure messaging app with some unique abilities. You can set a timer, so it self-destructs messages, whether that be after a few seconds or a few hours. It also has a shredder function which can irreversibly delete all data, such as texts, and social media chat.'

'Sounds like a good one to have if you're getting a bit on the side!' someone shouts out, much to the mirth of everyone in the room.

Frank resumes. 'Neither of the pair ever communicated by voice—always by text. With the MiI app, Bridges could track Zoe Clark wherever she went, night or day. He admitted he'd stalked her on five previous occasions, once before at Saltwick Bay, but aborted the kidnapping each time because of the amount of people around.

It just so happened that on Monday, the stars aligned for him. Emma Tolhurst was collateral damage, as he termed it. If he snatched Zoe, then he obviously had to take Emma as well.'

'And do we have the burner phones?' DC Hill asks.

'No. After Bridges rendezvoused with Miss Butler to transfer the girls, he dropped the dog off back at Miss Butler's home, then stopped near the cliffs at Robin Hood's Bay and threw the phone into the sea as Butler had instructed him to do. As you know, Carston Hall is only a five-minute drive from Robin Hood's Bay. As for the burner phone belonging to Miss Butler—if she had one—which is no guarantee, we haven't located it, and I doubt we ever will.'

Another hand darts in the air. 'Yes, DS Cartwright?' Frank says.

'Boss, it seems like an open and shut case to me. We've seen this sort of thing many times before in the past. Someone commits a crime, they deny any involvement, we confront them with incontrovertible evidence—in this case Zoe's hair tie found in the Kombi—then they fess up to one part of the crime.

Bridges is obviously trying to divert attention onto Tiffany Butler, probably still bitter at being ditched. This is his payback. But he's possibly already killed the girls, and he's pretending he doesn't know where they are. That way, he goes down for abduction instead of murder. He's trying to wriggle out of a maximum life sentence.'

Enthusiastic approvals support his declaration from many in the room.

Prisha takes the floor. 'I've interviewed Tiffany Butler for over an hour, and she's not as innocent as she appears. I've only fed her little snippets of the information Mark Bridges relayed to us. I've not even mentioned the dog yet. I'm saving that for our next interview. Tiffany Butler is cold, lacking in empathy and highly intelligent... and a damned good actor.'

'Unless she's telling the truth,' DS Cartwright comments, followed by a chuckle.

'True, and I haven't ruled that out. I still have an open mind, but she displays a lot of tendencies associated with psychopaths. Having said that, there's one part of this story that just doesn't add up,' Prisha adds as she nods to Frank to take over.

The room falls silent as Frank slowly paces back and forth.

'Indulge me for a moment,' he begins. 'I'll play the part of Mark Bridges and for this hypothetical scenario, we'll assume Tiffany Butler is as pure as the driven snow.'

'I like a good pantomime,' a uniformed officer calls out from the back.

'Widow Twanky, he's behind you!' another officer shouts out to much laughter

'Okay, okay,' Frank says with a grin. 'I appreciate your gallows humour, and God knows we need it sometimes, but let's be serious for a moment.

I'm Mark Bridges and I've been lying through my back teeth about Miss Butler's involvement. So here's how it plays out.

I've already admitted I built up a relationship with Zoe and Emma over the past year. Sometimes they came into my workshop on a dinnertime to chew the cud, or in winter get a warm next to the boiler.

One day, at the end of dinnertime, they head back to their classroom, but Zoe Clark leaves her phone behind. I download the MiI app into her mobile and link it to my burner phone. She's got hundreds of apps on her phone; she'll never notice one more.

I start to track her, and by my admission, I enacted the kidnapping plan on multiple occasions, hoping I'd find her alone in a deserted area at some point, but to no avail, each time aborting the mission. I even stalked her to Saltwick Bay once before, but all she did was sunbathe on the beach alongside her mother and Emma Tolhurst.

Then... last Monday morning, at ten o'clock, I check my burner phone and the MiI app. Zoe is near the abbey, then she moves along the Cleveland Way. I suspect she's heading to her favourite beach spot. It's a warm sunny day, so why not?

Again, I decide to enact my plan. I know the CCTV cameras at the school are out of action because of a thunderstorm on Sunday night which momentarily cut the power and reset the modem. I haven't yet got around to resetting it, therefore it's not recording to the Cloud. If I depart the school grounds, there will be no official record of me leaving—perfect. Everyone with me so far?' Frank asks.

He receives studious looks and numerous affirmations.

'Good. I jump into my Kombi van and take the back road to Saltwick Bay, avoiding the ANPR cameras on the A171.

Today could be my lucky day or it could be another aborted mission. I'm nervous, edgy, excited, and bloody frightened to death.

Driving along, I suddenly have a brainwave. I'll call at Tiffany Butler's house, hoping by some amazing miracle she has a white terrier puppy in her back garden. I can then borrow the puppy, knowing how much Zoe and Emma adore puppies, and use it as bait to lure them into my van.'

Frank stops and studies the faces of his team, which are a mixture of puzzlement and concern.

'Can you all see how utterly ridiculous and implausible that scenario is? How did Bridges know Tiffany was looking after her neighbour's puppy? How did he know Tiffany would be out? If she were home, she certainly wouldn't have let Bridges, her ex-boyfriend, the stalker, take the puppy.'

'That's my take, boss,' Prisha states. 'If we are to believe Tiffany Butler is innocent, there's no way Bridges would have known about the dog.'

'Are we certain the dog hair on the cliff top belongs to Tiffany's neighbour's dog?' DS Hill asks.

'Not yet. I got a sample from the neighbour earlier today and it's still with the lab. But the hair from the cliff top is white, belongs to a pedigree and is from a puppy, possibly a terrier, which all matches with the West Highland White Terrier belonging to Butler's neighbour. He left the dog with Butler on Monday. And anyway, whatever the outcome, it still doesn't explain how Bridges knew about the dog.'

'Hang on though,' DS Cartwright badgers, 'Bridges said he dropped the girls off with Butler at around eleven-thirty-five, at which time, Tiffany Butler was at Frodsham Spa. You said you checked her alibi, and it was kosha?'

Prisha shrugs. 'I know. That's the puzzling part. I'll pay another visit tomorrow and double check everything.'

'Right, questions?' Frank demands, becoming impatient. He stares rather irritably at the fleshy hand of DS Cartwright. 'Yes, Cartwright?'

'Have you brought the sniffer dogs in to check the boot of Tiffany Butler's car?'

'A pair of dog handlers are on their way from Northallerton, as we speak. They'll be helping with the search later, but yes, we'll get them to check the boot of Butler's car as well.'

'They're amazing those dog's,' Cartwright states with a certain amount of glee.

'They are, indeed, Cartwright. Unfortunately, they're not as amazing when they're put in the dock and questioned by a robust defence counsel.'

Laughter rings out as Cartwright blushes slightly.

'That's why we use humans for forensics. They seem to have better communication skills. Okay, that's enough for now,' Frank says, checking his watch. 'It's now five-forty. Everyone take a break, get some refreshment, relax and get back here by six-ten. We'll be mounting a search based on the timings that Bridges gave us. I'll go over the search area when you return.'

As the room disperses, Superintendent Anne Banks pulls him to one side.

'Frank, a quick word in your office.'

'Yes ma'am,' he replies, puffing his cheeks out as he shoots a dispirited glance at Prisha and Zac.

49

Anne Banks sits behind Frank's desk as he follows her in.

'Take a seat, Frank.'

Frank grits his teeth and sits down, as Anne leans back and places her hands in her lap.

'The new girl, Inspector Kumar... she's good,' she states.

'Aye, we snared a keeper, that's for sure. Mind you, Zac is doing a damn fine job too, ma'am.'

'Come on Frank, you don't have to stand on ceremony when we're alone. Call me Anne.'

'Sorry, Anne. Force of habit.'

'What's your gut telling you?'

'That I'm bloody famished!' he replies with a chuckle.

Anne frowns. 'Do you always have to make a joke about things? This is an extremely serious matter. I found your briefing highly informative, if a little unprofessional. It could do with less levity.'

'It eases the tension. You know what they say; if you don't laugh, then you'd bloody well cry.'

'And I also don't like the way you belittle your colleagues in front of other officers.'

'I don't belittle them.'

'Cartwright?'

'Oh, come on, Anne. It's simply light-hearted banter. Anyway, they can give as good as they get, believe me.'

'Really? Anyway, we seem to have gone off-piste somewhat. Where were we?'

'Gut instinct.'

'That's right.'

'I think Prisha is right. Tiffany Butler is up to her eyeballs in it. Mark Bridges is a smart man, but offshore bank accounts, ransom demands, kidnapping, I don't think so. Armed robberies on petrol stations is more his style. He's a pragmatic sort of chap, straightforward. A kidnapping like this takes a lot of planning and guile.'

'And yet you don't have a single shred of evidence against Miss Butler.'

'Not yet. But she'll have left a clue. Every criminal does.'

'If that old nonsense were true, then we wouldn't have any unsolved crimes, would we? Talking of which, any developments in the Shirley Fox murder?'

Frank squirms in his seat. 'Ahem, no. I'm hoping the upcoming reconstruction may bring in some fresh leads.'

'Possibly, but don't rely on it. You still need to be actively investigating it.'

'I bloody am! It keeps me awake at night, at least it did. The two missing girls have now taken over that job.'

'Do you keep in touch with Dudley, keep him in the loop of how things are progressing?'

'Yes. Not as often as I like, but the Family Liaison Officer calls around every few weeks as well.'

'Good. You realise Tiffany Butler's solicitor will be hammering for you to release her unless you come up with something soon?'

'I know. But we are entitled to keep her in custody for twenty-four hours without charge and that's what I intend to do.'

'It might be what *you* intend to do, but it's not what we *are* going to do.'

'What?'

'If you don't have any concrete evidence against her by eight o'clock tonight—release her.'

'But Anne, we have Bridges' testimony.'

'Ha! Can you imagine what a defence counsel would do with that? They'd rip him to shreds and you know it. Eight tonight... do I make myself clear?'

'Ma'am,' Frank replies, seething inside.

Anne walks towards the door.

'I'm heading back to Northallerton now. I have a dinner party to attend tonight, but if there are any developments, contact me.'

'Yes, ma'am.'

'And Frank, don't push your team too hard. They all look exhausted; we need to think of their welfare too.'

'We'll search until it's dark, then I'll send them home.'

'Good.'

———◦———

Frank dumps the paper bundle onto his desk and takes a seat as his phone rings.

'Ah, Meera, my love, how are you?'

'I'm good. You?'

'Oh, fair to middling.'

'Any news on the girls?'

'No. But we have a couple of suspects in custody. We'll be launching a search shortly.'

'You'll be home late then?'

'Yes.'

'Have you eaten?'

'I've just bought myself a pasta salad from the supermarket,' he says as he peels back the butcher's paper with his free hand and gawps at the golden pile of hot, fresh fish and chips and sniffs their heavenly aroma.

'Good man. I'm so proud of you.'

'Why's that?' he replies as he deftly peels back the lid on a small tub of curry sauce one handed and pours it over the chips.

'I know it's been incredibly stressful for you of late, and yet, you're still sticking to the diet. I'm just about to make myself a tuna salad.'

'That's nice, love.'

'Right, I'll let you go. I know you're busy. I love you.'

'And I love you. Don't wait up for me.'

'Of course I'll wait up for you. I can't sleep until you're home. And Frank, plenty of water, right?'

'Yes, sweetheart. I've got a bottle right in front of me. Bye.'

'Bye.'

He drops the phone on his desk and tugs at the ring-pull on a can of coke, then breaks off a piece of fish, dips it into the curry sauce and deposits it in his mouth.

'Oh, sweet mother of Mary,' he murmurs in ecstasy. 'I think I've died and gone to heaven.'

50

The incident room is dark. Heavy, black curtains block out any remaining daylight and also imprison the muggy, fusty atmosphere. A tired gentle buzz of voices, the only noise.

Zac flicks on the projector, which splashes a dazzle of harsh white light onto the back wall. He turns a knob and fiddles with the map until it comes into sharp focus.

Prisha, feeling refreshed from her shower, silently shakes her head, bemused by the archaic equipment. If she were still with the West Midlands Police, they'd have a giant computer monitor, Google maps, and each officer would be holding a tablet.

The glow from the projector illuminates Frank's stout frame. He picks up a ruler and points at the orange circle drawn on the map with a marker pen.

'Aislaby is our starting point because we have to start somewhere and it's the last known whereabouts we have of the girls, if we are to believe Bridges. The radius of the circle is 2.5 km, or 1.5 miles in old money. It covers an area of nearly 20 km. We split into two teams: the red team and green team.

Red team sets off in a clockwise direction, green team—you guessed it—anti-clockwise. We have six patrol cars, four unmarked vehicles, and two dog vans. Two officers in each car. You will need to search every road, every gravel track, every dirt trail, so you'll need to be in constant touch with each other via radio to let each other know what roads you've been down and what properties you've searched. As you call in your progress, I'll shade in the map.

Once you've come full-circle, we expand the circle to another 2.5 km and repeat. We keep on doing this until it gets dark. Sunset tonight is 8:20 pm, but we should have some light until nearly 10 pm if the thunderstorm holds off. You need to search outbuildings, abandoned houses, old halls, anywhere it's possible to conceal two captives. So, we're talking about places that are out of the way, isolated. Use your common sense. Good luck everyone.'

A rush of excitement suddenly permeates the room as the officers make haste for the exit.

'And remember what this is about!' Frank calls after them. 'Find those girls! Prisha, you need to get Butler back in the interview room. The superintendent insists we release her by eight tonight unless we can produce some evidence. Zac, you're in charge of the search. And remember...'

'Yes, Frank... keep you updated.'

'Smartarse. Oh, and let Special Constable Kylie Pembroke ride shotgun with you.'

'Why?'

'She's a bright kid and I don't want to lose her to archaeology.'

'What?'

'Never mind. Right, I'm going to have another crack at Bridges. There are a lot of missing details I need to get out of him.'

51

The micro-pub at the Malting Pot brewery is heaving with tourists, so Dudley heads outside into the beer garden, which is just as busy. Pushing through the throng, he snaffles a spot against the boundary wall and places his pint of bitter on top of an ancient stone coping, scarred and weathered from the salty elements. He fixes his gaze upon the abbey with the becalmed North Sea in the background as Tyson rests at his feet, panting.

It's the first time he's visited the Malting Pot since he lost Shirley. They used to have a routine. On the Sundays when they weren't out walking together, they'd come to the brewery for an hour as a roast slowly cooked in the oven. Dudley had two pints of Whitby Whaler and Shirley would have two halves of Abbey Blonde. Then they'd stroll the short distance back home, hand in hand, and work as a team in the kitchen to put together the roast dinner. Afterwards, Dudley would insist she put her feet up as he cleared away.

Simple pleasures.

'I haven't eaten a roast since. No point going to all that effort for one,' he murmurs.

There are a lot of things he hasn't done in the last six months, and some things he's started doing—none of them good.

Drinking too much for a start. He only used to have a tot of whisky on special occasions such as Christmas or birthdays. Occasionally, he'd have a nightcap after an exhausting day at work.

Ha! Work! He's not sure how much longer they'll put up with him being away, but he suspects he's pushing their limits. Work was a joy for him, a fascination. So close to a breakthrough as well. Another couple of months and the sequencing would have been perfected. They could have brought someone else in to finish the project, but it is top secret; they're probably cautious of being infiltrated.

Then, there's the talking to Shirley. He can't even remember when it began. But it's getting worse. It's completely insane, he realises as much, but he can tell when she's there, in the house. He experiences a tingle down his spine. That's when he knows she's sitting in her chair staring out at the abbey, or gazing at Tyson, or peering lovingly at Dudley. She chastises him for his drinking, lack of exercise, ready-made meals, and takeaways. She says he's going to pot. And she's right.

He finishes his drink and saunters home, stopping occasionally to let Tyson have a good old sniff at something. He tries to cheer himself up. There's a tender piece of Porterhouse steak in the fridge. It will go nicely with a batch of homemade chips and fried onions.

Tyson is in the back garden having one of his mad moments as he rolls in the grass, snuffling and growling. Dudley picks up his bowl. It makes the tiniest clink against the tiles. Tyson instantly sits up, ears erect, and stares at him through the open door.

Dudley chuckles. 'You don't miss a beat, do you?'

The dog scampers towards him as he empties a half can of dog food into the bowl and places it outside the back door. It's devoured before he's even finished washing and drying his hands.

In the sitting room, he takes his tablets, washes them down with a glug of whisky, then removes the pipet from the lithium bottle. The liquid drizzles onto his tongue. The added lemon juice makes him pucker. Another gulp of whisky removes the taste. The hairs on the back of his neck stand-up as he involuntarily shivers.

She's here!

'That young inspector called around earlier, Shirley. She's a pretty lass. Yes, I know... she's not a lass, she's a woman and I shouldn't describe someone as pretty, these days, it's judgemental. You always were politically correct. She only started this week. Moved from the midlands. Works under Frank Finnegan. If she was hoping for a nice quiet rest in North Yorkshire, then she can think again. What a baptism of fire.'

He tops up the tumbler with whisky and wanders into the kitchen to prepare his evening meal. Peeling onions, his eyes water.

'It's a hell of a warm day, Shirl. The town is heaving. Don't think I've seen it this busy in years. The abbey car park is chocker. I had a couple of pints at the Malting Pot, very nice they were, too.'

Placing the meat on the counter to come to room temperature, he starts to peel the potatoes.

'That young detective, she wanted a witness statement from me, you know, about the Kombi van with the orange door. Well, I couldn't do it. Why not? I'll tell you why not—because I'd have been lying. You know me, I'll not tell an untruth. Yes, you can mock and call me old-fashioned, but that's just the way I am.'

The deep-fat fryer is already primed with cooking oil. He plugs it in and sets the temperature.

'Steak, onion, and chips. No, I don't fancy a nice salad... who's eating this, me or you? I disagree, it's not unhealthy. Okay, maybe the chips are, but how often do I have homemade chips? It's a rare treat. Yes, yes, I'm going to start exercising on Monday. I might get myself to the gym for half-an-hour.'

With everything prepared, he ambles back into the sitting room, turns on the TV and hits the mute button, then sags into the settee opposite Shirley's chair.

'They have a suspect in the missing girl's case. That's why they wanted a statement—something official.' He chuckles. 'No, I know it's not a laughing matter. I'm not laughing at that;

I'm laughing at the look on the detective's face when I told her you had texted me the information about the van. It was a bloody picture. Her jaw nearly hit the ground, then she went all quiet. I thought she was going to pass out at one point.'

With dishwasher stacked, he sets it going then returns to the sitting room. On the small coffee table in front of the settee, he unfolds the map and peruses it.

'You see, the thing is, Shirl, I told her—the policewoman—I'd ask for your help in locating the girls. What? Sorry! Police officer, not policewoman. A slip of the tongue. Did you hear what I said about the girls? You did. Good. Do you need to look at the map? Okay, suit yourself. I must say, you're a tad grumpy today. If you want to help fine, if you don't then that's also fine. Just text me if you have anything.'

52

Some would say she carries herself with an air of dignity, refinement. Prisha thinks she's simply bloody arrogant, conceited, superior. She has thirty minutes left to get something out of Tiffany Butler, otherwise she'll have to let her go. But she still has her secret weapon—the dog. She opens the door and marches in.

'Inspector Kumar, you've held my client now for almost five hours—without charge, and without a single scrap of evidence. All you have is the statement from Mr Bridges, a disgruntled and pernicious ex-boyfriend. I really must insist...'

Prisha holds her hand up, cutting the solicitor off. 'I just want to clear a few things up. The sooner we get on with it, the sooner we can all get out of here.'

With rights read, and the recording live, she begins.

'Tiffany, when Mark Bridges took Zoe and Emma, he didn't use force.'

'At least that's something,' she replies curtly.

'He had a puppy with him and told the girls he had another two back in his workshop. That's how he got them into his van.'

'He deserves a medal.'

'We found what appeared to be dog hair near to the spot where Bridges first approached the girls. The lab confirmed it to be dog hair. White, from a puppy and a pedigree.'

Her face is completely emotionless as her eyes bore into Prisha.

'Before I arrested you, I'd been having a quiet chat with your next-door neighbour—Mr Lee. Nice chap.'

Did her eyes widen, or was it just wishful thinking?

'It's a lovely puppy he has. A West Highland White Terrier.'

She waits as they play a game of Mexican stand-off. Not once has she blinked; that's some effort. Her legs and arms are crossed defensively.

'I got a hair sample from Mr Lee's puppy.'

Still nothing. She must know what's coming.

'I've just had confirmation from the lab that the hair from the cliff top is an exact match to Mr Lee's dog.'

'Then maybe you should have arrested Mr Lee instead of me,' she snipes.

Prisha nods thoughtfully. 'Maybe I would have if he hadn't had an alibi. He told me you looked after the puppy for him on Monday, from about eight until late afternoon. Is that correct?'

'Yes.'

'So how did little Cooky get up onto the cliffs overlooking Saltwick Bay?'

'Obviously, Mark Bridges took him from my back garden. I left home at about nine-forty and put Cooky outside. He's not fully toilet trained. Bridges must have been spying on me.

I've already explained how he stalked me when I ended the relationship.'

'Oh, come on Tiffany! According to you, Mark Bridges just happened to be spying on you as you left the house and thought, oh, I know, I'll borrow the dog and kidnap two girls from somewhere, then return the dog.'

'According to me, nothing! I'm not the one who has to come up with a sequence of events. That's your job.'

'Bit of a coincidence though, isn't it?'

'Coincidence is not evidence.'

'No, but Mark Bridges' testimony is evidence. He said you messaged him on Wickr about dog-sitting, and to come and collect the dog as bait.'

'I never realised he had such a fantastical imagination.'

Damn her! Not a chink, not the slightest crack in her veneer.

Another twenty minutes fly by as Prisha throws everything at her. She doesn't budge an inch from her original statement.

'We can spend all night trawling over what Mark Bridges said, *acting* inspector, but as you are aware, I was at Frodsham Spa between ten and two. I'm sure you've checked that. If I was there, then how could I have met Bridges around eleven thirty to transfer the girls into my car? It doesn't matter what hypothetical theories you come up with; the fact remains, I couldn't have been in two places at once.'

Christ! Who's being interviewed here?

'Inspector,' her solicitor begins, 'unless you have any fresh evidence against my client, then I really think we need to wrap this up for tonight. Miss Butler has agreed to come back, voluntarily, at a later date to assist you in your investigation if required to do so.'

The chair legs scrape across the floor as Prisha stands up.

'Okay, I'm releasing you without charge. I'll send in the duty officer to do the paperwork. It won't take long. Thank you for your time, Miss Butler.'

She heads straight to the toilet and splashes her face with water. Her mirrored reflection paints a sorry picture. She heads back out into reception. Butler's solicitor is already scurrying across the car park as Tiffany emerges from the interview room. Prisha sidles up to her. There's no one else around apart from the desk sergeant who has his head down, busy with paperwork.

'I know you're involved,' she whispers leaning towards her. 'And I will get you if it's the last thing I do. People like you always slip up.'

She sneers. 'And your type always have a chip on your shoulder.'

'My type? What does that mean?'

'I'm sure you can guess.'

Prisha bristles at the implied racism.

'You're an arrogant, bigot,' she fumes pointing a finger at her. 'This isn't over, so don't think it is. I'm coming for you. Do you understand?'

'Is that a threat, inspector?'

'You can take it whatever way you want!' she hisses.

A weak smile spreads across her full lips. 'When will I get my car back?'

'When we've finished with it.'

'I see. The walk will do me good. It's a pleasant evening, by the looks,' she says, throwing a glance outside. 'Goodnight, inspector. I hope you find Zoe and Emma—safe and well.'

She struts across the yard, turns a corner, and is gone. Prisha slumps against a wall and pushes out an exasperated sigh. The desk sergeant looks up.

'Tough nut to crack?'

'You could say that. Is Frank out of the interview room?'

'Yes. He finished about twenty minutes ago. He's back in the incident room.'

'Any updates on the girls?'

'Not that I've heard. It's not looking good.'

'No, it's not,' she murmurs under her breath as she turns to leave. 'And that bitch is the only one who knows where they are.'

53

Frank's attention is divided by the map, and the strange words jotted on a scrap of paper on his desk. A police radio is perched on a filing cabinet. Occasionally, it crackles into life as officers from the search party update each other on their progress.

Prisha walks lethargically into the office. Frank gives her a cursory glance.

'I take it from your demeanour you didn't get anywhere with Miss Butler?'

'Is it that obvious?'

'Did you release her?' he says as he scribbles notes down onto a writing pad, clearly distracted.

'Yes. Without charge. It's that bloody alibi!'

'Don't worry about her, and don't let her get under your skin, although I think she already has. It can cloud your judgement. We'll cook her another day.'

'How's the search going?' she asks, taking a seat.

'They're covering the ground at a fair click, but nothing yet.'

He pushes the scrap of paper towards her.

'What's this?' she says as she picks it up and stares at the peculiar jumble of words which mean nothing.

303

'A love letter from Dudley Fox. He hand-delivered it to the front desk about an hour ago. The sergeant said he was a bit wobbly on his feet.'

'Just what we need. Another distraction,' she says dispiritedly as she studies the handwritten note.

"Sorry Frank. This is all that Shirley texted me. It's obviously some sort of code and I've spent the last three hours studying a map of North Yorkshire, trying to pinpoint the location, but I can't make any sense of it. Good luck, Dudley."

delta sewer egg ran

'The sign of a very delusional and troubled mind,' Prisha says thoughtfully as she drops the note back onto Frank's desk.

'Hmm...'

Prisha glares at the top of his head.

'No, please Frank! Don't tell me you're actually wasting time on this nonsense?' she cries.

'What?' he says absentmindedly as he jots more letters down then crosses some off.

'I've told you about the drugs and the hallucinations, mix that with the drink and we have a guy who is imagining things and is completely off his rocker!'

She leaps to her feet and slams her palm down hard onto the desk to get his attention. Frank stares at the hand for a moment, then leans back in his seat.

'Who was it who gave us the lead on Bridges' Kombi?' he says, calmly.

'So what? He was undoubtedly out walking, in a psychotic stupor, saw the van and it lodged in his memory. Then later he imagined his wife texted him the message. It was a lucky break, that's all.'

'And what if he really is communicating with his dead wife?'

Prisha drops her head into her hands. 'Please Lord, tell me I'm dreaming. I can't actually be having this conversation,' she whispers.

Frank smiles. 'Let me rephrase that. What if he *wants* to believe he's communicating with Shirley? Dudley Fox is no slouch. He's a highly intelligent man. Did you know he won Mastermind a few years ago?'

'And?' Prisha says, rubbing her forehead.

'Like I said... highly intelligent. Whatever he was working on at RAF Menwith Hill was highly confidential.'

Prisha resumes her seat. 'Isn't Menwith Hill a global communications tracking station designed to give us all a two-minute warning before the world is wiped out?'

'Supposedly. It also provides communication and intelligence support to the US and UK military.'

'Then why would a bio scientist be working there?'

'Exactly. Rumour has it the place is riddled with underground bunkers and labyrinths. When me and Zac interviewed Dudley, after Shirley's death, there was a JSTAT agent who sat in on every occasion.'

'JSTAT?'

'Joint State Threats Assessment Team. Part of MI5. They assess national security threats: assassination, espionage, interference in elections, that sort of thing. All very cloak and dagger. The Super had to sign the official secrets act, so she knows more than I do about what Dudley Fox was working on at Menwith Hill. The agent didn't have a name, just a number.'

'007?' Prisha questions cheekily.

Frank smiles. 'No. It was SE17.'

'Doesn't quite have the same ring to it,' Prisha says with a chuckle.

'No. It sounds more like a bloody postal code.'

'Or a boy band.'

'Whenever I asked a question to do with Dudley's work at Menwith Hill, he would look at the agent first before answering. If the agent nodded, Dudley would answer. If the agent shook his head, Dudley would reply—no comment.'

'Hell! I wonder what he was working on?'

'Not sure, but I could hazard a guess.'

'Go on.'

'A bio scientist, who also has a degree in botany and herpetology.'

'He told me about the botany, but what's herpetology?'

'The study of frogs, toads, reptiles. Many of them contain highly poisonous toxins. In my mind, it all adds up to one thing—nerve agents.'

'Holy crap.'

'Indeed.'

'You don't think Shirley's murder could have anything to do with Dudley's work, do you?'

'Why would it? It was Shirley who was murdered, not Dudley.'

'Maybe a warning by some foreign power to back off on whatever clandestine project he was involved with.'

'Then why not just kill Dudley? It's not like he lives in Fort Knox.'

'No... but he's not been back to work since.'

'And if your phantom international killer, working for some foreign government, had taken Dudley out—he wouldn't be going back to work ever again, would he?'

'I suppose not. Sorry Frank, I'm just thinking aloud.'

'That's okay. Thinking laterally has its benefits... sometimes. Anyway, back to Dudley's note,' Frank says as he leans over his desk again.

'He says he's been studying the map. What if somewhere in that brilliant but addled mind of his, he made a connection? He's not thinking logically, that's for sure, but it doesn't mean the information he's given us is invalid. The mind is a mysterious jungle, Prisha.'

She looks at the confusion of words again.

delta sewer egg ran

'So what is it? An anagram, or does each word represent a location?'

'Not sure yet.'

'Sewer could be a drain, and delta is an area of low, flat ground.'

The radio sputters as Zac's voice tells everyone they've circumnavigated the third search area and are now expanding it out another couple of miles, starting at Dunsley. Frank shades in another part of the map.

Prisha kicks herself. 'What am I doing? This is madness. I'm going to join the search.'

'Good idea,' Frank replies, distracted. 'Hmm... egg ran, could be grange,' he murmurs as Prisha leaves the office.

As she gets into the last remaining unmarked car, the rumble of thunder rattles the windows.

'I don't know who's the most insane, Dudley Fox or Frank bloody Finnegan—delta sewer eggs ran — ridiculous! Is this what police work has come to? I should never have left the midlands. I think they're a bit backward up here.'

Starting the engine, she releases the handbrake and the car moves slowly off. Before she pulls onto the main road, she comes down hard on the brakes and jolts forward as Frank's last word hovers in her brain like a piece of ripe fruit dangling tantalisingly from a tree. Quickly reversing, she parks the car and leaps out. She sprints back through reception and past the bemused desk sergeant.

The door is nearly taken off its hinges, as she bursts into Frank's office, the sudden incursion making him reel back in his chair.

'Hell's bloody bells, Prisha! I've told you before to knock.'

Panting hard, she struggles to enunciate her words.

'Egg ran... grange....'

'What of it?'

'Dud... Dudley Fox used to... sometimes... took kids out on the moors. Bot... botany. Ages ago.'

'So?'

'He said they had a place on the moors.'

'Who did?'

'The school.'

Frank jumps to his feet and picks up the police radio, readying himself. A booming crack, accompanied by a jagged spear of lightning, illuminates the ruins of the abbey high up on the hill. For a moment, it looks like the opening to a gothic horror film. The explosion of thunder makes them both instinctively duck their heads.

'Did he say what it was called?'

Prisha shakes her head as she takes in gulps of air. 'No. Just that it was on or near the moors,' she gasps.

'It is a rather large moor—nearly six hundred square miles!' Frank roars, nearly as loud as the thunder.

'When I interviewed Charles Murray, the deputy principal, he mentioned the school had a handful of buildings across the country, most of them in North Yorkshire. They use them for outdoor pursuits. One of them was called... something grange.'

'What grange?' he yells.

Prisha flaps her arms around. 'I can't... I can't remember,' she squeals.

'Think, inspector, bloody well think!'

'Something... dale.'

'Nidderdale, Wensleydale, Airedale, Gordale, Wharfedale, Swaledale?'

'No.'

'Ribblesdale, Teesdale, Kingsdale, Malhamdale?'

'No.'

'Jumping Jack Flash! Do you know how many dales there are in Yorkshire? Think, Prisha, think!' he implores.

'I'll ring Charles Murray. I have his number.'

As Prisha focuses on her phone, Frank frantically meddles with the remaining letters of—delta sewer. He removes the letters that form—dale and jots down the remainder.

Prisha pleads with her phone. 'Come on, come on, please let him answer.' There's a click as a voicemail message kicks in. 'Damn it!'

Frank freezes.

'Westerdale Grange,' he murmurs, barely audible as a smattering of rain stains the window.

'Yes! Yes! That's it!' Prisha exclaims, jumping up and down with a mixture of excitement and triumph on her face.

'I know Westerdale,' Frank adds thoughtfully.

He pokes his finger onto the map at Aislaby and traces it west.

'Westerdale,' he announces with satisfaction. 'It's about twenty miles east of Aislaby.'

He pulls the radio to his mouth.

54

DS Zac Stoker is speeding as fast as he dares, in the torrential rain, towards Westerdale Grange.

He turns to Special Constable Kylie Pembroke in the passenger seat, who is clutching her mobile in one hand, while clinging onto the Jesus strap attached to the inside of the roof.

'How far now?' he shouts above the roar of the engine and the pounding rain.

Kylie nervously drags her eyes away from the road ahead and glances at the GPS map on her phone.

'We should enter the village any moment now.'

'I hope Frank is bloody right about this,' Zac hisses. 'Talk about a wild goose chase.'

The road sign for Westerdale flashes by.

'And now?' he snaps.

'You better slow down. In about four hundred yards, there's a right turn. Looks like a private road. Quite long, maybe a half-mile.'

Zac squeezes the brakes with his foot as the wipers continue their frenetic, repetitive dance across the windshield. He swings the car hard to the right. It veers slightly, losing purchase with the road as Kylie yelps.

'Calm down, Kylie,' he says with a grin. 'I've done defensive driving.'

'Really? You could have fooled me.'

The car bumps and rattles along on an unsealed road. The full moon, which had offered a modicum of natural light thirty minutes ago, has now completely abated. It's as black as Whitby Jet outside.

'Don't suppose you have any wet weather gear in the boot?' Kylie asks, to which she receives another toothy grin.

'No. Looks like we're in for a bath. At least it's warm rain.'

'I like the way you always look on the bright side.'

The headlights illuminate another sign:

Westerdale Grange

Carston Hall Public Girls School

Private Property. Trespassers will be prosecuted.

'Elitist gits,' Zac mumbles.

Two hundred yards further on, the imposing outline of the grange comes into view. Two storey, Victorian era, built from old Yorkshire sandstone.

'Not bad for a school holiday retreat,' Kylie comments.

'We were lucky to get a day trip to Edinburgh Castle,' Zac replies as he brings the car to a halt outside the main entrance.

He surveys the scene. No lights, no cars. The place appears deserted.

'Okay, let's do it. You take a walk around the perimeter of the building and check for signs of life. I'll try to find a way in.'

Kylie stares back at him, mute.

'What's wrong with you?' he asks.

'I'm a scared.'

'What of?'

'It's dark and we're dealing with kidnappers.'

'The only two suspects we have are back in Whitby—one locked up in a police cell.'

'What about Tiffany Butler? What if she's lurking about with a massive knife like you see in those Hollywood horror movies?'

Zac sniggers. 'She'd have needed a time-machine to get from Whitby to here before us.'

'And what if someone else is involved?'

'Okay. I tell you what. We'll just go home, shall we? You're a police officer. Sometimes you have to go into scary situations and deal with nutters. It comes with the job.'

'I'm only a volunteer,' she murmurs.

Zac pats her on the shoulder and smiles. 'Remember the SAS motto—he who dares wins! Come on, let's go,' he says as he grabs two torches from the back seat and hands one to his junior colleague. 'And if anyone attacks you, biff them on the scone with your torch,' he says with a wry chuckle.

'Great,' laments Kylie as she opens the car door. 'I could be at home now watching Dancing With the Stars sipping on hot chocolate.'

'Ah, but you won't recall that in forty years' time, will you? Whereas tonight, you'll remember it for the rest of your life. You'll be able to tell your grandkids about this... if you survive, that is.'

'Will you shut up! You're not helping.'

Zac marches briskly up the steps to the double-fronted giant doors as Kylie sets off, rather tentatively, to circumnavigate the building, the bright beam of her flashlight leading the way.

Five minutes pass before Kylie returns. Zac is huddled against the front doors, which offer a degree of protection from the elements.

'Well?' he calls out to her.

'I'm soaked to the bone.'

'Any sign of life?' Zac shouts impatiently.

'Nothing. No vehicles that I can see.'

'What about mad-axe men or knife-wielding maniacs escaped from the local insane asylum?'

'Very funny. Have you found a way in?'

'Yes. I was waiting for you to return.'

He scampers down the steps and stares up at a row of windows sitting above head height. He crouches.

'Right, on you get,' he orders.

'What?'

'Get on my shoulders.'

'You mean sit on them?'

'Yes,' he says as he wipes water from his eyes.

'I thought you said you'd found a way in?'

'I have. Through the window. Now get on my shoulders.'

Kylie reluctantly obeys, gripping tightly to his ears as though they were reins. He pushes himself to his feet.

'Can you see inside?' he asks.

'Yes.'

'And can you please let go of my ears? I'm going to look like Dumbo after this.'

'Sorry.'

'What type of locking mechanism is on the window?'

'It's just one of those push-out bars that has holes in it.'

'Good. Right, now smash the window with your torch, put your hand through and push the bar outward. And don't cut yourself. The last thing I want to do when I get back to the station is fill out an incident report.'

'Smash the window?'

'Yes.'

'Isn't that illegal?'

'Not if I suspect a crime has been committed inside; and false imprisonment is a crime. Now smash the bloody window. My shoulders are buckling.'

A blinding streak of lightning blazes through the atmosphere, lighting up the old house and the surrounding, empty countryside, which appears foreboding and encroaching.

'I'm sorry, boss,' Kylie whimpers.

'For what?'

'I think I've just wet myself.'

'Charming. The window?'

The tinkling sound of glass can barely be heard as the heavens continue to unleash a fusillade of water.

'It's open.'

'Good. Now climb through.'

'I'm scared.'

'So what? It's only an emotion. It can't harm you. Go on... you'll be right.'

Kylie clambers unsteadily, head-first, through the opening and slides to the wooden floor inside.

'I'm in,' her disembodied voice cries out.

'Make your way to the front door and see if you can unlock it. Oh, and Kylie?'

'What?'

'Watch out for Freddy Krueger!'

'You bastard!'

55

A couple of minutes pass until Zac hears a scrabbling and rummaging sound and the wooden door creaks open.

'The bloody lights don't work,' Kylie declares in a forced whisper, eyes agape. 'The storm must have knocked the power out!'

'Or maybe they kill the main fuse switch to disable the electricity when no one's here,' Zac says as he steps into the relative humidity of the house. 'Right, you take upstairs, I'll take downstairs.'

'Not on your Nelly!' Kylie says, alarmed at the suggestion. 'I'm not leaving your side.'

Zac shakes his head and grins. 'Okay, scaredy cat.'

They trundle down a long hallway and head towards a door at the far end. Zac pushes it open and scans the room with his torch.

'Kitchen,' he says softly as he enters.

Kylie is directly behind him as she spins around, sending a flash of light down the hallway they traversed. It looks absolutely terrifying. Imagined ghosts and ghouls jump out from every hidden recess. She quickly closes the kitchen door behind her. Zac has already made his way to the stove and oven and is busily pulling open cupboard doors.

'They're hardly likely to be hiding in there,' Kylie states, bemused by his actions.

'No, but this is,' he says enthusiastically. 'The teachers' stash.' He pulls down a bottle of whisky and spins the top off.

'Isn't drinking on the job illegal?' she asks.

He puts the bottle to his lips and takes two thirsty gulps, then winces.

'Illegal—no. Against the terms of my employment—yes.' He hands the bottle over. 'Here, take a swig. You could do with some Dutch courage. They can't sack you—you're a volunteer.'

She puts the bottle to her mouth and takes a gulp. Her face scrunches up in obvious displeasure, but it doesn't stop her from having one more shot before handing it back.

'You're a bad influence. Come on, let's search the rest of the house. They're not in here, are they?' she says in a hoarse, throaty cough.

'No. But what do old Victorian kitchens usually have beneath them?'

'I don't know.'

'A cellar. In the old days, before refrigeration, that's where they used to keep all their perishables. And I suspect that door over there leads to a cellar,' he says, flashing his light towards a wooden panel in the corner. 'And what better place to hide a couple of captives,' he adds grinning.

'I think you're actually enjoying this, aren't you?'

319

'It beats paperwork.'

'And what if... you know... they're dead?'

'My highly tuned Gaelic senses tell me they're still alive.'

'I hope your highly tuned Gaelic senses are bloody right!'

They move quietly towards it as if walking on eggshells. Zac lifts the latch, but it's locked. He runs his hand along the architrave above the door and smiles as he locates what he's looking for and flashes it in front of Kylie.

'You could have been a burglar in a different life,' she proposes.

'There's not much difference between how a copper and a criminal think. That's how we catch them.'

Placing the key in the door, he gently twists it. There's a moment of resistance before it clicks, and he pulls the door open. He stands aside.

'Down you go,' he says, nodding towards the ancient worn steps entombed by whitewashed walls.

Kylie is aghast. 'You've got to be joking,' she hisses.

'Look at the state of me,' he says, deliberately shining the torch under his chin to highlight his features in a ghoulish manner. 'I'm drenched. I'm a man and I'm not in uniform, whereas you are a woman.'

'Glad you noticed.'

He ignores her. 'And you're in uniform. If they see me, they'll never sleep soundly again.'

Kylie doesn't look convinced.

'I'll be right behind you... honest.'

'You better be,' she says as she edges down the stairs, keeping the bright beam directly in front of her.

As they get halfway down, she comes to an abrupt halt.

'Did you hear that? It sounded like whispering,' she mutters.

Zac nods for her to carry on.

'Should I call out?' she asks.

'Yes. But do it in a nice reassuring voice.'

'What's that supposed to mean?'

'Nothing.'

'Hello, this is police officer Kylie Pembroke from North Yorkshire Police, Whitby. I have Detective Sergeant Zac Stoker with me. I'm in uniform, but he's not. Zoe, Emma, can you hear me? If you're down here, then please call out and let me know.'

There's no reply. The steps end as they turn into a cavernous room full of old wardrobes, tables, and other discarded items from the house. Kylie repeats her address. She stops again.

'I can definitely hear something,' she murmurs. 'Zoe, Emma, I'm the police! Please let me know if you're down here, as I'm beginning to get a little scared!' she yells again with a quaver in her voice.

'What do you mean—beginning to?' Zac mutters.

They navigate past more detritus; an old-fashioned blackboard, a chest freezer, a pile of plastic chairs stacked high, and a moth-eaten archery target. In front of them, a dozen old-fashioned tea chests stretch from one side of the cellar wall to the other, blocking their path.

'That's odd,' Zac whispers.

'Why?' Kylie replies, startled at her partner's comment.

'I don't know.'

'I thought you were supposed to be a detective.'

Kylie creeps forward and pushes one chest sideways with her knee as Zac closely chaperones her. As she passes the barricade a sudden movement to her right has her spinning around in a panic as a pulse of adrenalin fires through her nerves.

'No!' Zac screams.

56

Mark Bridges is sitting on the edge of his uncomfortable bed in his cell, head in hands, ruminating at his naïve stupidity. He knows there's a camera watching him, in case he should self-harm.

'I've been set up, big time. What a dickhead!' he mutters to himself. 'There's no way I'm going down by myself. This isn't over yet. I'm not going to spend forty years behind bars. There must be something I can think of that will pin the blame on her?'

Sarah Clark is crocheting, a hobby she took up a few days ago. She doesn't know what she's crocheting, but that's not the point. She rocks gently back and forth as she gazes at the mute TV screen.

John Clark stares at the page of his book, seeing nothing but a jumble of letters. It's been open on the same page for over an hour. He lifts his glass of red from a side table and takes a sip. He considers himself an amateur connoisseur of wine, but tonight it tastes like rancid vinegar.

———◦———

Emma Tolhurst's parents are surrounded by family who have travelled from around the country to offer their support in their time of tortured anxiety.

They do their best to offer words of encouragement, and talk about things like the weather, the football, the cost of living. They make a few light-hearted jokes occasionally to lift the mood.

Lenny and Rachel Tolhurst appreciate their efforts, they really do, but they'd prefer to be alone when they receive the news.

No more platitudes. No more cliches. No more bullshit. Just the cold hard truth served on a bed of slate.

———◦———

'Damn and blast!' Frank Finnegan explodes. 'Why hasn't Zac checked in yet?'

Prisha offers him a weary smile.

'Calm down, Frank. Zac is an experienced officer.'

'And what about Special Constable Pembroke? I should never have put her with Zac. I thought it would be good for her to get some experience with a senior officer. If anything happens to her, I'll never forgive myself.'

'I think you should have sent more than one car to the grange.'

'Hell, Prisha, this whole thing has gone belly up! We have one car out of action with *two* flat tyres. Another car bogged in mud. And one bloody police dog which has gone rogue, last seen chasing a flock of sheep across the bloody moors! I couldn't risk pulling any more patrols from the main search team on a whim and fancy provided by Dudley Fox.'

'Sorry, boss. Just saying.'

'Aye, well don't!'

Tiffany Butler turns the taps off and climbs carefully into the bath. She sinks into the warm water as the foaming suds engulf her naked body. She enjoys a long, luxuriating bath, especially on a warm night. It opens up the pores and flushes out the toxins.

Carefully picking up a chocolate truffle from a plate on a side table, she takes a half bite, enjoying the rich, velvety flavour of Belgian cocoa.

Returning the uneaten half truffle to the plate, she replaces it with a flute of expensive, chilled champagne.

'Oh yes, the simple things in life.'

———◇———

Charles Murray opens his wallet, pulls out two fifty-pound notes and hands them to the sex worker. She tilts her head to one side in a disappointed fashion.

'That's what our agreed price was,' he states nervously.

'It was, initially. But you couldn't help yourself, could you, and insisted on a little special extra. Or have you forgotten already?'

A bead of sweat creeps down his long nose as he pulls out another fifty.

'That's better,' the woman says as she greedily takes the money and opens the door for him. 'Goodnight.'

'Ahem... yes... goodnight.'

He hurries down the street like a stalked rabbit as the rain threatens to wash him away, unaware of the eyes following him.

———◇———

The lights are dimmed as "Save the Last Waltz For Me" blares out of the stereo in Dudley Fox's sitting room.

He dances around the room holding Shirley's hands.

'It was a little mean of you, Shirl. Why didn't you just give me an actual place name? It would have been a lot easier. Mind you, if anyone can solve that puzzle of yours, then it's Frank Finnegan. He reckons he's a dab hand at puzzles. Although, he's supposed to be a dab hand at catching criminals and murderers, but he hasn't caught yours yet, has he?'

As the music ends, he refills his whisky glass, and sups thirstily from it, as if it's water.

'What's that? Why don't I ask you who your killer was?'

He flops onto the settee and ponders the question, even though he knows the answer.

'It's because I'm afraid of what your reply will be.'

His phone vibrates. He stares at the message, a single letter in uppercase.

M?

'M? And what's that supposed to mean?

Me? Meera Finnegan? Mandy Dempsey? Charles Murray? Have I really got to go through all the people I know whose first, or surname, begins with the letter M?'

He sniggers, then guffaws, clutching at his sides as tears roll down his cheeks. The psychotic episode barely lasts a minute.

'I'll tell you what's so funny, Shirl... you, that's what's funny. You're so dramatic. It's like the old Hitchcock film, but with a modern twist. *Text M For Murder!*'

The tears flow again, but this time it's not because of laughter.

57

Zac reaches out and aggressively grabs the arm of the assailant as it begins a fast downward trajectory. His action stops the hand, which is clutching an arrow, inches above Kylie's head. Muted sobbing drifts from a corner. Kylie tries to catch her breath and assess the situation. The heavy curtains of fear and shock block her logic.

The seconds tick before she comes to her senses. Zac still has the girl's arm in a ferocious clinch.

'Emma,' Kylie says softly, 'I'm a police officer.'

'I don't believe you.'

'It's true. Look, this is my uniform.' She flashes the torch over herself. 'And here is my police radio,' she adds, tapping at it.

'Why's it not making any noise then?'

'We turned it off when we parked up outside, just in case there was a bad person here in the building.'

'Turn it on and prove it.'

Kylie turns the radio on, but there's only white noise as she flicks through the channels trying to pick up any sort of police communication.

'It's because we're underground,' Zac says. 'Emma, can you drop the arrow please?'

The girl releases the weapon. As it clatters to the floor, Zac kicks it away into the darkness.

'Emma, you've got to believe me,' Kylie pleads. 'I was the first officer to respond to Sarah Clark's call for help on Monday, at Saltwick Bay. We know who took you—Mark Bridges. He's in a cell at Whitby Police Station. Come on now, let's get you home. Where's Zoe?'

Emma nods sideways, defiantly, as Zac follows her direction with his torch. Huddled in a corner, with knees pulled firmly up to her chest, is Zoe Clark. Dread is creased across her tear-stained face.

Kylie drops to her knees and holds her arms out.

'Come on, Zoe, you're safe now. Let's go to our car and call your mum, yes?'

Zoe gets to her feet and inches forward, still reticent. Kylie pulls her into her chest as the girl sniffles and sobs.

'There, there... shush. It's going to be all right now. You're both safe.'

The girls relax a little.

'I need to ask you a couple of questions before we call your mums, okay?'

Both girls nod.

'Are you injured in any way?'

They shake their heads.

'That's good. And were you touched in any way—you know—sexually?'

'No,' Zoe says as her tears recede.

'No,' Emma confirms.

Zac and Kylie take a deep breath and sigh.

***

As they rush along the hallway, Zac issues orders.

'Kylie, get on the radio and break the news to the team. Tell them to get forensics over here asap and a couple of patrol cars to secure access. I'll take the girls to the car and call their parents. We also need the Family Liaison Officer to meet us at the station, and a doctor to give the girls a thorough examination... oh, and make sure it's a female doctor. They have been known to stuff up in the past.'

As Zac scurries through the pouring rain to the car with the girls in tow, Kylie stops at the entrance and shouts into her radio, forgetting all about the usual communication protocols.

'It's Special Constable Kylie Pembroke speaking... I have some fantastic news—we have found Zoe Clark and Emma Tolhurst alive and well at Westerdale Grange!'

***

Zac hands each girl a Mars bar, which they ravenously wolf down in silence as he taps at his mobile.

The phone rings twice before it's answered by the fractured voice of Sarah Clark.

'Sergeant Stoker... it's late. Please God... no!' she sobs.

'Mrs Clark don't' panic. It's not bad news, I can assure you. In fact, the opposite. I have someone who wants to speak with you.'

He passes the phone to Zoe as he holds two fingers up in front of her.

'Two minutes only, then we need to ring Emma's mum, okay?' he whispers.

She gives him a vigorous nod of the head and a cheeky grin.

'Mam, it's me, Zoe!'

Zac turns away and gazes at the puddles pooling on the gravel driveway. Sheet lightning bathes the bleak landscape in a wide swathe of hope, as it banishes shadows and dark monsters. Zac sniffs, then wipes the tears from his cheek with the back of his hand.

58

Friday 21st August

Frank readjusts his sitting position as he wearily stares at the grey hair on the head of Detective Superintendent Anne Banks. She uses her yellow highlighter pen again. It swishes dramatically across a sentence of Frank's report. She purses her lips as her tongue, unseen, brushes her front teeth. Frank studies the wrinkles around her mouth. They certainly weren't created by laughter.

Her elbows rest on the desk as she finally eyeballs her DCI.

'A job well done, Frank.'

'Thanks Anne.'

'There are still a few loose ends to tie up, but overall, this is a good news story.'

'There are more than a few loose ends. We still need to get a breakthrough on Tiffany Butler.'

Leaning back in her chair, she studies him with an air of impatience.

'Forget about Butler, we have our man—Mark Bridges. I want you to focus on him. Gather all your evidence together and make a watertight case to hand over to the Crown Prosecution

Service. Then we can put the case to bed and forget about it until it comes to court.'

Frank screws his eyes up, confused.

'But Anne, we know Butler is involved. We need more time to get something on her.'

'Drop it, Frank. You suspect Butler is involved—big difference from knowing. You're chasing shadows. I've read the report from the Family Liaison Officer. She interviewed Zoe and Emma last night, and there was no mention of Tiffany Butler whatsoever. The girls don't know who took them into the cellar at Westerdale Grange as they were blindfolded, but they assumed it was Bridges.'

'Assumed, that's right. With all due respect, the girls were exhausted and emotional last night. Given a few days to recover, they may remember something that's pertinent to the case.'

'You're not listening, Frank. I'm disbanding the incident team. And I want those girls and their families left alone.'

'But Tiffany Butler...'

She angrily interrupts. 'Tiffany Butler has a watertight alibi! You'll resume your normal CID duties. You still have a lot of work ahead of you—the armed robberies for one, and what Bridges involvement was, if any. And let's not forget the Shirley Fox murder.'

'But Anne...'

'I've made my decision, Frank. And don't sulk, it doesn't become you. Rejoice in the fact the case is solved, and the girls are home, alive and well.'

Frank's jowls harden. 'Apart from the mental scars.'

'Yes, and the effects of their appalling diet over the last three days. Imagine eating pot noodles for breakfast dinner and tea?'

'Indeed. I'm surprised the girls didn't expire from sodium poisoning.'

She peers down her nose at him, bypassing her spectacles, before relaxing back into her chair.

'I suppose we should be grateful Bridges provided them with food at all.'

'If he did,' Frank murmurs under his breath.

'I'll ignore that.'

'On a lighter note, I will give credit to Inspector Kumar. She was the one who put two-and-two together regarding Westerdale Grange. Although, if the penny had dropped earlier, we may have had the girls home sooner. But that's a small gripe.'

'Yes, ma'am.'

'Hmm... and also credit to DS Stoker and Special Constable Pembroke as well. Although, I do wonder why you put a community constable in the front line with a senior detective?'

'To gain experience, ma'am. I don't want to lose her to archaeology.'

'Pardon?'

'She's about to start her final year at university. She'll make a cracker of a detective. And let's face it, we need good people.'

She glances at her watch, then abruptly stands.

'Right, I have to go. I'm due in front of the cameras in fifteen, and I also have a meet and greet in York this afternoon with some high level officers from the Met on a work-related sabbatical.'

'Would you like me to front up to the media instead?'

'Thanks for your offer, Frank. But I can handle this alone.'

Frank kicks his office door open, cursing as he does so.

'My God, she's hard-nosed, pain in the backside!'

'I take it you're talking about the Super, boss?'

'Prisha, what are you doing here? I told you last night... or was it this morning... I didn't want to see your face until Monday.'

'Sorry, boss. I'm about to head over to Frodsham Spa to see if I overlooked anything in regard to Tiffany Butler's alibi, and I thought I'd swing by and see if there's been any developments.'

'Hmm... you can save yourself a trip. As far as the superintendent is concerned, the case is all but closed. She ordered me to line up all our ducks in a row against Bridges, then hand it over to the CPS.'

'And let Tiffany Butler off the hook?'

Frank pulls his tie off and hangs it on the hat rack.

'The Super has a point. We have nothing on Tiffany Butler apart from Bridges' testimony and our own suspicions.'

'What about the ransom money? That could lead back to her.'

'I spoke with the Serious Fraud Office earlier. The money has already been shifted somewhere else and the original bank account in the Cayman Islands has been closed down—absolutely no trace at the moment. And by the time they do find something the money will have been moved again. It's going to be a long drawn out paper trail, and it's up to the SFO now. We are to resume our normal duties.'

'But surely that proves Bridges wasn't working alone. How could he have moved money across jurisdictions while being locked up here?'

'Apparently, you can initiate these things in advance. Set dates, and what not, when to transfer funds. No different to your own online banking. On a good note, the Super acknowledged your contribution in locating the girls, so there's a feather in your cap.'

Prisha reflects silently for a moment. 'Did you mention anything to the Super about the cryptic message from Dudley Fox?'

'Did I hell!' Frank responds with some alarm. 'I'd have been drummed out of the force. No, there are only three people who know about his note and that's the way I'd like to keep it—understood?'

'Yes, boss.'

Frank relaxes as he pulls a wistful expression staring out of the window at the fishing boats moored up on the River Esk.

'How have you found your first week?' he enquires.

'Challenging, confronting... but as inappropriate as it sounds—exhilarating.'

He rubs at his chin as he turns to her.

'No, it's not inappropriate. Us coppers are a strange breed. We thrive on adversity, unanswered questions, the chase of the quarry. Right lass, get yourself home and enjoy your Friday afternoon off and the rest of the weekend. Put your feet up and relax. You've done a bloody sterling job in my estimation.'

Prisha smiles and checks her watch. 'It's nearly eleven thirty.'

'Aye, time flies when you're having fun,' Frank says absentmindedly, as he stuffs his sweat-stained shirt from the previous day into a plastic shopping bag.

'I was thinking...'

'About?'

'How about I treat you to dinner?'

Frank freezes, then eyeballs her. 'By dinner—do you mean lunch?'

'Yes.'

Frank smiles. 'What's on offer?'

'Well, as neither of us are supposed to be on duty, I reckon a couple of pints of Whitby Whaler accompanied by a few rounds of dripping on bread—lathered in salt.'

He grins. 'For me or thee?'

'For both of us. My shout.'

Frank erupts into laughter. 'Eh up, lass! Now yer talking!'

'As they say... when in Rome.'

'Aye... but not a word to my missus—right?' he says, appearing concerned.

'Yes, boss. Give me a moment. I need to powder my nose. I'll meet you in the car park and we'll walk if that's okay.'

Frank nods as she leaves the room.

He pulls a pair of scissors from a drawer and snips out part of a headline from a tabloid newspaper.

A faint smile creases his lips as he strides across the incident room. He rips the "MISSING!" tag from above the photographs of Zoe and Emma, takes the newspaper clipping, and jabs it with a pin into the board.

"FOUND!"

Author Notes

Dear Reader,

Thank you so much for joining me on the journey through Black Nab. I truly hope you enjoyed the story and found satisfaction in the resolution of the main mystery about the missing girls, Emma and Zoe. If you're wondering about the unresolved threads—like Who was Shirley's killer? What happened to the money? Was Tiffany Butler involved?—don't worry, you're not alone!

I chose to leave those threads open because they are deeply connected to the story in Jawbone Walk (Book 2), where everything will come together. Trying to fit everything into Black Nab would have turned it into a 700-page novel—quite an ask for a debut crime fiction book! It was never a premeditated intention or a callous marketing ploy on my part; it was simply a case of having too many ideas to fit into one book. For a new author, such a lengthy novel in this genre would have been extremely hard to sell or market.

I want to reassure you that my only goal was to keep the story at a pace and length that worked for the genre, and reader while ensuring all plotlines had the space they deserved. I hope this explanation helps, and that you'll consider continuing the adventure in book 2, Jawbone Walk.

Thank you again for your support!

Warm regards,

Ely North

Book Series Page

Also by Ely North – DCI Finnegan Series

Book 1: **Black Nab**

Book 2: **Jawbone Walk**

Book 3: **Vertigo Alley**

Book 4: **Whitby Toll**

Book 5: **House Arrest**

Book 6: **Gothic Fog**

Book 7: **Happy Camp**

Book 8: **Harbour Secrets**

Book 9: **Murder Mystery** – Pre-order (Dec 2024)

DCI Finnegan Series Boxset #1: **Books 1 – 3**

DCI Finnegan Series Boxset #2: **Books 4 – 6**

Prequel: **Aquaphobia** (Free ebook for newsletter subscribers)

*Note: All books are available from Amazon in ebook, paperback, and in **Kindle Unlimited** (excluding Aquaphobia). Paperbacks can be ordered from all good bookshops. **Boxset print editions are one book compiled from three books. They do not come in a box. *** Pre-orders only apply to ebooks.

Contact

Contact: ely@elynorthcrimefiction.com

Website: https://elynorthcrimefiction.com

Follow me on Facebook for the latest
https://facebook.com/elynorthcrimefictionUK

Sign up to my newsletter for all the latest news,
releases, and discounts.

Newsletter
Sign Up

Made in United States
Orlando, FL
13 October 2024

52595798R00192